A BOOK OF DAYS

Richard Snodgrass

A Novel

 Calling Crow Press

Pittsburgh

Also by Richard Snodgrass

Fiction

There's Something in the Back Yard

The Books of Furnass

All That Will Remain

Across the River

Holding On

Book of Days

The Pattern Maker

Furrow and Slice

The Building

Some Rise

All Fall Down

Redding Up

Books of Photographs and Text

An Uncommon Field: The Flight 93
Temporary Memorial

Kitchen Things: An Album of Vintage Utensils
and Farm-Kitchen Recipes

Memoir

The House with Round Windows

Published by Calling Crow Press
Pittsburgh, Pennsylvania

Book design by Book Design Templates, LLC
Cover design by Jack Ritchie

Printed in the United States of America
ISBN 978-0-9997700-7-8
Library of Congress catalog control number: 2020909634

For Ron Arias
and, of course, as with all things,
for Marty

I went there behind the crude but serious belief that you had to be able to look at anything, serious because I acted on it and went, crude because I didn't know, it took the war to teach it, that you were as responsible for everything you saw as you were for everything you did. The problem was that you didn't always know what you were seeing until later. . . .

Michael Herr, *Dispatches*

Contents

THE BOOK

—it's large for an orderly book of the period, 8-inches by 4-and-a-half inches though less than an inch thick, made for use at a garrison or carried in a haversack rather than tucked inside a soldier's tunic, bound in brown leather and hinged at the top—rests now in the corner of a trunk among old bed linens and blankets where it has been for more than a hundred and fifty years, placed there in the 1850s when it was discovered under a mattress thirty years earlier when a young boy on an iron plantation in Western Pennsylvania knew he should destroy the book or throw it away but couldn't bring himself to do so, the book forgotten as the boy grew to a man, had replaced his father as ironmaster at the blast furnace and then gone on to found his own company, a steamworks, had started his own family and built his own home on the slope of the valley's hill above the town, when the book and the trunk and other items from his father's house that no one knew what else to do with were moved to the new house and then stored in a dark corner of a cellar storeroom, handed down from generation to generation, or rather, forgotten about from generation to generation, until in the 1930s a fire destroyed the house on the hillside and the trunk was discovered in the ruins, still sequestered in the back of the cellar, intact and unscathed, moved again to the new home of the great-great-grandson of the boy who discovered it in its original hiding place, a blockhouse on the edge of the wilderness that was America, placed there in 1776 for safekeeping by a young woman and an ex-soldier without hands, the book placed there initially a decade earlier at the time of what became known as the French and Indian war by an Ensign of the 42nd Royal Regiment of Foot, the Black Watch, who had holed up in the blockhouse to write his story along with that of the mother of the girl and how the ex-soldier came to have his hands chopped off by Indians, the orderly book, a day book, a book of days, the days when it was written and the days when it impacted and changed the lives of those who touched it, all those years ago, hidden away in the corner of the trunk keeping its silence, waiting to be read to come to life again . . . waiting. . . .

THE BOOK OF LOVE
I

1817

There were crows in the trees, calling, calling. There were crows on the hillside, flying away. The boy and girl ran through the woods, both in their bare feet, the girl leading the way, running up the hill away from the river, the buildings close to the river. As they climbed higher into the woods, the boy, Colin, stopped to look back down the hill. Through the trees he could see the cluster of buildings of the ironworks below. The forge and the rolling and splitting mill along the bank. The stone furnace partially hidden, tucked away in a hollow. The Ironmaster's House, his house, built of the same fieldstone as the furnace, on a rise above the works. Thick black smoke from the furnace and the mounds to make charcoal plumed above the steep valley. And sitting among the other buildings in the mill yard, the old brick blockhouse. All that remained of some earlier conflict, a long-ago war. The abandoned building where he and his sister had found the Book of Love. The book he carried now, on their way to the secret place.

"Come on, Colin," Lydia called to him from farther up the slope. "Hurry up! I'll beat you there!"

She turned and ran on. Her long muslin dress like a vision, flitting among the maples and white oaks and hickory, in and out of shadow and sunlight, farther up into the forest. The trees were just beginning to bud in early spring, a frosting of green, like confection. Like something his mother might powder on a cake as a treat. The crows flew startled from the trees as his older sister passed. Then Lydia was gone, out of sight among the brush, beyond the edge of a ravine cut into the hillside. Where the secret place was. His heart racing with anticipation, Colin hurried on, clutching with his free hand for handholds among the low-hanging branches, keeping the book close to his side.

By the time he got to the secret place she was already inside. He got down on his hands and knees and crawled through the entrance. It was a tangle of blackberry bushes, tucked into the side of a dry creek bed, the branches pulled down from their own weight to form a tunnel several feet long. At the end of the tunnel, the interwoven vines formed a natural arbor, a latticework cave tall enough for a child of eleven or fourteen to sit upright. Sunlight filtered down through the vines, a green luminous shell. Lydia was sitting there waiting for him. Impatient. As Colin got situated beside her, Lydia took the Book of Love from him and opened it on her outstretched legs. She waited until Colin was still. Then she intoned, pretending to read the strange words:

"*Ba minik do sil Elis abeth so miba brea an sole.*"

"What does it mean?" Colin asked.

"It says the ways of love are wondrous and strange. That you must become an acolyte of love or it will turn you away."

"What's an acolyte? I thought I had to become a disciple of love."

"It's the same thing. Only an acolyte is more devoted."

"Then I'll be an acolyte. I believe," he said, quivering with excitement. Having played the game before.

His sister took the Book of Love and pressed the spine to his forehead. In response, he made a circle on his breast with two fingers, the way she told him the Book instructed. Then she leafed through the pages until she found another passage. This one seemed to particularly please her.

"*An brothar braya reedh riompi, glassara ar gach toby de.*"

"What does it say this time?"

"It says a brother who is a true acolyte of love is allowed to look at my bare legs."

"All the way up?"

"The Book of Love doesn't say. I guess it depends on how devoted you are."

Colin knew his heart overflowed with devotion, ached. If not for the Book of Love, at least for his sister. To him they were one and the same. As he scooted down into position beside her legs, Lydia put the Book to one side and leaned back on her elbows. Colin took the edge of her long skirt and started to slide it up.

"Slow. It has to be slow," Lydia said. "Or the Book of Love won't allow it."

The boy tried to contain himself. In the distance, below in the valley, he could hear the indistinct rumble and ring of the iron-works. The calls and whistles of the draymen with their loads of coal and ore. The low roar of the furnace in blast. He took the edge of her long skirt and slowly slid it up to expose her knees. Then farther, midway up her thighs. He touched her legs gently as she had instructed him to do according to the Book. Marveling at them, at her. After a moment he looked up at her face. He waited for her to say something but she only smiled. He leaned over and kissed her knee. When she still didn't say anything, he kissed her other knee. Then her thighs. They were soft, soft as the breasts of ducklings, but firm too. Her skin smooth even with the halo of light blond hair. Mystery of mysteries. She tasted salty, and something he had never tasted before, not at all like the taste when he once licked his own shoulder.

He looked at her again. This time there was something else in her eyes. He slowly lifted her skirt higher to expose the tops of her legs, and when she lifted her bottom so the material could slide under it, her stomach. The thin tangle of blond hairs in her crotch. He leaned forward and rested his check on her small puff belly. Turned his head and kissed it gently. He reached to put his hand between her legs but she sat up abruptly and pushed him away.

"That's enough for now," she said, pulling her dress back down and brushing past him. Crawling hurriedly down the tunnel. He watched her scurrying form fill the entrance, then she was gone. There was only the glimpse of dry creek bed, the slope and the trees and the brighter sunlight outside, though he could hear her, she was laughing to herself, and singing, her voice growing more distant as she called.

"Colin. Col-lin! Time to go home. . . ."

He picked up the Book of Love and glanced through the pages on his own. But the words meant nothing to him, without her. The Book clutched in his hand, the boy crawled down the tunnel and back into the sunlight. Squinting as he stood again, looking around as if he had just entered a new world. Wondering, What did I do? Why did she run away like that? What did I do wrong?

Colin thought of that day now, on a morning a few months later, as he stood on the front porch of his house. Squinting again, though this time not from the sunlight. The sun was above the ridgeline of the valley's hills, but it was only a white-hot circle in the morning haze. The butt end of a heated iron bar. Or as if he peered into the tap hole of the furnace. Thick smoke filled the valley, drifting among the buildings of the ironworks, as it did most days when the summer heat or the possibility of rain kept the smoke from rising, kept it contained within the cut of the hills. He had wakened this morning with an idea. He would take the Book of Love to Lydia again, to ask her to interpret what it said again. They hadn't looked at the Book, or been to the secret place, since that day in early spring. But for the moment his attention was drawn to what was going on in the yard.

His father was standing with several workmen near the old blockhouse. The men were digging two holes close to the rear wall of the structure, and a team of mules was dragging a large log up the hill from the river toward the site. As Colin stood there, scratching one bare foot against the other, trying to figure out what was going on, Margaret, the maid, came from inside the house and stood beside him.

"It's time for your breakfast, young Colin," she said in her thick Scottish brogue. "What are you staring at so steady?"

"What are they doing, Margaret? Down there, by the blockhouse."

"Aye, your father, the ironmaster, said 'twould be today." She folded her dumpling-like arms across her tummy and nodded, totally accepting. Her apron and her makeshift cap were cut of the same blue-flowered cloth. Beneath the apron she was wearing her traveling clothes.

"What's today? Tell me." He was starting to feel panicky.

"The day your father, the ironmaster, said he was going to tear it down."

"But why?"

"Aye, and why not? It's too small to store things in and it sits there like a lump in a pudding. Your father, the ironmaster, says he's going to use the bricks and stone for a new building and use the space to expand his mill, and that's for sure . . . Young Colin, come back here!"

He was away and running. Down the steps and down the hill, his bare feet slapping along the silvery, hard-packed trail, into the mill yard. Circling away from the blockhouse and the men, along the side of the mule and horse barn and past the blacksmith shop, staying close to the buildings to keep from being noticed.

The ironworks was a collection of large wood-frame buildings, positioned close to the river, with channels and watercourses cut from the river to power the waterwheels of the forge, the rolling and slitting mills. The thirty-foot-tall blast furnace sat back in a notch of the hillside against a bluff. Along the top of the bluff was an access road for the wagons of charcoal and limestone and ore; a wood platform extended from the edge of the bluff to the stack of the furnace, so men with wheelbarrows could feed the furnace. The smoke that filled the narrow valley came from the furnace and, from farther off in the forest, the mounds of charring wood for fuel. Colin had grown up on the iron plantation, as some people called it, the yard of the ironworks his playground since the time he could walk. But today, for reasons he didn't understand, his playground seemed different to him. Threatening somehow. Unyielding. Cruel.

It was a place where day and night changed places, the daytime drained of color and light under the shroud of smoke, while the nights roiled orange and red and yellow as the furnaces flamed and sparked. Standing out of sight near the open doors of the forge, he became aware of the noise around him. Noises that he had heard since birth but never really paid attention to before. The quick relentless flap of the huge bellows. The thud and ring of the power hammer as it fell on the iron being wrought. The splash of the water wheels, the creak of the wooden mechanisms. Inside the semi-darkness, the fires in the finery and chafery hearths burned brightly, the changing colors telling the smiths and forge hands the state of the metal being worked. As he watched, a fiery ball was dragged from a hearth across the floor to the power hammer. Showers of sparks erupted with each blow of the one-ton hammer, a stream of liquid fire suddenly arcing over the workmen's heads when the hammer hit a cavity in the metal. The men laughed at the near miss that could have vaporized any one of them on the spot, continued working.

Colin shuddered. As the son of the owner and ironmaster, he felt as if he was supposed to know what went on here. But it was all a mystery to him, as much a mystery as everything else

seemed in the world. There was so much to learn, about everything. How was anyone supposed to know it all? Know enough
to take his place among the men? Maybe the Book of Love could
tell him about that too. He had to get the Book to Lydia again,
to ask her to interpret more of it for him. Before she went away.

His father was still talking to the workmen, directing the activity along the back wall of the blockhouse. It was a five-sided,
two-story structure, with a foundation of fieldstone up to the
level of a row of gunports, and red brick above. The story went
that it was built before the Revolution, at the end of the French
and Indian War during Pontiac's Rebellion sixty years earlier, at
the time Colonel Bouquet lifted the siege at Fort Pitt and drove
the Indians into the Ohio wilderness. For a time the site in the
valley had carried the famous war hero's name, Bouquet's Woods,
but since Colin's father established the ironworks here along the
Allehela River, it had come to be known simply as Furnace. Now
his father's workmen were constructing a tripod of heavy logs,
almost as tall as the blockhouse itself, from which to hang a battering ram. The first two legs were in place, and a carpenter was
shinnying up one of the poles to guide the third log into place
and secure it. Colin didn't have much time.

He ran along the side of the slitting mill, then waited until a
wagon carrying ash and cinder crossed the yard, keeping the
wagon between himself and his father, until Colin was out of his
father's line of sight around the front of the blockhouse. The door
made of heavy timbers was unlocked, as it always had been when
he and Lydia came here. Inside it was dark and musty, but he
didn't dare leave the door open. He waited until his eyes got used
to the dark. From beyond the wall came the men's voices. His
father's voice. The sound of hammering and the creak of a block
and tackle. Around the perimeter of the single room, at shoulder
height for a Scottish soldier, the slits of the gunports glowed like
evenly spaced lead bars. When he could see again, he hurried to

the back wall, directly opposite the workmen on the other side, and pulled loose a couple boards from the shooting platform. Felt around inside the dark space, creepy with cobwebs—something shell-like scuttled around his fingers; Colin wanted to jerk his hand away but didn't—until he found the Book wrapped in oilskin. The hiding place of the Book of Love, where he and Lydia had first discovered it—it seemed like forever ago now.

He tucked the Book under his arm, ready to flee. Then stopped. A thrill coursed through him. He found an old crate and dragged it across the floor, onto the shooting platform. Stood on it, raising up slowly, the slit of the gunport descending into his view. Outside the workmen were hoisting the timber they were going to use as a battering ram into position.

"Come on, men, put your backs into it," his father commanded behind them.

Colin saw the looks on the workmen's faces as his father yelled at them, the looks they gave each other. His father moved closer, among the men to adjust the sling, then stood there. Turning his head to look at the wall of the blockhouse. For a moment Colin was on the same level as his father. Stared into his father's eyes. But there was no recognition from his father. Nothing Colin recognized as having anything to do with himself. The Book clutched under his arm, the boy jumped down from the crate and the platform and ran out the door, back across the yard. Giddy with triumph yet afraid, more afraid than he had ever been in his life. Behind him, he heard his father calling "Swing! Swing it, men!" followed by the heavy thud of the timber hitting the wall once, then again, the first sounds of the wall giving way. Colin ran on, between the buildings and up the hill toward the house. More determined than ever to find an answer.

IN THE SHADOW
OF THE VALLEY
I

1776

"D'no be afraid."

A black bear stood on its hind legs in the trail in front of her. Otherwise, there was no one in sight, the deep forest around her was still. There were only the songs of the birds, finches and cardinals and thrushes. In the distance, crows. Sunlight seeped down from the branches of the trees far overhead, spilling over the moss and ferns on the floor of the forest. The bear twisted its head, keeping its eyes on her, trying for the scent. The curious thing was, though she knew she should be afraid, she wasn't.

"Are you a talking bear? Did you just speak to me?"

"Och, the bear did no speak to you," said a voice off to her left. "I did."

He was in his late thirties or early forties, though there was something ageless about him, as if he was always very old or would always be very young. He was dressed in frontier muslin, a poorly made shirt, heavy britches, a shapeless hat. As he stepped from between the trees, Sara saw that he had no hands, only stumps at the ends of his arms.

"He's curious about you, 'tis all," he said, nodding toward the bear. "He does no ken enough to be afraid, he's young. He's probably never seen a woman before. Never seen the shape before, the long skirts and petticoats and bonnet. He's wondering if you're a ghost. A spirit."

"Would you tell him different? Before he decides I'm real enough to eat?"

The man smiled a little, one side of his mouth, wistful. He came closer to them, midway between Sara and the bear, standing among the ferns.

"Hold your bundle away from your body. Let him see your hands."

Sara slowly lifted her arms, her cloth bundle dangling from her left hand. The bear followed her movements, looked at the man.

"You see? I told you 'tis nothing there to be afraid of. Daft bear."

The bear huffed a couple of times, as if it were indeed feeling foolish, dropped back to all fours and trundled away through the ground cover and clusters of wildflowers, up and over a fallen tree trunk, the fur of its hindquarters shimmying, glancing back at the man and woman as if reproachful.

"Is he your bear?" Sara asked.

"No. The bear belongs to the bear. I've just become friends with him, since he included this stretch in his territory. I fear for him, I've tried to tell him that no everyone will be so accommodating to share this forest with a bear, but he does no listen. I fear the lesson will kill him. As lessons often do."

He was thoughtful for a moment, looking inward, then, apparently deciding that he'd said too much, or at least enough, turned and started back into the forest.

"Wait," Sara said. "You're the Seer."

The man stopped and looked back.

"They told me at Fort Pitt you lived in this area."

He considered something for a moment. "Aye. Is that what they know me as now? The Seer." He shook his head, smiled to himself, started to leave again.

"I've come to see you," Sara said hastily. With her free hand she adjusted the brim of her bonnet around her face, tried to smooth the front of her dress. To be more presentable. Then caught herself, afraid she appeared simpleminded. The man regarded her over his shoulder, studied her under his thick brows, heavy forehead. Waited for her to go on, if she would go on.

"They said you know magic. That you see things other people can't. That you know secrets."

"Magic. Secrets. I know a few herbs the Indians taught me. I helped a few people with minor ailments. Thus is a reputation born in this world."

"They said you have a book."

For a moment the man looked at the dark forest in front of him, as if he longed for its depths, its solitude and solace. Then slowly turned to face her. Resigned that she was here. "What kind of a book do they say I have?"

"A book in a strange language. An old language no one else can read. A magic book."

The man smiled sadly, looked away from her. "The settlers get strange notions. Word spread that I have such a book, at the same time that I know some medicines. So my magic must come from a magic book."

"I heard other things. I heard that the book tells what happened here." She nodded in the direction of the forest, the river. "At the outpost that was here."

"And if it does so, why would you care about such a book?"

"I believe my mother was at the outpost. I heard she died at the outpost."

"'Twas a soldier's outpost, no a settlement." He looked at her suspiciously. "Scottish soldiers of the Black Watch. Why would a woman be at such a place?"

"I heard she was here nonetheless. I heard it from a soldier at Fort Carlisle, who said he heard it from a soldier who was at Fort

Pitt. When I went to Fort Pitt I heard about the book. And about you."

"You came all the way from Carlisle? By yourself?"

"Yes."

"How old are you?"

"Eighteen. Anyway, I think it's eighteen."

"You're no sure?"

"I was born and raised with the Indians. Hurons, Wyandots. Before I was sent to live with missionaries in Carlisle. My mother was an Indian captive. I lived there in the Ohio wilderness with her until Colonel Bouquet came and made the Indians return all the whites. I'm as much an Indian as a white."

The man looked at his stumps. "'Twas the Indians who took my hands."

She took a careful step forward and, when he didn't move away, approached till she was only a few feet from him. Up close she could see that he had been a handsome man once, before the toll of the weather and his experiences took over. His features seemed worn like the rocks caught in the current of a stream, his eyes were in deep crevices as if hidden away. There was a darkness about him, his face, his expressions, even when he smiled, but she couldn't decide what caused it, it seemed more, deeper, than the loss of his hands. She realized that he was studying her closely as well.

"I heard you found the book in the blockhouse Bouquet built near here at the time of Pontiac's uprising."

"Aye. When the British soldiers at Fort Pitt heard there was such a book, they sent a detachment here with bayonets to retrieve it. But when they could no make sense of it, they left it. Daft." He shook his head at the folly.

"The last anyone saw of my mother," Sara said, "she was on her way to the outpost. They said that later on the entire detachment of the outpost disappeared. Maybe the book can tell me if my mother was with them."

"It's best to leave the dead as they are," the man said. "If they want to tell us something, there's better ways than through the pages of a book, and that's the truth of it."

He studied her a moment; she studied him in return. Then he looked down at the ground cover between them. Looked around at the dark forest. At the branches far above, the late afternoon sunlight filtering down through the net of leaves. With his stump he adjusted the tilt of his hat.

"It's getting on then. You should no be out here, wandering around this forest by yourself. A young lass. You can come stay at my place this night. But in the morning you need to be away."

Was it a trick? Another man trying to take advantage of the circumstances, to get her into a situation where he could use her body? She didn't think so, but you never knew. Though she wasn't concerned about fighting off a man with two stumps. She had fought off worse, stronger, full-bodied men; she had also let them have her, when it was to her advantage. What concerned her was her sudden tiredness—it washed over her without warning, she felt as if she were encrusted in lead. She had come so far to find her answers, been through so much. Now all she wanted to do was rest, and there was something restful about this man for all his darkness. She wanted to trust him, almost thought that she could, for reasons she didn't understand, but she had been duped before. Hurt before. She felt numb with indecision. For once she didn't know which way to turn. Which step to take. What had come over her?

The man had turned and was starting through the trees. He stopped again and looked back at her, waiting for her to follow.

"Think of this," he said. "There might be other bears on your way back to the settlement. Older, wiser, more experienced bears who already discovered that we're no spirits to them but meat."

He smiled crinkly at her, not unfriendly. Rubbed the knob of flesh at the end of his arm against his cheek to scratch an itch, brushed a midge away. Sara nodded and followed him into the forest.

There were oxen among the trees. Standing here and there. Great white muscular beasts, 150 stone or more, ghostly in the half-light of late afternoon. The man walked through the scattered herd, going to as many as he could and placing the stub of his arm on the beast's nose, rubbed its brow. Said something to each one in a language she'd never heard before. Before he reached them, the beasts were nervous and wary, not of him but of her, coming behind him, but the sound of his voice apparently soothed them and they returned to their foraging, nosing among the moss and wildflowers on the forest floor.

There were more oxen in the fields as they emerged from the forest, walking down the gentle slope of a hill toward a homestead near the river. A scattering of outbuildings, barn, chicken coop, pigsty, an open shed for sheep and goats. A larger log building that looked like the barracks she had seen at Carlisle and Fort Pitt. All carried the signs—scorched timbers, cobbled repairs—of being rebuilt after a fire. In the center a blockhouse of brick and stone. Surrounded by the remains of what had once been star-shaped fortifications, the embankments and ditches mostly leveled now through weather and neglect. The buildings all grouped among a small stand of sycamores and willows. Beyond the buildings a steep hillside thick with maples and oaks and chokecherry, a solid mass of green. As the man and woman approached, the trees of the hillside were suddenly alive with the sounds of crows, dozens of them, perhaps hundreds, calling, as if talking among themselves. The leaves quivered with the birds' activity. Sara followed the man across a small footbridge over a stream that meandered through the compound, draining toward the river. He shook his head apologetically, looked up at the hillside, the mass of trees.

"Oh hush, you noisy birds. It's all right, she means us no harm. At least I d'no think so."

The birds immediately quieted down.

"Is this the outpost? The blockhouse?" Sara said, looking around. "You live here?"

"Do you no think I could maintain a place like this when I have only these?" he said, holding up the stumps that were his hands.

A single crow that she hadn't noticed before, sitting on a thick branch of a sycamore near the creek, leaned forward and laughed raucously a few times before growing silent again.

The man looked at the bird, then at the ground in front of him for a moment, considering something.

"Aye, you're right. That was too harsh." He looked at her again. "Aye. This was the outpost, the blockhouse there. This is where it happened. Whatever it was that happened."

"And this is your place now?"

"'Tis no one else who wants it. 'Tis no one else who will come near it. The settlers all think the place is haunted." He thought a moment. "I think they think I'm the ghost."

"How did you end up here?"

They were standing beside the creek, the water gurgling softly behind them. In the distance she could hear what sounded like a falls in the river. He thought a moment, looked around at the trees, at the black forms of the crows among the leaves. As if asking them something, as if asking if he should proceed, what he should say. Then he looked at her again.

"Blame them, the crows there, them and their eternal squawking, noisy wee buggers. I would no have found it on my own. But there was no one here, living or dead, when I arrived. No sign that anyone had ever been here. Aye, true to your story, they say that after the trouble here the only body they found inside was that of a woman. But then the Indians came and took her body with them. I dinna know why, any of it."

"My mother. They must have been reclaiming one of theirs. They were taking her home."

The man looked away at the surrounding forest. Rubbed absently the wrist of one stump against the wrist of the other, like rubbing two sticks together to make a fire. The birds and the trees were still. As if there were no crows there at all. Sara began to wonder if they ever were there, if she only imagined them. She felt the world or her mind was starting to play tricks on her.

"I've talked enough," the man said finally. "Now I have my chores. You can sleep in the blockhouse, you'll be safest there. Use the pallet in the corner, I'll sleep in the barracks tonight."

"Can I come with you? To do the chores?"

"Why would you want to? It's only milking and such." He looked at her sharply again. "I d'no need any help."

"I never thought you did. It's just . . . it's been a long time since I've been around someone doing something ordinary. Like milking a cow."

"You must have a strange idea of pleasure," he said, regarding her carefully. "But come away then."

Sara hurried to catch up with him, following him across the lot to the small barn, surprised at how girlish she felt. Excited to see milking, chickens.

On the other side of the barn were two dairy cows, held in a separate pasture from the oxen, waiting for the man. He opened the door and they filed in, udders swaying, almost touching the ground, each one taking a stall on its own. The man lifted down a low three-legged stool from its perch on a dividing wall and, held between his two stumps, started to carry it toward the near stall. But as he passed Sara, the stool suddenly slipped from his grasp and Sara caught it. Laughing at the mishap. The man eyed her, started to take the stool from her again, when it slipped out of his grasp a second time and back to Sara. She laughed again, as if it were a game.

"This wee stool seems to have a mind to be with you," he said.

"Well, I do know how to milk a cow," she said. "If you'd let me."

The man regarded her from under his heavy brows.

"It would be fun," Sara said, going over and taking one of the tin pails. "You know, part of my 'strange idea of pleasure.'" She curtsied and headed toward the near stall.

"Not that one," the man said, nodding toward a brown Guernsey. "She's a one-man cow, and I'm her man. She's used to the pull of these stubs. But you can do the other one. If it so pleases you."

Sara was thrilled. Her energy had returned. Before he could change his mind, she hurried to the far stall and sat down beside the cow and began pulling on the teats. It seemed to her an untold, unmitigated joy. The cow looked around at the unfamiliar touch but decided it was all right, glad for the relief. The warm milk sang into the tin bucket, then the song turned into more of a gurgle as the level of milk rose.

On the other side of the divider came the sound of the man's milking. After a few minutes, his voice said, "I had a helper once, when I first came here. An Indian boy. He had trouble in the town around Fort Pitt, the place they now call Pittsburgh. Came here, I guess, because he thought he could hide out. I put him to work. He helped quite a bit to get me started. A godsend, you'd say, or whoever sends those things. The crows again perhaps. But eventually he went away. Everything does in this world, you know. Go away."

He seemed to be talking more to himself than to her, so she didn't respond. Didn't know what she'd say without saying something about herself, and she didn't want to do that. She felt she'd said too much as it was. Before she was finished with her cow, he was through with his and she saw his shadow cross the doorway, a flicker in the light, as he left to do other things.

When she finished milking, she took the two pails to the springhouse, then found the man in the barracks, heating a kettle of stew on the hearth. He directed her to get plates and flatware from a shelf and take them outside to a wood table and benches under the sycamore near the stream. As dusk grew deeper in the valley, the hills turning rose and then purple-black, they ate the stew and hardtack, sitting across from each other. He had grown reticent again and barely spoke, concentrating on the effort to manipulate the eating utensils with his stumps. She wondered if his eating always required such attention, or if he was preoccupied thinking of something else; she wondered if he was angry at her for something, that she didn't say something when he spoke in the barn, or if he was waiting for her to say something now. But she finally told herself that she couldn't worry about such things, she had other things to worry about. Besides she would be gone in the morning. Would never see him again.

When it was dark, after cleaning their dishes in the stream, the man went up the slope to the blockhouse and got his bedroll and headed toward the barracks. Sara called good night to him, but wasn't surprised when he didn't respond. The interior of the blockhouse was darker than the night, the only illumination once she closed the door from the row of gunslits around the walls, a chain of moonlight. She made her way carefully among the sparse furniture, a table and a few stools, barrels, an officer's campaign chest and a small stand, to the corner pallet and slipped under the cover of an oxhide, falling asleep before she was even settled.

She woke with a start. With a feeling that someone was there, someone near. She looked around quickly, but the blockhouse was empty. She was alone. The gunslits glowed with sunlight, small glimpses of the world outside; from what had to be the east wall, shafts of sunlight slanted down through the gloom, leaving a trail of luminous rectangles across the stone floor. The angle of the light told her it was midmorning and she hurried out of bed, straightened her clothes and tried to set her hair aright. She was panicky that she had missed something, that something important had happened without her knowing—what was wrong with her, she couldn't believe she had let herself sleep like that, to lay vulnerable like that for so long, anything could have happened to her. She hurried to the heavy door, half-expecting to find it bolted, that she was a captive, but the door swept open when she pulled on it, blinding her momentarily with the daylight outside.

The man was sitting at the table under the sycamore, a long unlit clay pipe sticking from his mouth, looking away at the distant hills. When he saw her approaching, he took the pipe in his two stumps and laid it on the wood table.

"I canna keep it lit now," he said, as if answering an unspoken inquiry, "but I fill it with tobacco and get some flavor sucking on it even so. Or imagine I do. So you slept then?"

She found she was still groggy and could only mutter, rubbing her eyes. He smiled.

"Your head is full of wee cobwebs. Go get you some tea and porridge. Perhaps they will help wake you."

Was he chiding her for sleeping so long? she wondered as she crossed the compound to the barracks. She didn't know what to make of him, though she was sure he didn't want her here, wished she had never come. The only reason he had offered a place to stay the night was out of kindness, he had made it clear that there was nothing for her here, that he could or would be of no help to her. She returned to the table with a tin mug and bowl, sitting across from him as she had the night before. The man had grown meditative again, so she ate in silence, trying to wake up, occupying herself listening to the calls of the songbirds in the meadow, the play of the water in the little stream. Grasshoppers launched out of the tall grass along the bank like brown rockets; high overhead a hawk or an eagle spiraled slowly down the sky. She was through with her breakfast, ready to go to the blockhouse for her things and prepare to leave, when he finally spoke again.

"D'you hear the creek talking? I wish I could understand what it is saying. The stories it could tell, the things it has seen."

"It is so peaceful here. So beautiful. Far away from the world of trouble. It's hard to believe that terrible things happened here."

"But 'tis the way of it, is it no? This thing we call the world. Full of both beauty and terror. In equal measure, it would seem."

She wanted to say that maybe it didn't have to be, that maybe it could be different. That maybe the beauty could win out. But she couldn't let herself start thinking that way.

"I need to be going," she said, gathering her dishes. "If I'm to make Fort Pitt by nightfall."

"Wait you a while," he said, putting the pipe back down on the table and standing up. He stood for a moment, looking off into the trees of the hillside—she wondered if he heard danger, she looked around, listened closely, but heard nothing beyond the birds and the creek—then realized he wasn't listening at all, or if he was, it was only to internal sounds, inner voices or a voice, he was making up his mind about something. "Wait you a while," he said again, softer this time, his own echo. Stepped over the bench and went up the slope to the blockhouse.

He returned in a moment carrying a flat parcel wrapped in oilskin, placing it on the table between them as he sat down again across from her. He opened the parcel, sliding clear the flaps of the oilskin with his stumps, to reveal a book bound in leather.

"I found this hidden under the boards of the shooting plat-form. When I first came to settle here."

"Is that the book they say is magic?" Sara asked.

"Och, magic," he said. "'Tis only an orderly's day book. And the old language supposedly meant to conjure with, 'tis only Gaelic. It takes no great magic to read if 'tis your tongue since birth."

He paged through the book awkwardly with his stumps, sliding one page to the next, glancing through the text as if considering one more time what he was about to do, before he continued.

"But it tells some of what happened here. It tells what happened to the woman you say was your mother, though I canna say whether she was or no. As for the rest, it leaves more questions than it gives answers. But I'll read it to you, if you like."

"Please," Sara said.

The man positioned the book in front of him, holding down the corner of the pages with his stump against the occasional touch of wind, and began to read out loud, slowly, making sure he translated the words correctly, a solemn, stately pace, almost an incantation. As the sound of his voice filled the morning air, a lone crow appeared from the trees on the hillside and alighted above them in the branches of the sycamore.

THE JOURNAL OF
THOMAS KEATING

Day the First

They are out there. Outside the walls. I can hear them, though they are too cunning, too cautious to show themselves. Not quite yet. Not until it is time.

I hear them, the low whisper of their voices. Indistinguishable from the distant sound of the falls in the river, the closer sound of the creek. I hear the brush of their moccasins in the grass on the other side of the wall. Indistinguishable from the rustle of the leaves on the bluffs of the tree-covered hills. Occasionally a shadow passes quickly across the rectangle of light of a musket port. Something large, quick as a crow's wing. A blink in the shaft of light where I sit in the otherwise darkness. Then it is gone again. Still again. In the distance there is only the call of the crows. Here in what the Indians call the Valley of the Crows.

I get up from my makeshift desk, an upturned flour barrel sitting on the floor. Leave my quill and mixture of ink, the blank pages of the untried Orderly Book where I have begun to write. Go to the row of musket ports that trace the perimeter of the blockhouse. I rest my face against the coolness of the brick. Position myself so the 1-foot x 4-foot recess fits across my eyes like a mask. Looking out at the rectangle of the burned and abandoned buildings of the outpost, the barracks and the barns and the sawmill down the slope toward the river. The grass of the commons still green from the spring rains, the green of the steep valley walls. The boundless green of this new land. As I stand there I half expect to see a pair of eyes appear. Eyes staring in at me staring out. Brown-black eyes, fathomless as twin wells. A face painted half-black, half-red, a feathered scalpknot crowning a shaved head. Delaware or Shawanese. Huron. But there is no one. Only the murmur of the falls, of the creek. The whisper of the breeze. The endless green, green. Though I know they are out there. Waiting for the time. Waiting for me.

No. I am wrong to write thus. I am an officer in service to His Majesty George III. This should be a proper Orderly Book:

Fort Bouquet 12 miles from Fort Pitt
Monday, 2 June 1766
Parole—Edinburgh
Countersign—Stephenssohn's Coffee House
Field Officer for the Day—
Ensign Thomas Keating   Engineer 42nd Royal Highland
    Regiment of Foot The Black Watch
Detachment to remain within Fortification until further
    Orders. Garrison to prepare their Provisions for three
    Days Bread and two Days Meat which they are to
    draw . . .

But what is the use? I am alone now. A garrison of one. A singular command, as it were. The Forlorn Hope, perhaps, as the advance guard is known when the army marches into perilous territory. Though in my current circumstances, it is impossible to tell whether I am in the vanguard of a larger attack, or at the rear. The detritus. I wonder what kind of Hope it is called when one is the only survivor of a command. When there is little hope at all.

　　She knew of hope. Of living when there is little reason to hope. Little reason to live. How else did she go on? She lay in a shaft of light coming from a gunport. The light washing over her sun-darkened face, the curls of dark hair straggling down her cheek. A loose strand trailing in the corner of her mouth. I told her that we should stay here in the blockhouse. That perhaps at Fort Pitt they would learn of what had happened here and send reinforcements.

"You are a fool, Thomas Keating," she said. Not angry. Almost a lament. "You are an engineer, but you don't know how the world is made. You can add the figures, but you cannot see the sum."

She reached out then and touched my cheek. Her hand moving through the shaft of sunlight. Dark to light to dark. Like cutting into water. But perhaps hers was a hope born of hate. A courage bred of desire.

Now the sunlight from the gunports extends across the darkness of the blockhouse. Like spokes, turning infinitely slowly as the late afternoon sun wheels toward evening. I follow their progress. Shifting my little desk and writing instruments across the stone floor. Pursuing the last light of day. Afraid to light a lamp or candle in case, rather than my shooting out, someone tries to shoot in. I found the blank Orderly Book in which I write among the stores kept here in the blockhouse by the late garrison. Along with quills and powdered ink. To mix the ink powder, there is fresh water from the spring tucked within the corner of the structure. Water as flowing as my flow of words.

This blockhouse is my refuge, my sanctuary, my prison. It is identical in structure and layout to the blockhouse Colonel Henry Bouquet built at Fort Pitt. To command the moat toward the Allegheny when he strengthened the fortifications there in 1764. This one built a year later to the same set of drawings. Erected to command the mouth of the Allehela River, close to where it joins with the Ohio. Five-sided, each side measuring 19-foot long. Two-storied, with a rubble masonry foundation to the height of five feet. To the first layer of squared and mortised timbers that form the musketry ports. Then red brick above to the second-floor tier of musket ports. Then the shake roof.

The plank door faces south. Toward the road leading up from the river, the outbuildings of the post scattered along the slope. The placement of the blockhouse determined in good measure by the discovery of the spring when staking the location. A spring-house to accommodate it constructed under the fifth corner of the structure. A brick cavern three steps down into shadows and coolness. Security for a long siege. Surrounding the blockhouse is a ditch 7-foot deep and 10-foot wide. Beyond which is an earthen bulwark shaped like an 8-pointed star. The 7-foot-tall glacis topped with shooting platforms sloping down to the terrain. All useless now with no one left to man the walls.

I was sent here five days ago by the present commander at Fort Pitt, Captain William Murray. To inspect these fortifications, make my recommendations on how to strengthen them. I expected to find the battlements in need of some repairs. Having weathered their first year of driving rains and heavy snows, hard freezes and sudden thaws. What I didn't expect to find was a command without its commander. A garrison of only leave-behinds. And I didn't expect to find the woman. Elizabeth.

She was tethered to a stake. In the commons between the barracks and quartermaster sheds and livestock pens. I saw her for the first time upon my arrival. As I climbed the bank after fording the river, on my way to the fort and blockhouse farther up the hill.

It had been an uneventful trip from Fort Pitt. Retracing the first 12 miles of the route Colonel Bouquet took a year and a half earlier when he led his army of Highlanders and Royal Americans into the Ohio wilderness. Taking an army where it was said no army could go. Pursuing the Delaware and Shawanese and other tribes he defeated at Bushy Run. To their villages beyond the frontier where they thought they were safe. Demanding peace and the release of their white captives. Since Bouquet's expedition the territory had been relatively safe. Though I was accompanied on my journey by an Indian guide, Turtleheart, a trustworthy Mohawk. He did not speak to me during the entire journey. Walking in silence 10 paces in front of me through the thick forest. We had started at first light, the day barely a glow in the eastern sky. Following what remained of Bouquet's road, always within sight of the Ohio River beside us through the trees. It was late afternoon as we rounded the base of a ridge. Started down the slope of the Allehela Valley. Turtleheart stopped and raised his hand. I froze, looking around wildly, musket at the ready. Unable to see anything among the darkness of the trees. After a few moments when Turtleheart hadn't moved, I walked up cautiously to join him. Through a gap in the trees we could see the buildings of the outpost below on the other side of the river, Fort Bouquet.

"What is it?" I asked quietly.

It was several moments before he responded. "Smoke. Smell it? Something burns."

I didn't smell a thing. Only my own sweat from the wool tunic. The Indian's leather hunting shirt. His strong musk. None of the buildings below were on fire, everything seemed intact. I felt foolish, sniffing the air like a dog.

"Maybe it's coming from the sawmill."

He gave a short quick snap of his head. "There is no one there, Highlander. No one works the mill. See, everyone is gone."

He was right. The place appeared deserted. No one was about, nothing stirred. Ominous.

Then the Indian shook his head again. "No. Turtleheart is wrong. Someone is there." He looked at me and smiled broadly. "The Highlanders at this place keep strange tame animals. A bitch on a lead."

"You mean like a pet?"

"Pet." He repeated the word. Nodding to himself as he put it away for future reference. I strained to see what he was talking about. The outpost still looked deathly quiet to me. Whatever it was, Turtleheart wasn't taking any chances. He led us off the trail. Picking a pathway for us through the trees and sandstone boulders the rest of the way down the hill. At the treeline on the bank of the river, Turtleheart motioned for me to stop again. We waited several moments, surveying the buildings on the other side. Up the slope. Before emerging from the dark tree cover into the glare of late afternoon sunlight.

We forded the river above the falls. The water only a few feet deep. Barely above our knees. The bottom of my kilt skimming the surface of the water. Billowing about me balloon-like. Though the dampness of the cloth, my waterlogged brogues and checkered stockings, welcome after the long march. But I felt increasingly uneasy as we climbed the opposite bank. The sawmill and bateau yard below the falls were deserted. Tools left on the ground where they had been dropped. A half-sawn tree trunk still on the cutting table. Either the outpost was kept in deplorable condition, or something had happened here. We freshly primed the firing pans of our muskets. Fanned out as we continued up the hill toward the fort. Then I noticed the woman. In the commons among the outbuildings. Sitting on the ground at the end of an 8-foot tether, her hands bound in front of her. Dressed in a simple muslin blouse and hickory cloth skirt. Both garments badly soiled and frayed. Her long hair tucked haphazardly under a drawstring bonnet. Sitting there, she worked with her teeth at the knot of the leather thong around her wrists. A sergeant carrying his musket appeared from the barracks. Talking to the woman as he crossed the grass.

"Here now, missy, we'll have no of that. Leave those knots alone or I must tie your hands behind you as before."

When he saw us approaching, he swung his musket our direction. At Turtleheart. Squinting. As if they had just wakened several dogs, mastiffs, appeared from among the sheds, hallooing. The sergeant relaxed a bit when he noticed I was with the Indian. My officer's tunic. Sent the dogs scattering before turning back to me.

"Aye, lad, would you no halloo before you come upon a man then? You half surprised this old heart to death."

"Would you no have sentries posted to tell you when someone approaches?"

The sergeant cocked his head, as if to take my measure. A slight smile playing at the corner of his mouth. Apparently bemused at something. He looked up the hill at the fort. Then back at me. Resting the butt of his musket on the ground. His hands gripped around the top of the barrel like a staff. Wagging his head as if regretful. Away from the falls of the river, I could hear a fiddle. Coming from somewhere beyond the battlements on the rise above us.

"Aye, sentries. Well now, that would be a lovely thing. . . ." He was in his forties or older. His face weathered from years of service in the colonies. His sandy sidewhiskers joined in an arc above his mouth. I trusted him at once as knowing what he was about. But I was certain he didn't trust me.

"What's going on here, Sergeant? Where is everyone? And why is this woman tied here?

"And you would be the engineer, lad, sent here to check on the fortifications?"

"I am an officer commissioned to His Majesty's 42nd Royal Highland Regiment of Foot. Ensign Thomas Keating."

The playful smile was back. But he apparently decided to go along with the young ensign before him. As the sergeant spoke, Turtleheart drifted away. Making a cautious survey of the nearby buildings.

"Sergeant Adam MacKenzie of the same. Aye, what's going on here, and where is everyone? The commander of the post, Lieutenant Stewart, has taken most of the lads upriver. Two days ago now. That morning our scouts came in with a report of a large column of smoke far up the valley, in the direction of the Onagona village 10 miles upstream. And they said they found signs of a party of warriors close to the post heading that direction. Lieutenant Stewart thought he should investigate what was going on."

"I don't know the Onagona. Have they caused trouble before?"

"Not a trace. There's only the one village, as far as I know, and they always keep to themselves. They didn't participate in Pontiac's uprising, but didn't side with the English either. Very peaceful people they are."

"Then why would warriors be headed their way?"

"The very reason why Robbie Stewart thought he should go upcountry and have a look."

"If he left two days ago, he should be back by now."

"That wee thought has occurred to me as well. Sir."

I looked to see the extent of his sarcasm. Despite the half smile under his mustache, his blue eyes were cold and deadly serious.

"How many men are with him?"

"Most of the garrison. Fourteen by count. Plus himself."

"And who is left?"

"Myself and three of the lads. The injured, and those . . . well, sir, not fit or ready for duty."

I wanted to ask him exactly what he meant but my attention was drawn again to the woman. Sitting on the ground.

"And what of her? Why is she tied there?"

"Orders of Lieutenant Stewart before he left."

I must have looked questioning at him because he went on.

"Och, a sad story it is. She turned up here a few days ago, the day our scouts saw the smoke from up the river. She wanted to see Robbie Stewart, and she wouldn't take no for an answer. I don't know what all went on between the two of them before, but she wouldn't leave when he refused to talk to her now. Then when the business with the smoke and the Onagonas started and Lieutenant Stewart said he was going to investigate, the woman said she wanted to go with him. So he told me to tie her there, in case she took it in her head to follow. 'Tis for her own good."

"Sitting there day and night?"

The sergeant seemed hurt as well as indignant. "Och, I would no do such a thing. I take the wee darling back inside every night. I fixed a room for her in one of the storage sheds. A room with a lock. I set her out here in the day to get some air."

"I'm sure the wee darling appreciates it. But release her now."

"I canna do that. Lieutenant Stewart left an order."

"Lieutenant Stewart is no here. But I am, I'm the ranking officer, and I said cut her free."

I must have made an impression of some sort. Because the sergeant nodded and said "Aye. Sir." But before either one of us could move, Turtleheart appeared behind the woman. Reached over her and cut the leather bonds with one quick motion of his hunting knife. The woman gasped. Unaware that the Indian was behind her. Spun around to face him. Turtleheart studied her. Reached out and touched a strand of her long black hair from under her bonnet. Rubbed it between his fingers as if testing its quality.

"Here now," the sergeant said. Hurrying over to her. Musket pointed.

Turtleheart smiled. At the woman. At the sergeant. Then at me. And moved away. I joined the sergeant beside the woman. Offered my hand to her.

"Allow me to help you to your feet."

She looked at my hand. Ignored it and stood on her own. "I don't need your help, if that's what you're thinking, Ensign."

The sergeant smiled in spite of himself. Walked a few paces away, looking at the hills up the valley. The woman dusted herself off. Then regarded me. She was younger than I first thought. Only in her late twenties. With fair skin toughened from exposure to the elements. Green eyes the color of the trees on the hills. I asked her name and she said Elizabeth Cawley. But she continued to stand there defiant. As if at any moment she might try to strike me.

"I told Sergeant MacKenzie to release you because I thought you were smart enough to stay close by to the post. Unlike your Lieutenant Stewart, I d'no care if you go traipsing off into the woods on your own. But before you do, I'd consider that there seems to be a large party of unknown Indians moving about out there. I'm no sure they'd welcome you with the same intention that you find here. But the choice is up to you."

My bluff apparently worked. She softened a bit. Rubbed at the marks left on her wrists from the leather bonds. But she kept her head lowered as she spoke so she didn't have to look at me. "Thank you, Ensign. But you were right in the first place. I'm smart enough to stay close to the post. On my own."

The sound of a fiddle was still drifting down from the battlements above. From near the blockhouse farther up the slope.

"Sergeant, you should introduce me to the rest of your garrison."

Sergeant MacKenzie continued to look up the valley for a moment. At the river curving out of sight among the abrupt green hills. As if trying to will Lieutenant Stewart and the others to appear. Then he sighed. Looked back at me. Cradling his musket. "Aye. It would seem we may need to know each other very well before this time is over."

I looked around for Turtleheart. But he was nowhere to be seen. Elizabeth moved off a ways. Taking up the vigil. Looking expectantly up the river. At the shadows of the valley. The distant hills darkening as the sun lowered toward evening. The sky bannered with streaks of pinks and purples. Shadows lengthening around us. I followed Sergeant MacKenzie up the hill toward the blockhouse.

The entrance to the fort was simply a cut in the embankment that surrounded it. A diagonal ramp cutting into the glacis leading up to the ramparts. Totally exposed, without so much as a wooden gate to slow an attacker's progress. I made a mental note. It would be one of the first issues I'd need to address in my assessment of how to strengthen the fortifications. The music was coming from the top of the bulwark. A private sitting crosslegged on the parapet. Fiddle propped against his chest. Head bent in concentration. His eyes, though, aware under his heavy brow. Watching us as we approached. He was working through the variations of a pibroch. A dirge usually heard on the pipes.

"Is this your sentry then, Sergeant MacKenzie?"

"Such as he is. This is Duncan Murchie. They call him Black Duncan. Or the Black Lad."

"Why do you let him play the fiddle if he is on duty? He should be keeping watch, particularly if you have bands of Indians roaming around these woods."

Murchie watched us though he didn't raise his head. Didn't stop his playing. The sergeant regarded the soldier. Listened for a moment to the keen of the lament. Before addressing me again.

"'Tis enough for me that Dunnie is here at all. That he agrees to keep the watch in any fashion."

"Agrees? He is a soldier of the King. The security of this post is—"

"The lad has the second sight. He sees things that no one else can see. And he has said he will no fight again."

I stood dumbfounded. "He will no fight? What are you talking about, Sergeant? If that's what he's said, the man should be court-martialed and flogged with six hundred lashes of the cat. Colonel Bouquet shot deserters for such an offense."

The sergeant lowered his head slightly. Regarded me with cold steady eyes. Voice barely beyond a whisper. "The lad is no deserter. He agrees to sit here and 'tis enough for me and 'tis enough for Lieutenant Stewart. And you do no evoke the name of Colonel Bouquet to me, Thomas Keating. You did no serve under Colonel Bouquet. You were no there at Bushy Run. You were no there into the Ohio, at Muskingum. As was every man at this post. As was the Black Lad here. And keep this in your mind, young ensign, no one will touch this lad for any manner as long as my lungs hold breath."

The sergeant continued to fix me with his eyes. A long moment. Then turned away. Started back down the embankment. Black Duncan watched him go from under his brow. Then abruptly stopped playing. Raised his head to look at me.

"Do you see the crows?"

"What?" I said. Still lost in the sergeant's words. Incredulous that he would say such things to an officer. With such fierceness. Incredulous now that the private was speaking to me. As if nothing had happened.

"The crows. See them there in the trees? The crows are the ones with the second sight, 'tis no me. One for sorrow, two for joy, three for a girl, four for a boy. That's the song my mother taught me. It's no quite right, the numbers aren't important, but the general idea is. There are always crows when something important is happening. They know."

I started to turn away. But he spoke again. "The crows are for you, Thomas Keating. For you and for me. They say we are going to die."

"Everyone dies, Black Duncan."

He sat listening for a moment. Listening to the crows in the trees at the edge of the clearing. Cocked his head to look up at me. His face matter-of-fact. "I may die in service to you, Thomas Keating. But you will die alone."

"And is that why you play the lament?"

He looked at the fiddle in his lap. Smiled. "Och, no. The laments are for while we are still alive. Because we have no learned enough yet."

He began to play again. Lively this time. A strathspey. The figure of the melancholy reel unwinding like thread from a spool. Then Turtleheart was there. Off to one side of the rampart. And began to dance. An Indian dance. Moccasins pounding in the dust. Arms extended like just-opened wings. Swooping and twisting about. Face rigid with concentration though his body was alive with motion. Eyes focused somewhere only he could see. I cradled my musket in my arm. Turned away. Crossed the drawbridge over the dry moat and entered the blockhouse.

While there was still light, I spent the rest of the afternoon and evening trying to acquaint myself with the fort. Its layout and garrison. The outpost where I found myself to be senior officer. In addition to Black Duncan, there were two other privates who hadn't accompanied Lieutenant Stewart on his expedition. Neil MacNeil was as fair as Duncan Murchie was dark. Sandy, curly hair, a bright eager face. Full of jokes and good cheer. MacNeil had been knifed in the leg during a skirmish after the regiment returned from the Ohio wilderness. At a time when the fighting was supposed to be over. An irony that seemed to amuse Neil MacNeil. The wound hadn't healed properly and left him with a bad limp. Donald Fraser had been kicked in the head by a horse on the return from the Muskingum. For which, as I was to learn was his nature, he blamed himself, not the horse. He continued to suffer severe headaches, and noises like screams in his head. So loud at times he said he could hear nothing else. With the rest of the garrison away, the two men took care of the animals. Pens of cows and pigs and sheep. MacNeil fulfilled the duty as his duty, with his usual good cheer. For Donald Fraser, the animals were the only company he could tolerate. After the chores were finished, he stayed the rest of the evening in the sheep or cattle pens. The animals accepting him among them. Donald Fraser sitting on the ground reading. Or holding his head. Listening to the roar and cacophony only he could hear.

I avoided Sergeant MacKenzie after our confrontation. Suspecting that he would want as little to do with me as possible. But as evening came on and sunlight drained from the valley, he sought me out. As if nothing had happened earlier between us. To let me know that the evening meal was ready. I looked for Turtleheart, but he preferred to eat alone. Squatting by himself near the treeline, roasting a rabbit he had snared over an open fire. The little garrison ate together in the barracks common room. Including the woman, Elizabeth. Before he sat down Mac-Neil loaded a plate with food and took it to Black Duncan. Still on sentry duty, such as it was, on the rampart. Mutton stew, pan-fried cornbread. Fresh greens I was told Black Duncan grew in a garden near the river. As we ate, the sergeant told me the history of the outpost. After Bouquet raised the siege of Fort Pitt in 1763, and led an army into the Ohio wilderness to set the terms for peace with the Indians and set the white captives free, he set about to strengthen the chain of forts from Philadelphia. To protect his supply line across the Alleghenies. As well as to keep track of settlers on their way to the frontier. Bouquet's treaty with the Indians kept the westward territories for the Indians. No whites were to settle beyond Fort Pitt. Accordingly, Bouquet also directed this fort and blockhouse constructed. Here at the mouth of the Allehela, 12 miles downstream from Fort Pitt. The outpost called Fort Bouquet. The surroundings sometimes referred to as Bouquet's Woods. To help make good on the treaty. To help make sure no whites settled in the area. As well as to provide an early warning. If for some reason the Indians came boiling up the Ohio River.

The Onagona, however, were never a concern. Inconceivable that they might come boiling out of the Allehela. War and aggression seemed no part of their nature. The Delawares and Shawanese called the Onagonas the "Ancient Ones." A recognition of how different the Onagona were from other tribes. The Six Nations of the Iroquois considered them either crazy or sacred. Or both. But no matter, they traditionally left them alone. The French when they inhabited the area called the chief or sachem of the Onagona Colonel Berry. A corruption of what they thought they heard when he said his name. For better or worse, the name stuck. When the Scottish soldiers erected the outpost at the mouth of the Allehela, Colonel Berry was the only one of the Onagona to make contact with them. Traveling down the valley occasionally to trade furs or food.

"The cornmeal you've been eating came from Colonel Berry," Sergeant MacKenzie said as we sat around the table afterward. The sergeant and Neil MacNeil lighting pipes. Donald Fraser had listened for a while, then headed back to the animal pens. "Berry was here only a few weeks ago," the sergeant went on. "'Tis one of the reasons Robbie Stewart thought he should go up the valley when we learned about the smoke in the direction of their village. If there was trouble, he wanted to aid him."

Elizabeth had redd the table and was cleaning up the cooking utensils and dishes. Across the room when the sergeant mentioned Lieutenant Stewart's name. She raised her head quickly and for a moment she and Sergeant MacKenzie looked at one another. She left the dishes where they were and went outside. The sergeant shook his head.

"Our lassie canna even bear to hear Robbie Stewart's name. There's something no right there. Something no right."

"Maybe it's because she's so concerned about him."

"She thinks Lieutenant Stewart is another kind of Indian," Neil MacNeil grinned through a haze of pipe smoke. "She wants a Highland lad to replace the native one she had in the woods. She wants to be his woman and follow him around."

The sergeant gave him a sharp glance. Thought about something for a moment. Spreading his fingertips across his upper lip to smooth the ends of his mustache. I asked him what MacNeil was talking about.

"Our Elizabeth was one of the captives that Colonel Bouquet freed when he took the army into the Ohio wilderness. She was married to an Indian there, some said she was married twice."

"And she didn't want to come back from there either," Neil MacNeil put in. "She wanted to stay an Indian."

"Aye, 'tis true. She fought to stay there with the Indians. Her real family, she called them. The darling even broke away twice and the lads had to go get her again. On the march back, it was Robbie Stewart who helped guard her to make sure she did no run away again."

"And her Indian husband followed her. We'd see him off there in the woods, beyond the flankers. At night he'd come into camp with fresh rabbit or deer for her. Robbie, Lieutenant Stewart, let them sit together sometimes in the evenings."

Sergeant MacKenzie nodded. Stoked his pipe. "The Indian stayed with her all the way back to Fort Pitt, but then the other whites threatened to kill him and he disappeared again. It was then she started to be around Robbie Stewart all the time."

"They said she married the second Indian husband when her first one died. She was probably looking for a new husband again," MacNeil said.

"That's enough talk of Lieutenant Stewart now. Until he comes back again."

"Do you think he will come back, Sergeant?" I asked.

The sergeant looked at me through narrow eyes for a moment. Before he spoke to MacNeil. "Aye, Private, it's time for you to relieve Black Duncan on the rampart. That's a good lad now."

MacNeil's face lost some of its usual cheerfulness at being cut out of the discussion. But he gathered up his flint and tobacco and left the room. His injured leg dragging. When he was gone, the sergeant looked back at me.

"I d'no want to have that talk in front of any of the lads."

"I understand. Though I'm sure they've thought of it themselves."

"They are soldiers of the King, and what's more, Highland soldiers. You canna know what they think."

From his expression, it was apparent the remark wasn't about the secret thoughts of Highland soldiers. It was at my personal inability to understand them. The first time I had a glimmer that Sergeant MacKenzie's chariness of me might have something to do with more than my age or inexperience with the regiment. But I let it pass for the time being.

"If it's been two and a half days now since you've had any word of Lieutenant Stewart and his men, we have to face the possibility that they've run into serious trouble."

"Och, you think I d'no know that, man?" The sergeant slammed his fist down on the plank table, making the tankards and silverware jump. He stepped free of the bench and went to the window. Staring out at the distant cut in the hills. "I should no have let him go up the valley without me. If we d'no hear anything tomorrow, I'm going up there myself and find out what's going on."

"With all due respect, Sergeant, I d'no think one man would make much difference. If Lieutenant Stewart and his men have stepped into harm's way."

The sergeant came back and stood across the table, looking at me with flat blue eyes, his voice almost a whisper. "One man might no help Robbie Stewart and the lads. But it would help me."

"I canna allow you to do that, Sergeant. You're too important here. If we d'no hear anything tomorrow, we'll send a message to Fort Pitt requesting reinforcements and then send a company of men upcountry to find Lieutenant Stewart. We'll need reinforcements here regardless, if the Indians are rising up again."

"That could take three or four days before reinforcements get here. It would be too late."

I stood up from the table. To meet his eyes at his level. To let him know the discussion was finished. "Sergeant, you know as well as I do, if we d'no hear from Lieutenant Stewart by tomorrow, the chances are it's already too late."

It was evening. The valley plunged into deep shadow. Though the sky above the valley's hills retained an afterglow, a richer blue. A sense that light still existed somewhere in the world. Somewhere, but not here. Across the slope of the settlement, fireflies lifted from the grass. Tiny miracles, stars come to earth. An occasional candle-lantern moved among the buildings as the men finished the chores of the day. Elizabeth made ready for the night. A surprising chill in the evening air. Reminder that winter wasn't that far behind, that summer was still ahead. The garrison, if you could call it that, had continued to sleep in the barracks after Lieutenant Stewart took the rest of the men up the valley. Privates MacNeil and Fraser dividing sentry duty between them on the ramparts of the fort through the night, Black Duncan taking sentry duty through the day. With the probability that Stewart had encountered trouble, and signs that bands of warriors were moving in the woods, I made a command decision. Instructed Sergeant MacKenzie to move everyone into the blockhouse overnight.

"Aye, and what of the sentries then?"

"There is no need of anyone. If we're attacked, I'm sure we'll know soon enough. And this way all the men will get a good night's rest. We need to be on the alert now."

"And the woman?"

"She'll sleep on the second floor. The men will sleep on the first. Have one of the men help her move her bedding and the cooking utensils. We'll all move into the blockhouse until we learn one way or the other about Lieutenant Stewart."

The sergeant wouldn't admit it, but it was apparent he thought it a good idea. As he went to instruct the men, I went to find Turtleheart. He was still up the hill, squatting close to the treeline. The butt of his musket planted on the ground between his legs, his cheek resting against the upraised barrel. When I told him of my plan and that he should join us, he shook his head. The pendants dangling from his ears rattling softly.

"Turtleheart will take his chances in the woods. I will have more corners to hide in than you."

He grinned and I realized he was making what he thought was a joke. But the fact that he didn't want to join us gave me a moment of doubt. For some reason, having traveled here with the man, I felt I could trust him. That there was some sort of bond between us. "Do you think it's a bad idea, moving into the blockhouse?"

The question, or that I would ask it of him, seemed to surprise him. He studied me closely in the gloom. "No one can tell you what will happen, Highlander. About anything in this world."

He rose to his feet in one smooth motion and moved off into the trees. Becoming a shade among shades. Then was gone. I fought the urge to hurry, to run, as I returned to the blockhouse to join the others.

Now it is close to that time of evening again. As I sit here and write this, the sky is still light above the dark hills. A glow seeps through the gunports. Enough light to dimly see the interior of the blockhouse around me. This five-sided room, the paper where I write. For a moment I leave my writing instruments on my barrel-desk and stand at the gunports. Looking out. Fireflies once again lift from the grass, the dark line of trees at the edge of the clearing. But no candle-lanterns move among the buildings as they did a few days ago. I make a tour of the musket ports around the perimeter of the room. Looking for movement, signs of life among the piles of charred logs and ashes, the few buildings that still stand, the remains of the outbuildings of this post.

Then I go up the twisty wooden stairs to the second floor. Repeating the exercise at the gunports. Searching the slits of landscape, only a more encompassing view, elevated. The panoramas of the surrounding hills. The river winding out of sight in the dusk deeper into the valley. I had realized something while I was writing. I had grown used to the stillness without the lowing of the cattle calling to be milked. The voices of the sheep and pigs in their pens that we heard when we returned from up the valley. Before the Indians slaughtered them or took them away. But now the barking of the dogs is stilled too. The dogs of the outpost that had continued to run free among the buildings while we holed up here in the blockhouse. Now there is only the sound of the crickets in the grass. The wrens and finches in the trees. The distant call of the crows, always the crows. They must have driven off the dogs, or slaughtered them as well. Ate them, after roasting them over slow fires. . . .

My mind drifts, returning to the stories I have heard since I came to this wilderness. The story of Lieutenant Gordon. At Fort Venango. A blockhouse surrounded by fortifications, very much like this one. The story of how the Indians gained entrance to the fort. Pretending to be on a friendly mission. Simply walked in, and before the garrison knew what was happening, closed the gates behind them and slaughtered everyone inside. Everyone, except for Gordon. First making him write down the grievances they dictated to him. Then, slowly, over several nights, tortured him. Burned him over a low fire. Roasted him alive. But not too quickly. Cutting chunks from his flesh and eating them in front of him. Keeping him alive on purpose. To draw it out as long as possible. Until he mercifully died. . . .

I cannot think such things. I will not now. I hurry back down the steps and drag my humble desk and writing instruments close to the wall. To catch the last glow of the day from the gunports. To put down here one last thought before the room goes black around me. A memory of that first day when I arrived here at this outpost. A memory of Elizabeth.

I joined the men that first night here in the blockhouse. Our bedrolls spaced around the walls to help us hear if anyone moved outside. But I could not sleep. I lay on the floor in the darkness of this room, looking up at the lighter darkness of the row of gunports. A chain of dark sky. A necklace of stars. Listening to the men snuffling in their sleep. Breathing in the darkness. As if the blockhouse itself were breathing. Straining to hear the slightest sound from outside. Wondering how they could sleep at a time like this. In the presence of such danger. To ease my own uneasiness, I repeated their names to myself. Adam MacKenzie. Duncan Murchie. Neil MacNeil. Donald Fraser. So that I would be sure to know them in the days to come, these men whose fate I now shared. Whose lives had become tied to mine. Mine to theirs. An invocation of sorts. An involuntary litany.

Unable to bear it longer, I got up. Intending to look out the ports to see if I could see anything stirring among the buildings on the slope below. Moonlight filtered through our quarters in a blue-black haze. My eyes gradually adjusted to the gloom. I could make out the huddled forms of the men wrapped in their plaids along the walls. In the half-light their faces glowed with a deathly pallor, waxen. I was concerned to stand too close to the walls, for fear of disturbing the men in their rest. I decided to try the second floor. Slowly eased my way up the wooden steps.

The second floor of the blockhouse was nearly empty of stores. Only a few barrels of powder brought here earlier in the evening in case we needed them for an attack. A supply of paper cartridges and extra flints. Elizabeth curled among her blankets in the center of the room. I moved quietly to the row of gunports and viewed the night outside. The buildings on the slope below the fortifications in the bluish darkness. A slice of moonlight on the river. The blue-black wall of the valley's hills. In one pen the ridged backs of the cattle. In another, clouds of sheep. Something moved in the shadow beside the barracks. Moved stealthily across the open area toward a storage shed. But it was only a small animal. Fox.

"I'm not the regimental whore, if that's why you're up here, Ensign," the woman said behind me.

I turned to look at her in the darkness of the room. She had raised up on an elbow from her bedding on the floor. Her black hair tumbled to one side of her face. Her breasts loose, without stays, beneath her shift.

"I did no think you were. I could no sleep."

"Because it could seem that, I know. But I'm not. Your whore."

"I came up for a look at the outbuildings. To see if anyone was about."

She lay back down and appeared to stare at the ceiling. Her bare arms folded outside her blanket. Her sun-darkened skin glowing in the faint moonlight. I started to turn back to the gunports when she said, "I remember you, Ensign. From Fort Pitt."

"Yes. I thought it was you. That night outside Suckie Sly's. In the lower town. It was dark that night, I was no sure. . . ."

"Yes. It was me." She thought a moment. "That night wasn't what it seemed either. I didn't want you to think. . . ." She left it unfinished.

"I did no think anything. Then or now."

"Och," she said dismissively. "I'm sure you have your thoughts."

"If it concerns you, sometime you can tell me what did go on that night."

"I would, if I thought you'd listen."

"I would listen."

She spoke again quickly. Still looking away from me at the ceiling, but as though the thought was on her mind all along. "Did Sergeant MacKenzie say what Indians made the tracks the scouts found in the woods?"

"No. I d'no think he knows. He would have said when he—"

"They are Huron."

"How do you know?"

"The sergeant will go after Lieutenant Stewart. There will be no way to stop him, I know that about him. And because he'll go, the men will go with him. That means you'll have to go as well. You'll have to lead them." She raised up on her elbow again. Looking at me across the darkness of the room. "You must promise to take me with you."

"No one's going after Lieutenant Stewart. Not if I give the order not to."

"Don't fool yourself, Ensign. Sergeant MacKenzie will only follow the orders from you that he would issue himself. You may wear the same tartan, but he breathes the difference."

"What difference? What are you talking about?"

"Be mindful of what I say. And be mindful of Sergeant MacKenzie." She lay back down. Looking at the darkness of the ceiling above her, as if she had nothing more to say. I started for the steps, but she added in a softer voice, almost as if speaking from another time, "You were kind to me that night outside Suckie Sly's. At a time few people showed me kindness. Now I have to ask you one more kindness, that you take me with you when you go after Lieutenant Stewart."

I didn't answer. I continued down the steps to the lower floor. The musket ports now aglow with moonlight. As I passed where Sergeant MacKenzie lay, I saw his eyes were open in the darkness. Watching me to my bed.

The man stops reading and rubs his eyes with the stumps of his arms. "'Tis no like any Orderly Book I've ever seen. This Keating, a regular storyteller he is." Then he looks at her. "I'm guessing this woman must be your mother. Are you sure you want me to keep reading?"

"Why wouldn't I?"

"I've got to go relieve myself."

Sara sits for a few moments at the table, thinking about the story, then realizes she should take advantage of the break as well. She goes across the little footbridge over the stream and down the bank, squatting out of sight of the buildings. When she comes back, he is at the table again, a bucket of water with a dipper beside him to ease his throat.

"Because," he says as she gets settled, picking up the thread of his earlier remark, "you may no be as ready as you think you are to learn what you're going to about this woman."

"What is it that you think I'm going to learn?"

He doesn't answer. He takes a sip of water, contorting himself as he manipulates the dipper between his forearms, clears his throat, spreads the book open again, holding down the pages with his stumps against an occasional breeze, and begins to read again.

A Book of Days

Day the Second

In my dream, they are out there. There is nothing I can do. Nothing I can do to stop the Indians from entering the blockhouse. I latch the door with the heavy timber. Drag a plank table across the room to place against it. Pile in front of the door boxes of supplies, barrels of gunpowder and flour. Even the barrel I have been using as my desk. But to no avail. The Indians sweep it all aside. Burst through the door as if there is nothing there and grab me. I struggle against them. Try to pull away. But they are too strong for me. They have me by my arms. Drag me outside into the glaring light of midday. Yelling their hideous war cries. I look in their eyes and see sheer joy. Not an ounce of pity. Total rapture at my terror. The paralyzing fear that engulfs me. I am dragged to their village where everyone turns out to see their latest victim. The day's excitement and enjoyment. An entertainment only. Nothing human. The crowd surges forward. Strikes at me. Spits on me. Poking me with sticks. The whole time laughing and encouraging each other. The women issuing piercing trebling cries. Then the women grab me and pull me into their own circle. Strip my uniform and kilt from me. Stand me in the middle of their circle. Laughing at my nakedness. My fear. Then I am on the ground. They are attacking me with needle-like splinters. Piercing my arms and legs. My testicles and penis. My screams of pain only making them laugh and enjoy themselves the more. Stake me spreadeagled on the ground. And I think they can do no more to me. Think that I have reached the barrier where pain cannot increase. I do not even feel the point of the knife that slices into my wrists, my ankles, my thighs. I am only vaguely aware of the laughing naked man painted half-red, half-black who bends over me. With meticulous care he separates a tendon in my wrist from the bone. Slices it and wraps the end of the sickeningly white fibrous cord around a stick. And pulls. Rips the tendon and muscle from within my arm. Repeats the operation on my other arm. My shoulders. Legs. Severing the ligaments as he goes. Leaving me only a gelatinous mass. The women cut me free from the stakes and giggle. Kick at me. Roll me this way and that over the ground. A bag of loose bones. Now I have traveled far beyond the realm of human care and regard. Into a land where there is pain and only pain and nothing but pain. Nothing more to fear. I wake drenched in sweat. Tangled in my plaid. Afraid that I have screamed out loud. That someone has heard me. Discovering to my joy that I can still lift my hand. Move my fingers. That I am still whole. Still alive. . . .

That morning we ate in the blockhouse. Sitting around on barrels and crates, our plates balanced on our knees. The light of the open doorway the only illumination. A breakfast of jerked beef and cheese and leftover cornbread. Before the men dispersed to go about their duties. Sergeant MacKenzie said little to me. Made no mention of my wanderings in the night. Nor of his own wakefulness. Neither did Elizabeth give any indication of our late-night encounter. She in fact seemed to take special care to ignore me. To not show that anything had ever passed between us. She would not look at me as she served the food. Kept her eyes lowered as she sat across from me. When the others left, I lingered a few moments as she straightened things. I was curious if her attitude would change. If she would say anything more to me if no one else was around. I noticed that today she wore tall Indian moccasins under her skirt and petticoats—the day before she wore buckled shoes. I wondered if she often wore the moccasins. If she had grown used to them during the time she was a captive. Or if there was another reason she chose to wear them now. I was also aware, after having seen her in her shift in the middle of the night, that she did not wear stays under her blouse during the daytime. Like the loose women I had seen in the lower regions of Edinburgh and London. Or the Indian women she had lived with for so many years. As she leaned to retrieve a knife, she caught me looking at the open neck of her blouse. Only then did a slight smile play across her lips. A faint sign of recognition flicker in her eyes. But they were gone just as quickly. She turned away, presenting only her back to me. After a few more moments, I left the dark musty interior of the blockhouse. Stepped out into the day.

Morning sunlight had just cracked above the hills farther up the river. Splintering down through the silhouettes of trees along the ridgeline into the valley. In a delicate blue sky as crystalline as water, an eagle hung suspended. Hovering motionless above the river. Watching for anything that moved. From the forest surrounding the outpost came the sounds of birds and animals I had never heard before. In an endless land I never could have imagined. A land where to reach a promontory meant only the ability to see more hills. More forests. Stretching away forever. Before, in the travels of my young life, there had always been a definition to the land. A destination to a journey. A *there* to reach from a *here*. But in the land America, there was nothing beyond the treeline of the frontier. Nothing and everything. On the edge of this limitless wilderness, there was not the sense of a continent of solid possibilities before me. Rather, I was standing on the brink of a leafy void. A green emptiness. Ready to swallow up anything that strayed. That stayed too long within it. Absorb it like a fallen log digested into the forest floor. Though the morning was bright and warm, a chill ran through me. I did not like to think that it could be fear.

I was wakened from my thoughts by Black Duncan. Coming up the hill from the river with his fiddle. On the way to his vigil on the embankment wall. As he approached, he said, "They were here last night."

"Who was? How do you know?"

He looked at me from under his dark brow. Grinned. "'Tis not the second sight this time, Ensign. You can see for yourself."

He nodded toward the buildings farther down the slope and continued on to the ramparts. I hurried down the hill. Found Sergeant MacKenzie and Neil MacNeil looking at something on the ground behind the blacksmith shop. At their feet was one of the mastiffs that had come over the mountains with the regiment years before. The dog's throat had been ripped open. Its blood soaked into the ground around the body.

"I d'no hear anything last night. Did you?" MacNeil was saying to the sergeant as I joined them.

"And what of you, Ensign Keating? Perhaps you had the occasion to hear something in the night," the sergeant said. Turning his gaze steadily upon me.

"I had the occasion to see a fox around the barracks," I said, trying to come back at him in kind. "I d'no hear or see anything else."

Neil MacNeil wagged his head. "It would take more than a fox I think to kill a dog like that. A bear, maybe, or a lion. . . ."

"Och, it was a human animal that did this, and that's the truth of it. Poor beastie never had a chance. She was gentle as a newborn lamb, for all the size of her."

"But whoever did this would no know that about her, would they now?" MacNeil said. "They'd only see this great lumbering beast coming at them in the dark."

"Aye, the darling was probably only trying to lick him hello when the bastard slit her throat."

"It would explain why the other dogs did no raise more of a kafuffle," MacNeil said, looking around. The other dogs of the post were keeping their distance from the scene. "Once they saw what happened to this one, they ran."

Sergeant MacKenzie continued to keep his eyes on me. Unconvinced about something. Or expecting something. I decided I needed to exert my presence as senior officer.

"Are there any other signs that someone was about? Anything missing?"

Neil MacNeil started to speak. But the sergeant interrupted him. "No a thing. I had a walk around myself. There's no a hair out of place. It must have been someone passing through in the night. Some renegade settler perhaps who knew he was no supposed to be in the area in the first place. He got afraid the beastie would attack him so he attacked it first, and that was the end of it. He went on about his way. I would no concern yourself about it further, Ensign."

Now I was the one unconvinced. The sergeant seemed too willing to slough it away. On the ground the carcass had attracted clouds of flies. Maggots squirmed in the open wound. A trail of ants led into the dog's nostrils. I looked away, back at the sergeant.

"Nonetheless, I think we need to be on our guard more than ever. Something is going on in these woods, and we have no a clue what it is. Make sure the men carry their muskets with them and that they're primed at all times."

The sergeant started to say something but I cut him off. "And let's get this body out of here. Before it starts to smell. Aye, Sergeant?"

The sergeant cocked his head at me. As if he wanted to give argument about something. Then thought better of it. He nodded to MacNeil and each took a back leg. Dragging the body across the yard to the waste pit. Not wanting to continue the discussion with the sergeant, I went in search of Turtleheart. If someone had been around in the night, I thought the guide might have seen or heard something. Perhaps had some idea who it could be.

I went up the slope past the fort. To the place where I talked with Turtleheart the night before. But now there was no sign of him. The ashes in the fire pit where he roasted a rabbit were cold.

The grass where he had squatted to keep watch on the outpost below had straightened again. I stood at the edge of the treeline. Where I had seen him disappear the evening before. Peering inside as if into a great room. Morning sunlight slanted down through the deep leaf-cover overhead as if through clerestory windows, the columns of the massive tree trunks filed away up the slope. Becoming one with the shadows and the bluffs farther up the hillside. But there was no one there. Not that I could see. It occurred to me that, if someone were there, I was a perfect target. Standing there silhouetted against the light of the clearing behind me. I did not risk calling out for Turtleheart. For fear of drawing attention to him or to me, if an enemy was watching. I turned back down the hill. Stopped at the blockhouse to get my own musket. Before returning to the outbuildings below. On the ramparts, Black Duncan was again sitting crosslegged with his fiddle. This time playing "The Lads with the Kilts."

"Where's your musket, Private? I gave the order to Sergeant MacKenzie that everyone on the post was to be under arms."

"Sergeant Mackenzie was here and told me," the Black Lad said. He continued to play, the fiddle braced against his chest.

"Then where is it? Stop your playing and get your weapon. That's an order."

Black Duncan stopped playing and looked at me. Not with deference, or anger. But with sadness.

"I will no carry your firearm, Ensign. Because I will no use it. I told Sergeant MacKenzie that and I told Lieutenant Stewart that and now I will tell you that. And d'no bother to threaten me with the cat or court-martial or the like. I d'no care. I will be dead before the cat or noose can touch me, so it does no matter. I will sit here and try to help you by keeping the watch. But I canna do more than that."

He looked at me with genuine regret. I found I had no answer for him. No response. I turned away and headed down the ramp, the road toward the river. Black Duncan began to play again, "All the Blue Bonnets Are Over the Border." This time, the beat of the march in time with my footsteps. I stopped and looked back up at the ramparts at him. He stopped playing and saluted me with the bow. As I continued down the hill, he started to play again. The tune in time with my footsteps again. Until I was out of his sight among the outbuildings. My face stinging as if I had been shamed.

I decided if, as it appeared, I lacked as a commander of men, I could at least fulfill the job I had been sent to do. That of an engineer. But I needed a helper. Rather than confront Sergeant MacKenzie again, I determined to get one on my own. Went in search of Donald Fraser. I found him in the pen with the cattle. Cleaning out the dung and spreading fresh straw. He was in his shirtsleeves. Waistcoat draped over the fence rail along with his haversack. Musket propped nearby. Sticking out from the haversack was the edge of a book.

"Are you a reader then, Private?"

"Aye, that I am."

"May I have a look?"

He shrugged and nodded. Continued on with his work. It was a collection of essays by David Hume.

"A weighty book, I would say. For a man employed as you."

"D'you think such subjects are only for the likes of gentlemen and ensigns then?"

"You misunderstand me," I said, leafing through the pages. Engulfed for a moment in memories. "I was referring to the disagreeable work you're doing at the moment, no to your intellectual abilities."

"Aye, the work is no bad, for a' that. 'Beauty in things exists in the mind which contemplates them.'"

He did not look at me as he said it. But I could tell he was proud of himself. For working in a quotation from Hume. A kind of test for me, I supposed.

"It is undoubtedly whatever one gets used to," I said, replacing the book in his haversack. "'Custom is the great guide of human life.'"

He stopped and rested a moment. Leaned on the handle of the pitchfork. Having recognized the statement from Hume's *Enquiry Concerning Human Understanding*. He kept his head at an angle. As if looking at me from under a shelf. Because of his headaches I supposed. His eyes squinty with the constant pain. Sweat ran from his mass of dark hair. Either from his exertions or his pain or both. His lips cracked and parched as if from a fever. "So you know the man's work, do you?"

"Perhaps no as well as you. But I have studied him, yes. And I had the opportunity to speak with him a few times. A friend of a friend, when I was at university."

"Aye? In Edinburgh? I never had the chance at schooling myself. But my family were readers and I like what the man says about the world, and that's a fact. And 'tis a comfort to me at times, to hear a voice from home even on a page in the middle of this dismal wilderness. Sometime I'd like for you to tell me the cut of Mr. Hume and what you talked about."

"We'll do that. But right now I need your assistance. To help me take some measurements. Are you as good with numbers as you are with ideas of human understanding?"

He hesitated a moment, then came over closer to the fence. Looking around to see if anyone was about. Wincing when he turned his head too quickly. "I would be glad to help you with your measurements. Sir. But know you, I was told no to speak with you."

"Who told you that?"

"Sergeant MacKenzie. When I talked to him before breakfast. He said he did no want any of us talking with you, more than we had to."

"And did the sergeant say why he did no want you talking with me?"

"Aye. That he did, sir. But I d'no think I care to tell you."

"And suppose I order you to tell me? With the promise that if you d'no tell me, I'll remove you from taking care of the animals. I can do that, you know. I am ranking officer here."

Donald Fraser looked alarmed at the very mention of the prospect. I disliked having to threaten him so. But I was certain there was no other way to get the information from him. It took a moment for the man to work up his courage. To tell me what I asked.

"The sergeant said that he did no want to bother the wee man with trifles he would no understand. Those were his words, and that's a fact."

I could feel myself color at the words *wee man*. But I worked hard to keep my composure in front of the private. Forced a smile.

"And what exactly were the 'trifles' that he did no want to tell the 'wee man'?"

His tongue ran across his cracked lips. "Two sheep are missing."

"Are you sure?" It was a foolish question. I realized the moment I said it.

"Of course I am sure. I know my animals. And the pen was damaged and you can see where they dragged them away."

I thought for a moment. Why would Sergeant MacKenzie want to keep such information from me? It meant the sergeant had lied to me. When I asked him earlier if there were signs that anyone was about in the night. And why wouldn't he want the men talking to me? I wondered what MacKenzie was up to. If I could trust him at all.

"Well, Private Fraser, thank you for telling me. I w'no let on that you told me anything."

"It would be appreciated. The sergeant is a good sergeant, but he is no the man to cross."

"I will deal with Sergeant MacKenzie. And I see no problem with you assisting me in my work. We will say it is an order, and that you believed you would face the cat if you refused."

"Aye, that's the way of it then," Donald Fraser said. Rested the handle of the fork against the fence. Put on his waistcoat, gathered up his musket and haversack. "Mr. Hume also says that a wise man proportions his belief to the evidence. And I believe the evidence in this case is that I have no choice. What is it you want me to do?"

I led the private back up the hill to the fortifications. I did not have my transit and other proper surveyor's tools with me. But I did have a measuring chain. With Donald Fraser holding the one end, I set about to make some preliminary measurements and calculations. First for the gate I thought necessary at the entrance to the bastion. Then we began to document some of the damage the embankments had suffered over the fall and winter of the past year. My recommendations for repairs. It was pleasant work. Once I was engaged with the problems involved, I was in my element. Felt more like myself. The sun was full in the sky by this time. The June morning warm and bright. Green, everywhere green, a hundred shades. The forests on the hillside. The hills of the valley. The land seemed an Eden of peacefulness. The songs of the birds. Blue jays, cardinals, finches. English robins, like at home. The murmur of the falls of the river. I had to remind myself of the dangers around us. That a detachment of men had disap-peared into this wilderness. Swallowed up without a trace. The same for my guide Turtleheart. That bands of Indians, perhaps hostiles, roamed these woods. Perhaps had visited our outpost in the night. That the collection of misfits and cripples left at this outpost was totally incapable of defending it.

As I took my measurements and wrote them in my notebook, Donald Fraser and I said little to each other. Black Duncan continued to sit on the edge of the ramparts with his fiddle. This morning favoring quick marches and reels. "We Will Take the Good Old Way." "The Brown-Haired Maiden." "I Am a Poor Man." After a time, I sent the Black Lad down the hill. To take up his watch closer to the bank of the river. Giving as my reason that Fraser and I were on the embankment and could keep watch as long as we were there. Duncan would have a better view below of anyone coming down the valley. The truth was, however, that I had some further questions to ask of Donald Fraser. I was afraid he wouldn't answer them if anyone else was around. If he thought there was a possibility of such discussions getting back to Sergeant MacKenzie. I was greatly bothered that the sergeant had lied to me about the missing sheep. Tried to lessen that someone had been around the outpost in the night. Seemed to be trying to protect something or someone. I wanted to try to find out what or whom it might be. I sat on the edge of the embankment to make a few sketches in my notebook. Fraser sat near me. Bent over, elbows propped on his knees. Resting his head in his hands. I waited several moments. Continued to work on a drawing. Before I spoke to him.

"Your headache is back, Donald Fraser?"

"Och, my headache is always, Ensign. I wish the horse that kicked me had finished the job when it had the chance and put me out of my misery."

I continued to sketch, not looking at him, as I said, "How long have you been at this outpost?"

"Since it was built. They sent me here to take care of the animals. Because I'm no much good these days for anything else. Lieutenant Stewart asked for me when they assigned him here.

But I think it was more from Robbie Stewart's pity than anything else."

"Yet, you are good with the animals. And he must have known that."

"Aye, I am that. And always have been. Long before the pain came upon me. It was no the horse's fault that kicked me. The poor darlin' was spooked by a rattlesnake. I was fool enough to get in the way of its hooves while trying to protect itself."

"Lieutenant Stewart sounds like he was a good leader of men."

"Is." Fraser ran his tongue across his cracked lips. "We should no say 'he was' and tempt Fate until we know for sure. He *is* a good leader of men."

I continued sketching. Not looking at him. "And how did Robbie Stewart and Sergeant MacKenzie get along? Any rough roads between them, do you know?"

"They got along fine, they did." He fell silent. Waited until I raised my head to see why he didn't say anything further. "Excuse my saying so, sir," he went on. "But if you have something to ask me about Lieutenant Stewart or Sergeant MacKenzie or whatever, you should just out with it. I am no good these days at the dance around."

I hoped my cheeks hadn't colored. That my intentions were so obvious. I paused a moment to get my thoughts in order. "I need to know more of what happened. Why Lieutenant Stewart decided to take the men up the valley, rather than send his scouts. Or why he did no send for reinforcements from Fort Pitt before venturing upcountry. And I need to know why Sergeant MacKenzie is trying to keep me out of things now."

Donald Fraser held his head in his hands. Rubbing his temples as if to wring the noises and pain from his skull. Before looking at me again.

He told me he thought the reason Lieutenant Stewart went up the valley had to do with the visit they had a few weeks earlier from the sachem of the Onagonas. The chief they called Colonel Berry. The same visit when Colonel Berry brought the cornmeal we had at dinner the night before. Colonel Berry came to the outpost to tell Lieutenant Stewart that the Onagona were preparing to leave the valley. Continuing a migration their ancestors had started generations earlier, heading somewhere to the west. The chief told Stewart that he feared for the safety of his people. The other tribes had threatened to massacre the Onagona if they tried to leave.

"Why would the other tribes do such a thing?" I asked.

"Because the Onagona are the Ancient Ones, the other tribes consider them sacred. The keepers of the spiritual heart of the land, they are. The other tribes would rather have them dead in this place than move away to someplace else. At least then the Onagonas' spirit would remain here."

"Did he expect Stewart to protect the Onagona?"

"Aye, 'twould seem so." Donald Fraser squinted up at the sun overhead. As if to blame it for its brightness, before continuing. His tongue trying to moisten his damaged lips.

"'Twould seem Colonel Berry hoped our Lieutenant Stewart would give them safe passage through the Ohio territory. Past the villages where the Delaware and Shawanese are living now. But of course Lieutenant Stewart could no do that. It would take another army the size of Bouquet's to get the Onagona through, if all the other tribes took it in their heads to attack them."

"And you think that's why Stewart took the men up the valley?"

"The man was no in the habit of telling me what a lieutenant thinks or why he does what he does. But aye, 'twould seem to be the way of it. When the scouts saw the smoke up the valley and found the tracks in the woods, Robbie Stewart thought the Onagona must be under attack. There was no time to send to Fort

Pitt for reinforcements. If he was going to help the Onagona, he needed to get there as quickly as possible."

"It's commendable, no doubt. But rash for all that, would you no say? What could fifteen men do against a large war party?"

Donald Fraser looked at me, his hands on his temples framing his face. "You did no ask me if I thought he should have gone. Only why he did."

"How do you know so much of why he did then?"

"I was there, when Colonel Berry and the lieutenant had their talk. Och, I have said too much already. You must excuse me, Ensign. I can no more."

It did not add up to me. Was the lieutenant that conscientious? That he thought he should go to the aid of the Onagona, even if it meant risking his command, the lives of his men? Or was he that foolhardy, to think himself invincible? From all I had heard at Fort Pitt, Lieutenant Stewart was more intelligent than that. A more intelligent soldier. Donald Fraser's reason for the lieutenant's actions was essentially the same as the one given by Sergeant MacKenzie. And would explain why the sergeant was trying to keep the details of the expedition from me. Trying to protect his lieutenant, to keep what had happened from the command at Fort Pitt. To keep Stewart from reprimand. If by some chance the lieutenant was still alive.

I had finished my sketches. The repairs necessary to the northwest bastion and my preliminary drawings for the new gate. Talking to Donald Fraser had raised as many questions as it had answered. But I thought it unwise to try to pursue the topic with him further, demand answers as an officer. All it would do was further alienate him from me. Entrench him against me. And I sensed I would need as many contacts and supporters among the men as I could secure. Before this was over. I led the way around the ramparts to continue our work through the morning. This time on the southwest bastion that had washed away badly in the spring rains. Due to a poor arrangement of the sods facing the earth wall. Toward midday we stopped again while I made new sketches. Donald Fraser falling asleep with his back against the wall of the firing platform. I suppose I should have wakened the private. Reprimanded him for napping while on duty. But I took pity on him. Decided to let him rest. Apparently discipline at this outpost had its own customs and order. It wasn't worth another confrontation with Sergeant MacKenzie.

The truth was I welcomed some time alone. Without having to make responses. Without having to give orders or directions. I carried my notebook a ways along the rampart. Sat on the edge of the grassy embankment near the entrance through the glacis. A view of the outbuildings farther down the hill toward the river. Enjoying the beauty of the day. The peace. Processions of clouds, like squadrons of tall ships, moved stately across the sky. Edge to edge above the cut of the valley. The forest of the hillsides under the midday sun sparkling green. Within the forest, it was always dark. Or at least muted, sunlight barely able to wedge through the thick layers of leaves high overhead. A shadow world. An underworld. As if underwater, underground. Where life moved in silence and shade, with dangers and rules all its own. But looking at it from without, the layers of green on green were puffy and inviting. The outlines of the hills as rounded as a woman.

Below the fortifications among the outbuildings, Elizabeth had strung a line between the wall of the barracks and one of the storage sheds. Nearby a tub sat on a stool. I watched as she filled the tub with buckets of water from a stream that ran down the hill toward the river. Watched as she washed some of her articles of clothing in the tub. Hung them on the line to dry. Watched the way she moved. Remembering the maid at my grandparents' house washing clothes in a tub. Hanging them to dry in the closed backyard at the house in Perth. Remembering Jean walking along the narrow cobbled streets below the castle in Edinburgh. Her skirt and petticoats swinging as she walked. Canting back and forth, like the toll of a silent bell. Wearing her beloved tricorn hat.

Elizabeth was in a shift the color of rust, open in front over her several petticoats. A large white apron. Her bonnet perched on the back of her head. A few times she turned and looked up the hill in my direction. But I thought nothing of it. Only that she must be looking at the hills behind the fort, the sunlight on the forests. The mild spring day. I didn't suppose she noticed me sitting there. So I was surprised when, after gazing up the hill for a few moments, she left her washing. Started up the hill toward the fort and blockhouse. Toward the top of the embankment where I was sitting. Looking up at me looking down at her. As she came along the ramparts, she seemed pleased with herself about something. The sharer of some common knowledge. Her petticoats whispered as she walked. Her moccasins silent. I stood as she approached, though my puzzlement was obvious to her.

"I thought as long as you're going to watch me, Ensign, you might as well do it at close range."

"What makes you think I was watching you?" I said, thinking she referred to guarding her. Keeping watch on her so she didn't try to run away.

"You shouldn't try to deny it. I saw you as plain as day. I saw the way you watched me at breakfast too. You couldn't keep your eyes off me."

I realized she was talking about something quite different than guarding her. I felt foolish. And angry.

"D'no flatter yourself, madam. If I was looking in your direction, it was only because you reminded me of someone else. I would have no reason to look at you in such a manner."

If she was embarrassed, or taken aback, she didn't show it. She laughed a little, a kind of scoff. Then looked away, out at the river and the valley. Keeping her dignity. "If that is true, then she must have been an exceptional woman. To attract your attention so."

"Aye. That she was. She was bonnie."

She smiled to herself about something. "Then I shouldn't be bothering you. You and your reveries," she said, gathering her skirts and turning to leave.

"No, wait," I said. Before I realized I was going to say it. She looked back at me, and I was struck again by her eyes. Green, like emeralds. Set wide in her face. As if she were more aware of what went on in the world around her. "I mean, you can stay if you like. I mean, you d'no have to go. . . ."

Now she was smiling openly at me. My confusion in trying to explain myself amusing her. Though in sympathy, as a friend or companion would.

"I didn't mean to interrupt you. Or presume upon your good nature."

"I d'no know anything about my good nature. I was only finishing up some sketches, while my assistant gets a little rest." She followed my eyes to where I was looking. At Donald Fraser sitting asleep along the banquette. His knees upraised, his head buried in the crook of his arm. We turned and walked together. A little ways farther on so as not to disturb him.

"I would think the fact that you're letting the man take a rest at midday while on duty is proof of your good nature. Most would have him flogged."

"I know he suffers terrible headaches from his wound. It would seem an unusual cruelty to drive the man beyond his endurance. Especially when I know he has been trying his best to assist me this morning. But then perhaps I'm just a poor leader of men. Perhaps I should show more mettle in these situations. I fear the men will no respect me."

What possessed me to say such a thing to her? A woman I had barely spoken to. Why did I think I could trust her with such a confidence? I had been thinking out loud. Perhaps airing my inner thoughts to see how they weathered the light of day. She stopped and looked at me. Studied my face.

"The only thing you have to fear, Ensign Keating, are thoughts such as those. And displaying them for others to see."

She was right, of course. I knew better. Though to recover I knew only to attack. "Is that the way your Lieutenant Stewart handles himself? By never displaying his concerns?"

"He is not *my* Lieutenant Stewart, Ensign." She smiled knowingly. Apparently able to see through me. "But 'tis true. He did not make a practice of showing his thoughts or concerns. At least to me."

"And yet he did no hesitate to show his concern for this Colonel Berry and the Onagonas when he thought they were in trouble."

"I don't know what you mean."

I looked away. Off toward the river. The cut through the distant hills. The glimpse of further hills, endless forests. Close to the river, Duncan Murchie sat on the bank playing again on his fiddle. The strains drifting up the slope to where we stood. "When Lieutenant Stewart heard about the smoke up the valley, he evidently thought the Onagona were in trouble. He showed his concern for the chief and the village by risking his own men, taking them up the valley. Rather than looking after what should have been his first responsibility, the safety of his command. I wish I knew more what Colonel Berry told him the last time he was here. If there was something Berry said that helped cloud the lieutenant's judgment."

"Doesn't Sergeant MacKenzie know what Colonel Berry told the lieutenant?"

"Och, how would I know? I get no answers from Sergeant MacKenzie. For whatever reason, the sergeant keeps his own counsel as far as I'm concerned. I had to go to Donald Fraser there. It seems he was present when Colonel Berry talked to Stewart. He knew that the Onagonas planned to leave the area and were afraid the other tribes might attack them on account of it."

"Was that all Berry told Lieutenant Stewart?"

"I d'no know. I d'no think so, but Donald Fraser did no want to talk about it further, and I decided to no press him on it. I may later."

Elizabeth looked at the private asleep, back along the ramparts. Concerned for him, I thought.

"Perhaps that was enough for Lieutenant Stewart," I added. "If he is a man of conscience."

It was Elizabeth who looked away this time. At the valley and the hills. "Yes. He is that. A man of conscience." The morning sunlight backlit her face. Haloed around her high cheekbones. Full mouth. Sculpted chin. Glinted blue-black through a curl of hair that had escaped the scalloped edge of her bonnet. I hadn't realized before, or allowed myself to consider, that she was very beautiful.

"I would think that would please you."

"And why is that?"

"That he was of such strong conscience that he would go to help the Onagona."

She turned her gaze full upon me. Eyes that had turned to flint. "Meaning I would be pleased that he would show the same degree of conscience for Indians that he would, say, for white settlers?"

I was puzzled as to her meaning.

"Pleased, because I am an Indian lover? Because, as they said at Fort Pitt, I am a white-Indian? Because I am part savage now myself, eh Ensign?"

I was at a loss to respond. She turned and walked a few steps away. Turned and came back again. Her expression not of anger, but of patience.

"Let me tell you a story, Thomas Keating. In case you should ever search your heart and find such sentiments there. When the Indians took me, I was fifteen years old. First I witnessed them shoot my father as he ran from the fields, trying to get to our cabin to protect us. Then my mother panicked and ran for the woods. They caught her from behind by her hair and split her head in two with a tomahawk. My younger sister screamed and they cracked open her head as well. I carried my baby brother in my arms as they led me away through the forest. When the baby started to whimper because he was hungry, one of the braves took him by the foot and smashed his brains out against a tree trunk. When people call me an Indian-lover and white-Indian and savage, they don't know what they're talking about."

"Why are you telling me this?"

"I am telling you so you will understand. There are more mysteries as to why people do what they do than you will ever fathom with all your rules and measurements and calculations. I am telling you so— Oh, I don't know why I am trying to tell you."

She looked again at the hills. As though ready to turn away and leave. I was surprised at the degree that her words affected me. The degree that I wanted her to stay. To continue talking. Tell me more of herself.

"Was there such an incident the night I saw you at Fort Pitt?"

The smile slowly returned to her face. "Perhaps you understand more than I give you credit for."

"I know a man was stabbed and that mob was ready to grab you. I know they somehow blamed you for it."

"The man who died had tried to help me. He stepped in when several men tried to solicit me and then decided to take what they wanted by force. They thought they could because, as they said, I was a white squaw. Indian meat. That was before you happened along." She thought a moment. The coquette. "You were very gallant. Quite the dashing figure, actually. You with your sword drawn, holding them at bay. But you must beware, Ensign. I seem to bring bad luck, and worse, to those who choose to help me."

"A kind of curse?"

She shrugged, noncommittal. Perhaps a little pleased, to think to have such power.

"And was that your fear for Lieutenant Stewart?"

"Lieutenant Stewart thinks he is appointed to save the world. He thinks he is like Christ, and he may well end up like Him."

"So that's why you wanted to go up the valley with him. To try to protect him from falling victim of your curse."

She looked at me. Her head slightly cocked to one side, a wondering smile on her face. A kind of disbelief. I thought in appreciation of my understanding of her. Of her motives. . . .

Duncan Murchie had stopped fiddling. The birds had quieted also. I realized how still the world had become. There was only the distant murmur of the river. As if the world held its breath. Along the ramparts Donald Fraser was awake and on his feet. Looking out across the valley. Across the river. He called, "Ensign!"

I looked to where Donald Fraser was looking. Coming along the opposite bank of the river was a file of Indians. A dozen or more warriors. In war paint, their bodies painted red and black. As they came, they watched our outpost across the river. Muskets and long rifles carried at their sides, tomahawks and war clubs tucked in their belts. As if they were more curious than intent.

I looked quickly at Elizabeth. "Huron?"

She hesitated, then nodded.

"Private, stay with this woman!" I called to Donald Fraser. Elizabeth laid a hand on my arm, as if to warn me. Keep me from leaving. But I hurried down from the ramparts, down the hill. Running toward the outbuildings. The dogs appearing from among the buildings but not hallooing now in warning. Growling only, deep in their throats, but not advancing, staying close to each other. Duncan Murchie continued to sit where he was. On a stump on the bank as if transfixed by the sight. Ghosts from the forest. Spirits among the trees. Sergeant MacKenzie and Neil MacNeil appeared from different directions across the commons. Fixing their bayonets to their muskets as they ran.

"Hold! Hold!" I shouted at them. I realized I had left my own musket on the ramparts.

"Are you daft, man?" Sergeant MacKenzie replied as I joined them. "Those are savages there."

"They're Huron. We are no at war with the Huron."

"Aye, and will you be sure to tell them that?"

The three of us watched standing in the middle of the road up from the river. As the group of warriors reached the ford, they fanned out and started across the river toward us, splashing as they came, in no hurry but determined, their weapons still at their sides.

"Hold," I said again. Though my voice faltered now.

"It is too late regardless," the sergeant said under his breath. "They have us now."

"They will no," Neil MacNeil said, starting to raise his musket. But Sergeant MacKenzie motioned with his hand. MacNeil lowered it again.

The Indians had gained the bank and started up the slope toward us. Without hurry. Making neither signs of friendship, nor of attack. Approaching as if already acquainted with this place. Already possessed it. As they passed Black Duncan, one of the warriors reached down to touch his fiddle. Black Duncan pulled it away. For a brief moment the Huron looked as if he would try to take the instrument, or strike the Black Lad. Then passed on. When they got a few yards from where we were standing, the Indians stopped. The one who appeared to be their leader said something. The others laughed. He was naked except for tall buckskin leggings and breechcloth. His chest bedecked with strings of beads like trophies. Face painted black with finger streaks of red. I knew no common language with them. I desperately wished Turtleheart were here to translate. Then the attention of their leader was drawn to something farther up the hill. I turned and saw that Elizabeth was coming down the slope from the fort. Stopped a few yards behind us. Her hands gathered inside the waist of her skirt. Donald Fraser trailing helplessly behind her. The Indian said something, a deadly smile on his face. Started toward her. As if to claim her. I stepped in front of him. My hand on the basket hilt of my sword.

"No."

The Indian looked at me. Surprised at first. Then the smile became deadlier. His eyes deepened. The Indian said something. Again that I could not understand.

"No," I repeated, shaking my head. He made as if to go around me. I took two sidesteps to block him. "Leave her be."

The Indian studied me. Then looked at Elizabeth again. After a long moment he turned and walked back to the others. Saying something as he went. Reluctantly they turned and followed him back down the hill to the river. Looking back over their shoulders at us. As they splashed through the water, they began to give their war cries. Hallooing, shaking their muskets in the air. Their cries continuing as they disappeared into the forest on the other side. Echoing against the hills. Becoming fainter. Then stopped abruptly. The forest and hills around us silent again. Only the murmur of the river, hiss of the falls.

I turned to look at Elizabeth. But she had gathered her skirts and was hurrying back up the hill toward the fort. Donald Fraser watched her go. Undecided momentarily whether he should follow her or not. Then came on down the hill to join us.

"Are they gone then?" he said. To no one in particular.

Neil MacNeil kept his musket leveled in front of him. Watching the woods on the other side of the river. Waiting for them to reappear at any moment. On the riverbank, Dunnie touched his fiddle. Examining it, not quite believing its presence in his hands.

"Did you no see?" Sergeant MacKenzie said to me.

"See what?"

"Two of them wore our red coats," Neil MacNeil said.

"They might have been from sometime before," I said.

The facings were blue," Sergeant MacKenzie said. "They were Black Watch coats."

"But I didn't see a lot of scalps. If they attacked our lads, you'd think. . . ." Neil MacNeil trailed away. Unable to say more.

"There were others wore our belts and sashes," Duncan Murchie said. Coming up the slope from the river.

"They were from our lads. You can no tell me different," Sergeant MacKenzie directed at me.

I had no desire to tell him different. I hadn't noticed the jackets or other articles that might have been taken from Lieutenant Stewart's command. I hadn't noticed the lack of fresh Highland scalps. I only noticed the single fresh scalp they did carry. Dangling from the end of a long rifle. A topknot with a spray of hawk feathers. Like Turtleheart's.

"I am going up the valley," Sergeant MacKenzie said to the others. "To find our lads. Dead or alive. You can come with me, or you can stay here with Ensign Keating. I do no care. It is your choice."

"If you are going, Sergeant, I am going," I said.

Sergeant MacKenzie shrugged. Perhaps a bit surprised. The others quickly agreed they were going as well.

"Even you then, Dunnie lad?" the sergeant said.

Black Duncan nodded. "I will no carry a musket. But I may be of service to you." He looked at me, as if we had an understanding.

Sergeant MacKenzie looked at the sky. The sun just past its zenith, into afternoon. "We leave at once. We can still get a good start to the Onagona village this day."

"What about those Hurons?" I asked. Nodding toward the hillside across the river. Where the Indians who were here had disappeared.

"Were they Huron then?" MacKenzie cocked his head. Looked from me then up the hill where Elizabeth had gone and back again. As if he had just learned something of interest. Having to do with more than Indians.

"They could have attacked us while they were here and did no. Let's hope that means they're taking their savage business elsewhere. We'll have to take our chances." To the three privates he said, "Get your kits. But don't load yourselves down. Rations for three days. We leave within the hour."

"Hold on, Sergeant," I said. Stopping the men in their tracks. "The post needs to be secure while we are gone. Private MacNeil, you will remain here to tend the facilities and the animals. If we do not return in two days, you are to go to Fort Pitt and tell them what has happened."

Neil MacNeil started to protest but the sergeant silenced him with an upraised hand. "Do what the ensign says now, Private. That's a good lad."

As the other men dispersed, Sergeant MacKenzie regarded me.

"Yes, Sergeant?" I said. Expecting the worst.

But he wagged his head. Deferential. "Och, nothing. You were right, of course, about the safety of the post. I was no thinking.

And Private MacNeil is a good choice for the one to stay."

"I thought he was the strongest of the lot, despite his wounded leg. And it will take someone strong to be here on his own." I did not tell him my real reason, that I wanted Donald Fraser with us. That I thought I might have more of a chance to get information from him than any of the others. Including the sergeant himself.

"Aye," the sergeant said. "And what of the woman? Does she come with us then?"

"She can, if she chooses. And I am fairly sure she will choose so."

Sergeant MacKenzie studied the flintlock on his musket for a moment. Then put the butt end of the weapon on the ground. A staff to lean on. Faced me head-on.

"When you told us to hold as the savages came across the river, I thought you were a coward, Ensign Keating. But was a brave thing you did there, stepping in front of the woman. Blocking the Indian from her. A brave thing indeed."

"I did not want him to get any idea of taking her."

The sergeant nodded. Working with his tongue at something in the back of his mouth. Thought a moment. "But there is something I must tell you. Do no get the idea that it was the fierceness of your visage that turned the savage away."

"I d'no know what you mean."

"I was watching the woman, when you stepped in front of the Indian. She shook her head at him when he was ready to go around you, or kill you. She shook her head at him, and he stopped."

"You canna be sure of that. Maybe she was shaking her head because she could no stand the thought of going with him, of being dragged back into the wilderness again."

"You think what you will, Thomas Keating," the sergeant said. Taking up his musket. Cradling it in his arm. "I know what

I saw. You would be wise to keep in mind who and what she is. And to sleep with your eyes open. We leave as soon as we can get ready. Ensign."

He turned and headed up the hill. To the blockhouse to get his kit and rations. I looked up at the fort. Elizabeth stood on the ramparts, looking down at me. A blanket and a canteen for water in her arms. Certain, as she told me the night before, that we would be going upcountry. To find what happened to Lieutenant Stewart. Certain, without my having to tell her, that I would take her with us.

I stand once again at a musket port. Look out at my rectangle on the world. My rectangle *of* the world. Hume says all we can know of the world are our impressions of it. Impressions the subject of knowledge. Experience the boundary of knowledge. Or to phrase it another way, no knowledge exists beyond what we experience. The idea that is at the heart of why I am here in this New World. Why I am an engineer in the service of the King. A soldier of the Black Watch.

And yet the problem. If our impressions alone are the immediate objects of knowledge, passage outside of those impressions is impossible. You can't know the world by just looking at it. Ultimately, it means you can know nothing of the world at all. Of God. Of the soul. There are only the impressions. This rectangle of the world before me.

What exists beyond the five walls of this blockhouse? What is out there? Who? I can't know beyond this rectangle imposed upon the world.

Thomas Hutchins has his own idea of a rectangle imposed upon the world. Or in his case, a square. Many squares. Bouquet's engineer when the siege was lifted at Fort Pitt, and later when Bouquet took his army into the Ohio wilderness. The engineer whom I replaced at Fort Pitt when Hutchins left to map the further regions down the Ohio River and beyond. Hutchins sees the flatlands beyond the Pennsylvania hills divided into squares. A grid of 6-mile squares. Each square a township, to be further subdivided into 36 one-mile squares or sections, each of 640 acres. Square after square after square, unrolling across the wooded landscape. A convenient way to keep track of who owns what. And who lives where. When these lands are opened to settlers. As eventually they must be.

An interesting idea, to be sure. And Hutchins a better engineer and surveyor than I will ever be. But how to fit a wilderness in a square? How do you contain the wildness of this country, its savagery and beauty, within equidistant boundaries? It would seem more appropriate, more probable, to contain a windstorm in a saltbox. A demon in a gossamer.

Savagery and beauty. This country takes its count in equal measure. But why would they link so? Is beauty always coupled to brutality? Love with loss?

"Don't talk to me of love, Thomas Keating," Elizabeth hissed. "You know nothing of it. Nothing." The knife in her hand. Blood still dripping from the blade.

"Do you no love me, Thomas?" Jean said.

We had climbed the hill to the castle from the university. Standing on the tower wall in the late afternoon. The gray day, clouds in layers overhead. And below us. Toward the Firth of Forth there was rain in the valley. Clouds of rain drifting across the plains. Sections of the view blotted out, smudged. I had told her what I planned to do. To join the Black Watch. Then I tried to change the subject.

"Someday soon they will drain these marshlands in the valley. They say they will build a new town here. With beautiful brick homes and gardens."

"Why do you tell me that, Thomas?" Jean stood looking out at the same view I looked at. Her hands hidden in her muff. Her brown eyes tearing, perhaps from the wind and the chill. Perhaps from what she saw of us.

"Because it is of the sort that I want to be a part of someday. Something grand."

"Then stay here in Edinburgh and help them build the new town. Why must it be the army? Why America?"

I didn't know why. Not yet. Not then. I only knew the words then. "'Tis the way David Hume describes it. If there can be no knowledge of anything beyond experience, then I need to seek more experience. It is a matter of honor. Of honesty with myself. I need to seek the experiences that will teach me the world is real. So I know I am real. So I know what I think and feel is real."

"Aye, you are real, Thomas. Believe me. When you kissed me that day along the shore, I learned all I need to of reality in the press of your lips. That day I was made real for the first time in my life."

"But I need more than that, Jean."

She looked at me then. Her brown eyes liquid. The eyes of a young doe, watchful. The animal within her ready to bolt at the signs of danger. I added quickly, "I need more, to be more for you."

Did I believe that then? Did she? She said, "Aye, and you will find you in the dark kilt of *Am Freiceadan Dubh* then? You are a builder, not a destroyer."

"The Black Watch serves the interests of King George and his kingdom. They protect the expansion of the British Empire, and thus the expansion of civilization itself."

"Aye, I have read all about the Black Watch. At Ticonderoga. Where even their officers could no call them back from hurling themselves on the French abatis. Hundreds and hundreds killed. All for the sake of revenging their fellows, their clansmen. But

what of you, Thomas? You are no Highlander. No Highland laddie. Which clansmen will you fight for, Thomas? Which clansmen
will fight for you?"

I had no answer for her. Having no answer for myself. A
builder, not a destroyer, she said. I knew that I was a builder, of
course. But I also knew since the losses in America, the Black
Watch recruiters were hungry for new men. Otherwise, they
would have never considered me. But the attending question for
me was whether I could be a fighter as well. For the sake of honor,
I thought I needed to know that. To live the experiences that
would tell me that. Though I did not consider the consequences.
If I should discover that I wasn't.

"I thought you were a coward, Thomas Keating. When you told
us to hold as the savages came across the river." Sergeant Mac-
Kenzie looked at me. His blue eyes steeled. The sunlight glinting
in his sidewhiskers. The arc of his mustache across his lips. Moving with his lips. As if a visual echo of his words. "But 'twas a
brave thing you did to step in front of the savage. A brave thing
indeed."

But was it? Perhaps Sergeant MacKenzie didn't hear the
waver in my voice when I spoke the word. But I did. He couldn't
know the watering of my bowels as I stood there. When I con-
fronted the eyes of the Indian. When I saw in his eyes all the
hatred in the world. For me alone. He couldn't know the tremors
that ran through my limbs. The fear in my heart. How brave is
the man when he is afraid he could be the coward? It was a
question I had come many thousands of miles from home, from a
woman I loved, to find an answer to. But all I have done it seems
is to live the question. Again and again.

I stand at my portal, searching the confines of my world for
signs from the past. For indications of life, friend or foe, in the
present. As I watch, a plump squirrel scampers across the roof of

the corncrib. What remains of the corncrib, the scorched roof collapsed in upon the burnt timbers beneath it. But the squirrel knows nothing of fire or the anger of its beginnings. It is happy at the source of food it has discovered. The scattering of cobs and grains among the ashes. It sits up on the broken ridge beam, enjoying the treasure of a kernel, chattering to itself. Tail flicking. Blissfully unaware, and I cannot warn it, of the eagle taking flight. From the top branches of a tree across the clearing behind it. The great wings beating slowly. Flicking between the trees. Descending forever across the open space. Legs extended. Talons bared. A look of equal joy or fulfillment in its eye. The huge bird swooping down. Snatching the unsuspecting squirrel from its perch. Lifting it away into the blue and sun-filled sky. The doomed animal still clutching in its paws its treasure.

Heartsick at this lovely and uncaring world, I return to my makeshift desk. My writing. Remembering that it was at this time of day, past the middle of the day, when our little patrol—Duncan Murchie, unarmed, as our Forlorn Hope in the vanguard, followed by Sergeant MacKenzie, myself, Elizabeth, and Donald Fraser as rear guard—crossed the ford of the Allehela. Started up the trail along the river. Threading our way into the green darkness of the forest. Deeper into the shadow of the valley.

"So, the sergeant, he has his suspicions of the woman from the beginning," the man says. *"But the ensign takes her with them all the same."*

"He has his suspicions," Sara puts in quickly. *"But that doesn't mean there's anything to them."*

"You're only thinking about the woman, lass, your mother. The woman you think is your mother. You're no thinking about the safety of the command, the peril she might lead them into.

You're as blind as the ensign here, and the sergeant too. If he thought such a thing he should never— Och, what do I know? I've had enough, I can no more of this. I've got chores to do."

The man gets up abruptly from the table, knocking over the bucket of water on the bench beside him, the water running in rivulets toward the base of the sycamores, then disappearing quickly into the dark earth. The waste of the water, his own clumsiness perhaps, angers him further, and he storms off across the compound, stopping in the barn only long enough to take an axe, then heads across the field, up the slope into the forest.

Sara continues to sit at the table, after watching him go. Thinking of the story. Yes, he was right, she was thinking only of the woman whom Sara is certain now is her mother. Did Elizabeth know the Indians who came to the outpost that day? Most likely she did, if they were Huron they could even be kinsmen. But what did they want? To take her back? Why didn't she go if she had the chance? Her life—their life, mother and daughter—had been miserable since they were taken from the Indians. Brought back to so-called civilization, the frontier settlements, to be among those whom others declared were their own. After the initial greetings and huzzahs at their return, Sara and her mother were forced to live in squalid quarters in the shantytown beneath the ramparts of Fort Pitt, the garrison animals had better conditions. With no way to provide for them and no husband, her mother had sold the only thing she had, her body, to give them something to eat. Mother and daughter despised by soldiers and settlers and Indians alike.

"I'm sending you east to Carlisle," her mother said the last time Sara saw her. Her mother throwing the few clothes the eight-year-old had into a cloth bundle. "There's a wagon train leaving within the hour, I've made all the arrangements."

"I don't want to go to Carlisle," Sara said. "I want to stay here with you."

A Book of Days

"There's nothing for you here. Do you think I'm going to stand by and watch them turn you into a whore as well? There are people in Carlisle who will take care of you, maybe you'll even find relatives if any survived. When you get there, find the pastor of the church, tell him your story. Tell him you were separated from your mother, that you have no one. The good Christian women of the congregation will hopefully take pity on you. They're more civilized closer to the coast than the animals in this place. It's only the white rabble that comes over the mountains to the frontier."

"But I belong here."

"We both belong with our Huron family. But that can't happen now. We both belong nowhere now. Faraway governments have decided our fates and made orphans of us, you and me. Don't ever forget that."

Her mother grabbed her and pressed the child to her, holding her tight for a moment, then pushed her roughly away, taking the child with one hand and the bundle of clothes with the other down the street to the wagon train forming up. Once Sara was placed on the back end of a freight wagon, her mother turned and walked away, through the mud and slop of the street, never once looking back.

Sara looks now across the open field, at the sunlight sliding slowly down the distant hills as the afternoon wears on. Nothing much has changed she thinks, there is still nothing for her here. Anywhere. Despite her mother's efforts to set her on a better path, the good people of Carlisle, led by the pastor and the elders of her church, the good family who adopted her, eventually made her their servant and private whore in exchange for her room and board. The spread of so-called civilization, the gobbling up of the wilderness by land-hungry whites, was for her only another name for servitude, exploitation. She had hoped that finding out what happened to her mother would help her know more of what to *expect from this New World, an indication of how to live her own life in the face of overwhelming odds. So far, the story told in the orderly book does not hold much promise. This world seems meant for other people, not for the likes of her and her mother. The wilderness more of a refuge and safe haven than the world of tidy towns and tilled fields. And yet it is so beautiful, so peaceful here with the man with the stumps for hands, this place devoted to raising oxen, this sanctuary for songbirds and crows.*

The afternoon continues on; the dairy cows begin lowing from the barn. Sara goes and does the milking, feeds the chickens and takes care of the pigs, then returns to the barracks. In the morning they had cornmeal boiled in water for breakfast, a kind of mush, the most a man could do easily without hands. Now she takes cornmeal and makes a kind of johnnycake. She is busy at the hearth when a shadow fills the doorway. A figure with an axe balanced across his shoulder.

"You did the milking," he says.

"Yes."

"Even the brown Guernsey? She did no mind?"

"She started to. But I spoke to her, as I heard you do. And she quieted down."

"And now you're making fry bread."

"It'll be good with a little syrup. I saw you had some."

She thinks her efforts will please him, but the black mood he had when he left earlier in the day continues while they eat at the table under the sycamore. As the sun disappears behind the hills of the valley and the compound fills with afterglow, Sara redds the table and cleans the dishes in silence as the man continues to sit there, staring down the darkling valley, listening to the evening calls of the cardinals and finches, the whistle of a goatsucker overhead, the crows settling in for the night on the hillside. When she is finished she goes back to the table and stands across from him.

A Book of Days

"I'll be going at first light. I want to thank you for your kindness—"

He stops her with a wave of his stump. "You canna go."

"And why can't I?" she said, ready for a fight.

He looks up from under his heavy brows. The wry smile plays
on half his mouth. "We have no finished your story. Go get the
book and the betty lamp and bring them out here. We can still
read a little more this night. I thought you wanted to know what
happens to them."

She hurries into the blockhouse, more puzzled than ever at the
man, but wanting to take advantage of the offer while he is still
willing. She lights the small lamp with a brand from the hearth
and carries the light and book back outside. As she sets the lamp
beside him, she notices the skin on his forearms.

"You're hurt."

The man holds up the two stumps so that his loose sleeves slide
back on his arms. The skin on his forearms is enflamed from
where he held the axe and is badly nicked, some of the cuts bleeding, some of them scabbed over.

"Och, a wee scratch or two. I tried to clear away some nettles,
but it seems the bushes won the day."

"Some of those are more than wee scratches. Where is your
balm?"

He tells her where to find it in the blockhouse and she brings
it back to the table, covering the worst of the scratches for him.
He puts up with the attention for a while, then waves her away,
gets himself settled to begin reading again. Holds the pages of the
orderly book between his stumps so they catch the light. His voice
taking on a certain rhythm of the narration, like a song to the
darkness that quickly closes in around them. And as she sits there,
though she can't see anything, she feels the presence of things
outside the circle of light that surrounds them, as if the animals
of the forest, rabbits and foxes, deer and wolves, raccoons and

*mountain lions, as well as the oxen from the fields and yes, a
young black bear, have all gathered, sitting together in the darkness to listen to the man's voice. To listen to the story.*

These are the things we carried.

Sergeant MacKenzie, Donald Fraser, and myself each carried
a regulation .78 caliber smooth bore musket. The Brown Bess as
it is known, perhaps because of its walnut stock. The barrel 46
inches long, the overall length 62 inches. Weight 16 pounds. Because I am an officer, I had the choice to carry a lighter-weight
fusil of my own providing. But once here in the wilderness, I chose
the Brown Bess as my companion. I already carried too many
distinctions from the rest of the men of the regiment to worry
about differences of ammunition and flints and the like. And after
listening to the stories of the veterans, I also wanted the power
of a Bess. She is fussy. She is temperamental. Known to often
misfire. It is said the men do not aim the Brown Bess. They point
her in the general direction of the enemy and hope for the best.
But the toll when her ball impacts is horrible. Not piercing the
body but smashing into it. Tearing out chunks whole. The Pennsylvania rifles with their grooved barrels that some of the Indians
carry may be more accurate at a farther distance. But the Bess
is faster to load and fire, up to three rounds a minute. In this
land where Indians can appear at any moment among the trees,
I have come to love her. To trust my life to her.

In his hands, Duncan Murchie carried nothing. True to his
conscience or whatever drove him. In her hands, Elizabeth carried
a cloth bundle. A blanket into which were rolled a few essentials.
Her ration of food and canteen of water. Her apron, change of
undergarments. She had changed back to the clothes I saw her in
the first day. A simple blouse, plain skirt. As she walked through

the woods, she often lifted the front hem of her skirt so she wouldn't trip. With a flash of the bottom of her petticoats underneath. Her moccasins. Hands at her waist, with her bundle sometimes tucked under one arm. Sometimes held in front of her as if it were a child. Later Sergeant MacKenzie fashioned a length of vine into a sling for her, so she could carry the bundle over a shoulder or across her back.

Each of the men, including myself, was dressed in regulation uniform. Regulation inasmuch as it has become adapted to service in the woods of America. Short jacket of a dull, rusty-red color. With cuffs and collar trimmed in the blue of a royal regiment. A waistcoat of the same rusty-red cloth. Cut down actually from an older jacket that had otherwise worn out. Checkered shirt because it doesn't show the dirt. A *feilidh beag*, or "little kilt," of the somber green and black Government Tartan. Cut down after a couple of years from a "great plaid." The 12-foot by 5-foot cloth that originally served as both kilt and cloak in Highland dress. That now serves as blanket or cloak for a Highland soldier. The great plaid, because the nights at this time of year can still be cold, kept close at hand. Belted at the waist and hanging down the back from the left shoulder like a cape. Red-and-white-checked hose. Sturdy buckled shoes. Blue bonnet topped with a red ball and red band. With a strip of black bearskin not to exceed 5 inches. The badge of the Black Watch.

When Bouquet's troops marched over the Alleghenies and later into the Ohio territory, each soldier carried sixty pounds of equipment. On our little patrol, we carried less. No extra sets of clothes, no camp equipage. Expecting to be gone only two nights. Three at best, at worst. Yet it was enough, in the heat and humidity of early summer. Dressed in our heavy woolen uniforms, each man sweating within a short time. One of the reasons why the men prefer their kilts though they could wear linen breeches. One of the reasons.

The shoulder belt was black leather, 2-and-3/4-inches wide, supporting a basket-hilt sword. The waist belt also black leather, 2-inches wide. Supporting on the right hip a heavy cartridge box carrying twenty-four preloaded rounds. Each round a rolled paper cartridge containing six to eight drams of powder, and a one-ounce lead ball, the ends of the cartridge tied with pack thread. In addition to the cartridge box, each soldier carried on his waist belt a hanger and 17-inch bayonet. A dirk supplied by each soldier. A light infantry tomahawk supplied originally by Colonel Bouquet. Sometimes a second bayonet, sometimes, such as myself, an all-metal flintlock pistol—as much as twenty pounds of equipment. From a cloth strap hung a kidney-shaped tin canteen. From a leather cord hung a powder horn. Donald Fraser's powder horn hung from a beaded Indian strap. Sergeant MacKenzie's canteen hung from the remains of a crimson worsted sash once meant to delineate his station.

On the march the men would have carried in the kits on their backs an extra pair of shoes, camp kettle, leather tools for shoe repair, extra shirts and leggings, and other extras. On our mission, we carried a haversack with only the essentials. Three days' supply of dried beef and ship biscuit. An extra pair of stockings. I carried the few surveyor's tools I brought with me to the outpost. A measuring chain, compass, rule. My notebook—I don't know why. Donald Fraser carried his volume of Hume. Sergeant MacKenzie carried a set of undergarments he never wore. Each of us carried a comb. In compliance with Bouquet's order of 1763 that each man must daily comb his hair. Along with washing his hands and face. A razor and a piece of soap. Flint and steel for making a fire. In a smaller leather bag we carried the tools to maintain our muskets and pistols. Tin bottle of oil and cleaning rag. Folding patch knife. Extra flints. Pick and whisk to clean the firing hole and pan.

In a wooden case, slung across his back like a musket, Duncan Murchie carried his fiddle and bow. Extra strings. A small cake of rosin. At the beginning of our journey I had the concern, the fear, that at some point as we walked along, he would remove the fiddle and start to play. Lead us through the forest like the Pied Piper. Concerned because I didn't know how I would stop him. Or if I should. Later when he did exactly that, played us through the forest, he may have saved our lives. As for Elizabeth, I had no way of knowing what else she carried in the folds of her skirt.

Below the waist belts of the men hung their sporrans, made of badger skin. There each man carried his most personal belongings. Donald Fraser carried letters from his mother. A packet of herbs an Indian scout had given him to help his headaches. A stamped metal impression of Saint Andrew. A pair of bone dice. Sergeant MacKenzie carried a ribbon he had won once in a test of strength at a local fair back in the Highlands. The papers ordering his advancement to sergeant. A broadsheet folded down that told how to obtain land on the frontier. A deck of cards. Duncan Murchie's sporran carried not a thing. It was said the day he announced he would fight no more, he stepped to the fire and emptied the contents of his purse into it. In mine, I carried the iron pin my mother gave me the day I left to enter the King's service. The bodkin her father had used in the Highlands to pin his own great plaid to his shoulder. A drawing torn from a newspaper, wrapped in onionskin to try to protect it, of the castle at Edinburgh from the plains below. The sky above it much the same as the day Jean and I stood together on its ramparts. And I carried a small silhouette of Jean. A black cutout mounted within a small metal box. Made by a craftsman on one of the last days Jean and I went walking. Her long hair cascading down beneath her jaunty tricorn hat. The open neck and wide folds of the lapels of her tunic. A melancholy Jean. Her head looking down, as if in reverie. I often wonder if I am the subject of such reveries for her now. Thoughts of what might have been. Wonder if she thinks of me at all. I think of her more often than I should.

The men carried the attitude of Scottish soldiers. In my sporran was an article from the newspaper I had seen at the time I decided to pursue a commission in the famous *Am Freiceadan Dubh.* An article describing an author's ingenuous impressions of soldiers of the Black Watch. A reminder of what I wished to become. What I thought I wished to be. "The men possessed the attractive beauties of a soldier; sun burnt complexions, a hardy weather-beaten visage, with a penetrating eye, and firm expressive countenance, sinewy and elastic limbs, traces of muscles strongly impressed, indicating capacity in action, and marking experience of service." An impressive sight, to be sure. Though I don't know how applicable such descriptions would be to our hobbled little band. Making our way upcountry along the Allehela. When the Black Watch first landed in America, the Indians thought they were another tribe of Indians. In that they weren't far wrong. Soldiers from the Highland tribes. As barbarous and savage to the English as the Indians were to us. Then when they heard the keening of the pipes, the Indians decided the Scottish soldiers, the *petticoat warriors* as they called them, were actually creatures from another world. Figures from an apocalypse. As to what eventually became of the Indians' lands and way of life, they weren't far wrong in that either.

Duncan Murchie. Adam MacKenzie. Thomas Keating. Elizabeth Cawley. Donald Fraser. That sunny afternoon when our little group started off into the wilderness, we carried other things with us as well. Other intangibles. Fears. Hopes. Wishes. Secrets. Things we weren't necessarily aware of at the time. Any more than the Indians watching the Black Watch for the first time parade through Albany were aware of what they saw. That day we carried with us our own revelations. Our own apocalypse. We carried death.

My light is failing. I can write no more this day. If I live through this coming night, I will continue our story tomorrow. If not, the devil already has my soul.

Day the Third

I awoke this morning to glory. A brilliant gold light filling my eyes. A shaft of light aimed at me where I lay on the floor. Blinding me, startling me awake. Thinking for one brief instant that I had indeed passed over. That I was witnessing the heralds of the beatific vision. Angel light. The rays sprocketing through the darkness of the interior of the blockhouse. Barely awake, I got up from my bed of straw and went to the musket ports across the room. Outside, the trees up the slope from the river were topped with gold. A brilliant yellow as if in autumn. The same for a swath of trees on the bluff across the valley. I moved to another port along the wall. Where I could see the morning sun just breaking above a notch of the valley's hills farther up the river. Though the sky itself was brilliant orangish-red. The red of hot coals, a furnace. What they say of hell. Then in an instant it was gone. The sky a milky blue. The trees their normal spring green. A sign only that it would probably rain during the course of the day. Red in the morning, a sailor's warning. No more than that. After standing there a moment longer, watching the ordinary world without, I fixed myself my morning meal. Cheese, mealy bread, a dram of rum. Set about once more to tell what happened here at this outpost. This lost command.

The trail followed the river. Close along the bank, for a half mile or so, until the river wound out of sight of the outpost. The river's meandering course within the end of the valley. Then the trail climbed the valley wall as the walls on both sides of the river grew steeper. Entering deeper into the forest, the river only occasionally in view down the abrupt slope among the trees. Single file, maintaining a distance of a few yards from each other. Our muskets at the ready. Following Duncan's scarlet tunic 50 yards or so ahead among the dark trees. To give us plenty of warning should he encounter something. We walked in silence. Listening for sounds of danger. The crunch of our footsteps along the forest floor. The drum that usually kept the cadence for the march supplied by the beat of our own hearts. Though at one point I was surprised to hear furtive voices behind me. I turned to find that Elizabeth had dropped back and was walking with Donald Fraser. Speaking avidly about something. I stopped to wait for them and Elizabeth hurried forward.

"What's wrong?" I asked.

"Nothing. Nothing at all," she said as we started to walk again. "I had a question about the animals back at the post, that's all. We shared some of the chores, Donald and I. You know how Donald frets about his animals."

"It can wait till we stop to rest."

Sergeant MacKenzie, ahead of us, turned and glared his disapproval. We all became silent again. Fell into line and focused on the act of walking again. The succession of our footfalls. Taking us further from what was known to what there was to learn.

The trail ascended the valley wall. Across and then above the sandstone bluffs to the ridgeline, turning inland. Keeping parallel to the river, a falling away in the near distance. A sense of light and space to our left through the dark trees. Entering a dark cathedral of trees. The massive columns of sugar maple, beech, yellow birch. Trunks like sculptured granite, too large for three men to circumvent with linked hands. Their branches formed the tallest canopy, high overhead. The sky replaced with leaf cover. The intertwined boughs allowing only cracks of sunlight to filter down through the gloom. Cracks of sky. Lower was a second layer of cover. Though never so full, of white oak, red maple, red oak. Our checkered stockings brushed through trilliums and mayapple. Maidenhair and Queen Ann's lace. Elizabeth's skirts and petticoats swept over cancerroot and liverwort. Away from the river, the world became hushed. Muffled. The air close. As if we had entered a great hall. The world of shades. In the muted light, a swallowtail butterfly danced in and out of a shaft of sunlight. A chipmunk sat on a fallen branch to watch us pass. From a viburnum bush came the sound of a warbler. A cardinal picked among the ground cover. High above came the echoing calls of crows.

Sweat trickled down my chest inside my shirt. Pulled against my neck by the weight I was carrying, the stiff wool tunic of my collar chafed my skin. Heat rash. I couldn't seem to get the strap of my haversack positioned so it didn't dig into my shoulder. We had gone only a mile or so when Duncan's red jacket turned. Came back through the trees toward us along the trail.

"What is it, lad?" Sergeant MacKenzie asked as Duncan approached.

"Aye, we are being watched, Sergeant."

"Are we then?" Sergeant MacKenzie said, looking around, not particularly concerned. "And how would you know such a thing?"

"The forest has eyes. It is looking at us everywhere."

"Aye, I would think it is. We are quite a sight to behold."

"And there's something or someone flanking us. Away there in the brush," Duncan said, looking off at the trees. Away from the river.

"Out there, is it?" the sergeant said. Looking where Duncan looked. Still not seemingly concerned.

"Aye. I can see the movement sometime out of the corner of my eye. Catch a glimpse of it when I d'no really look at it. I know there's something out there."

"Then that's the way of it. Try to keep an eye on it and let us know if it moves closer."

"I will. That I will." Duncan looked off again. At the forest leading away from the cut of the valley. The endless trees. The impenetrable gloom. I followed where he was looking. Strained to see. The idea that something was out there watching us, following us, disturbed me greatly.

Sergeant MacKenzie nodded to Elizabeth. "Are you all right, missy? D'you need to rest awhile?"

Elizabeth looked at him coldly. Shifted the cloth bundle she carried higher against her hip. "Don't worry about me, Sergeant MacKenzie. I'm an Indian lass, remember? I will walk you into the ground."

Sergeant MacKenzie cocked his head at her. Unamused. Turned back to Duncan. "Off you go then, lad. Back to your place. But d'no get so far ahead that we lose you."

"I am there, Sergeant MacKenzie."

"I know it. That's a good lad."

Duncan started up the trail to take his position again in front of us. I took Sergeant MacKenzie by the arm before he could turn away. "You d'no seem very concerned that something's out there, Sergeant."

MacKenzie looked at my hand on his arm, then looked at me. Waited until I removed my hand before he answered.

"The Black Lad has the gift to see things that others canna. Then there are times he sees things 'twere never there at all."

"How do you know the difference?"

"You canna. That's why we all need to keep a close watch ourselves to see if there is anything out there."

"What if it's the Hurons we saw earlier?"

Sergeant MacKenzie shrugged philosophically. "If it should be that band, it will no matter. We could do little against the likes of them."

I looked at Elizabeth. For insight or opinion. For an instant her eyes flashed anger at me. Then softened. Remembering perhaps that she was the one who talked to me about the Indians earlier. "If there are Huron out there, you wouldn't see them. Unless they wanted you to see them."

"Why would they want such a thing?"

She looked away. To the place Duncan had looked at. Didn't respond. While we stood talking, Donald Fraser had walked off into the brush a few yards. Hiked up his kilt. Urinated on the ferns. He came back, a worried expression on his face. "Did you see something, Donald?" I asked.

He shook his head gingerly. Reclaimed his musket from where he had propped it against the trunk of a tree. "Och, no. I was just hoping that Neil MacNeil remembers the one goat has a sore teat. 'Tis all."

"My babies," Sergeant MacKenzie said. Motioned to the distant figure of Duncan Murchie through the trees. "On we go."

We continued our trek along the trail. Following the course of the river, parallel to the distant ridgeline. The lightness through the trees that marked the edge of the valley. But with an increased sense of foreboding. Of danger near. Was someone indeed shadowing us? I continued to strain my eyes as we walked. Squinting. As though that would help me see through the gloom that marked our trail to the right of us. To the trail in front. Watching for any untoward movement. A sudden fly-up of a bird or scurrying animal, signaling someone's presence. But there was nothing. Only the slow parade of trees wheeling by as we made our way through the forest. The endless dark forest. I began to question again our mission. Particularly my role in allowing it to happen. A stronger, more experienced officer would have challenged Sergeant MacKenzie when he first said he would go. Would have denied permission. Rather than simply chime in, "If you're going, I'm going with you." My cheeks burned with inner shame, thinking of it. How could I expect the men, the sergeant, to respect me? Follow my orders? I hefted my musket in my hands. Hoping yet for a chance to prove myself. To be worthy of the dark tartan. The regimental name I bore. The battle cry. *Nemo me impune lacessit.*

I looked behind me, to see if the two following were all right. As if she read my thoughts, Elizabeth smiled at me. Walking along, her cloth bundle tucked under her arm. The bottom edge of her petticoats kicking out as she stepped over lichen-spotted rocks. Exposed tree roots and spiny ferns. A smile of understanding and companionship. A smile that filled me. An unexpected happiness.

In a few miles the trail led back to the edge of the valley. Then down through the trees. To a large stream feeding into the Allehela. The day was starting toward evening. The sun lowering above the cut of the hills. The valleys starting to fill with darkling shadow.

"We'll camp here for the night," Sergeant MacKenzie said, after we had forded the stream. Indicating a grassy area along the bank. In view of both the stream and the river.

"What about a fire, Sergeant?" Duncan asked.

Sergeant MacKenzie turned to Elizabeth. As if to ask her preference. Or to inquire if it was advisable under the circumstances.

"Don't look at me, Sergeant MacKenzie," she said. "I know no more than you what is out there in the woods."

"I d'no say you did. Aye, how could you know such a thing, eh missy?"

For a second the sergeant and Elizabeth looked at each other. Something passing between them. Before Elizabeth looked away.

"No, no fire." Sergeant MacKenzie gazed around. At the hills rising in front of us across the stream. At the sweep of hills beyond where the stream drained into the river. "There's no cause to announce our being here. If someone has no learned it already."

We chose our places in the grass and unloaded our gear. Got settled for the coming night. Took rations from our packs and ate. Upstream a trio of beavers worked at the first stages of damming the flow of water. Waddling back and forth on the opposite bank. Flat tails dragging in the mud. Over the water a dozen goatsuckers provided an aerial circus. Whistling and swooping in repeated passes. Feasting on mosquitoes and river flies. All of it like a dumb show, an entertainment, displayed in our honor. Here in the middle of nowhere. As the evening settled, bullfrogs thrummed along the shoreline. A constant rumble. Like the sound of a distant cannonade.

After he finished his provision of jerked beef and hard biscuit, Donald Fraser wiped his hands in the grass. Took his book from his haversack. Settled back against a tree trunk to read. It seemed part of a regular routine with the men.

"Aye, Donald, and what does Mr. Hume have to say this evening?" Duncan said. Stretched out on his side on his plaid. His fiddle in its case close beside him. Tucked in against him like a pet or lover.

"Mr. Hume is still discussing the origin of morals," Donald Fraser replied. Taking time to run his tongue over his dry, split lips. Moisten them to ease the pain of speaking.

"Och, he's been worrying the problem for months now," Duncan said. "You'd think he'd know where they came from by this time, would you no?"

"Aye, the man will worry the subject to death and that's the truth of it," Sergeant MacKenzie said. He had taken out his folding knife to eat with. Now he sat crosslegged playing mumble-the-peg in the dirt in front of him. "It's enough to make you wonder if he has no morals himself, to make such a kafuffle out of searching for them."

"It is no the fault of Mr. Hume," Donald Fraser said, looking a bit wounded. "It is because I am a slow reader that he takes so long."

"Aye, so you would have us believe," the sergeant said.

"I will only say that the birth of Mr. Hume's morals is longer than that of my father's dray horse," Duncan said, shaking his head in mock wonder. "And seems destined to drag a heavier load through life."

Elizabeth sat off a little ways from the men. Closer to the stream, her legs tucked under the folds of her skirt. Her long black hair loosed from its bonnet. Combing it as it cascaded about her shoulders. Though turned toward us slightly, listening to the banter. Occasionally smiling at me. Meeting my eyes when she caught me watching her. When I caught her watching me. I wished there was some way to talk to her. To get up and go over and sit next to her. Get to know her better. But that was impossible. Worse, pointless. What did I have to talk to her about? Or she to me? I chided myself for being foolish. For letting my imagination run away with me. I was seeing interests and attractions where there could be none. Acting daft as a schoolboy.

Donald Fraser thumbed back through several pages looking for something. "I marked a passage to read you. Now where is the darling . . . aye, here it is. Mr. Hume says, 'The minds of all men are similar in their feelings and operations.' What say you of that?"

"Did he write that then?" Duncan said.

"Aye, he did. 'Tis right here on the page."

Duncan looked around at us. Waiting to see what someone else might say about it.

"It seems pretty obvious, does it no?" Sergeant MacKenzie said after a moment. Poised to flip the knife from his right ear. "I mean, if we're all men, we all think alike. 'Tis no great insight there."

"Except that he says it to explain the origin of morals. Where morals come from."

"Is he saying that because we're all the same, we all have the same morals?" Sergeant MacKenzie said. Flipping the knife in turn from his left ear. "Mr. Hume never lived in a barracks then, did he? Och, I'm afraid the man must think we all came up the river Clyde in a tin bath."

"I d'no say I understood it. I only said 'tis what the man said. 'Tis for the likes of Ensign Keating to understand more of what Mr. Hume says. He knew the gentleman in Edinburgh."

Sergeant MacKenzie and Duncan looked at me with new interest. As did Elizabeth.

"Are you friends with Donald's Mr. Hume then?" Duncan Murchie said. Rolling onto his stomach so he could see me more directly. The sergeant paused in his game to regard me. Holding the folding knife at his right eye. Before proceeding to flip it into the ground in front of his legs.

"I only spoke to him a few times," I said. Uncomfortable that everyone's attention was suddenly directed at me. Uncomfortable as well at the memories. "He was the friend of a friend. Someone I met while at university, 'tis all."

"So what is the man saying then?" Duncan said, picking at the tufts of grass in front of him. Then looking at me again. "The sergeant's right. I've known a lot of men, and just because we were all men d'no mean we thought the same or that our minds worked the same."

"If we all thought like you, Black Duncan," Donald Fraser said, "'twould be a fearsome thing."

Black Duncan nodded in agreement. Elizabeth was watching me around the drape of her hair. As if from beside a curtain. Waiting for my response to Duncan's question. I noticed that Sergeant MacKenzie, resting the point of the knife on a fingertip before flipping it into the ground, listened also.

"I think Hume is saying that because all our minds work the same, we can have sympathy for one another. We approve of the actions of others because we have sympathy for them, as if the actions were our own. And we approve of our own actions if we think those actions will meet the approval and sympathy of others."

"Sympathy, is that the way of it?" Duncan said. Picking at the grass again.

"Aye, so he says."

Duncan watched his fingers cropping the tops of the blades. "I have said I will fight no more. And that does no meet the approval of my fellows or the rest of the English army, though Sergeant MacKenzie and Lieutenant Stewart would no discipline me for it. Does that mean that because I will no fight that I am immoral for it?"

"You d'no have to say more, lad," Sergeant MacKenzie said. The knife stuck in the ground for *plowing the field*. Ready to slap it with his palm to flip it into the ground again a yard or so away.

Duncan ignored the sergeant. "I would think it would be immoral to take another life. Because of the sympathy I have for the other man. A man like myself. 'Tis a strange philosophy that turns the world so on its head."

I remembered my own encounter with Hume and his philosophy. My own quandaries and doubts. And the verbal drubbing I took at the quicker man's logic. I hoped my face did not color at the memory, though it felt so. Or if it did, that it was not noticeable to the others. And could say nothing to answer him. Sergeant MacKenzie whacked the handle of his folding knife sticking in the ground. The knife skittered over the earth and landed on its side. He leaned forward to retrieve it. Addressing me, though not looking at me.

"Keating. 'Tis an Irish name."

Elizabeth had turned away. To look at the stream in the glow of early evening. The lowering sunlight topping the rise of hills on the other side of the river. A lighter green than at the base. The river like liquid silver. But she looked sharply at me now.

Her eyes as if signifying an importance to what the sergeant said. A warning.

"'Tis. My father was Irish. My mother is purebred Highlander. Clan Donald."

"Clan Donald. Aye." Sergeant MacKenzie nodded. Cleaned the dirt from the blade of his knife with the edge of his kilt. Before speaking again, still not looking at me. "The Black Watch has known many a fine officer from Clan Donald, and that's the truth of it. So, how is it a lad with an Irish father found himself in a place to join a Highland regiment?"

"Normally I would tell you, Sergeant, that it's no business of yours. But it obviously concerns you so I will tell you. My father was a merchant in Sligo. An importer, of fine Scottish woolens. He met my mother in Perth, the daughter of his largest supplier. They married but he died in a crossing of the North Sea before he could move her hence, so my mother and I remained with her parents where I was raised. Despite my father's lineage and name, Sergeant MacKenzie, my upbringing in the Highlands was the same as yours."

"I doubt strongly, Ensign, that my upbringing had much in common with yours. Me being a country lad, not a city gentleman. Unless in the streets of Perth you tended cattle in midwinter snows wrapped only in a plaid for sleeping." He looked at his folding knife, weighed it in his hand. "'Twas a time when only men of Highland birth could serve as officers in the Black Watch. To say nothing of the men themselves. The day may come, my darlings, when we will see Lowlanders and even English in the ranks of the Forty-Twa."

He looked around at Duncan and Donald Fraser. Pulling a face at the thought.

"It will depend, I suppose, if the recruiting parties can fill their quotas with Highland volunteers," I said. "And if there are men in the Highlands who can qualify for such vacancies as surgeon and quartermaster. Or even engineer."

The sergeant looked at me then. Head cocked to one side. He smoothed the ends of his mustache with the tips of his thumb and forefinger, starting under his nose and working outward. Like calipers spreading. Allowing a slight smile. An acknowledgment of the truth of my point. But only a slight acknowledgment.

"Let me tell you a story, Ensign Keating, about a Highland laddie," he said. "About the Black Lad there. Though whether it speaks to the moral concerns of your Mr. Hume, I canna say. Duncan was with us in the West Indies, at Martinique, and on Guadeloupe when the lads got impatient and we drew our swords and rushed the entrenchments at the river Licorn. The French were terrified of the *Sauvages d'Écosse*, the Savages of Scotland they called us. They thought there were thousands of us, because we led every attack and no one could escape us. Duncan was with us on the hilltop at Bushy Run when Colonel Bouquet had us pretend to fall back as if we were retreating, then circled around a hill and swept over the Indians' flank, chasing the bastards two miles through the woods. The Black Lad was beside me as we ran them down, when we'd catch up to one of them and hamstring him and go on after the next. He was there when we came back through the woods with our swords and axes, the pipes playing, following the trails of blood to where the savages were trying to hide in bushes and thickets. It was the same Duncan on the march with Bouquet into the Ohio who was sent looking for lost sheep in the woods, and came back hours later carrying a wounded grenadier corporal across his shoulders. Had carried him miles through the forests with the man's scalp half-hanging off him so the Indians would no finish the job. The same lad who sits there now with his fiddle. The lad you only know as the one who will no fight."

What there was of a smile on the sergeant's face had gone as the memories came to him. He looked at me steadily, his head slightly lowered, from under the ridge of heavy sandy brows. All humor gone from him. Why was he telling me this? I wondered. What message was he trying to get across to me? Before I could ask him, Duncan spoke up.

"Och, people say I see things that others canna, that I have the second sight. But 'tis not the reason I will no fight. 'Tis because that day in the forest with the grenadier corporal I saw with clarity the world of the everyday, the world as it really is. With no illusions. No ghosts or bogles. I see that world still, and I will no fight in that world."

"What did you see that day?" I asked.

Duncan looked at me and smiled. Without malice. With sympathy, it occurred to me. "I can no tell you. Nor would you believe me if I did. You must see it for yourself, Ensign Keating. And I believe that you will."

"Tell me this, then. Whatever you saw trailing us in the woods today. Was that real?"

"I d'no know if it was real or no. I do know that it crossed the stream with us, a hundred yards or so up the ravine. I know that it sits out there now in the woods listening to our voices. But if it is real or no, I canna say."

I was confused and irritated. The man was talking in circles. If there was something out in the woods, I needed to know about it. What it was, or who. Certainties. Not bogles or visions. I looked at Elizabeth and met her eyes. She seemed to be watching me, to see what I would do. But before I could do anything, Donald Fraser slammed his book shut and stood up. Wincing with his headache from the sudden movement.

"It is impossible to read with all your blathering. I'm going to go find us some berries before the night sets in."

"I would no have you go," Sergeant MacKenzie said. Stroking the blade of the folding knife across a whetstone. His dirk laid out in front of him, waiting its turn. "The Black Lad says there's something out there and that's enough for me. I d'no want to lose you to it."

"Aye, and the Black Lad also said he d'no know if it is real or no. I would no go far. Just to have a look."

"There may be things I canna tell you, Donald Fraser," Duncan said. He was sitting up now, holding the case of his fiddle in his lap. Like a mother would a child. Aching to play. "But there are a few things that I can. Such as it's too early for berries. Though maybe the wild strawberries."

"Wild strawberries it is," Donald Fraser said. Twisting his kilt back and forth to get it settled on his hips. "Och, now I've got a hunger for them."

"I'll go with him, Sergeant," I said, getting to my feet. "If there is something out there, I want to know more about who or what it is."

"Aye, now I've got the two of you out there thrashing about," the sergeant said. "I will no come to rescue you, do you know?"

"I would never expect you to," I told him. We looked at each other a moment. Each a student of the other. "We will no be long."

Elizabeth's eyes were worried but she said nothing. Turned away. Busying herself by fussing with her apron, the folds of her skirt as she sat there. Donald Fraser and I put on our waist belts again. Checked the pans and flintlocks of our muskets. Attached our bayonets. And headed off into the brush. A foolish venture no doubt. But I had other reasons besides chasing after berries or bogles. I wanted the chance to talk to the private alone. We fanned out, a few yards apart. Made our way up the gentle slope of the hill away from the stream. Looking for the darker regions.

The thickets and ravines where there might be tangles of vines and berry bushes.

As soon as we were beyond hearing of the camp, I asked him, "And how is it with you, Private? Are you still worried then? About the animals back at the post?"

"Why would I be worried so?" he looked at me. Wrinkling his forehead. Wetting his cracked lips. "Och, because I said that about the goat's teat, is it? No, I just thought of it, 'tis all. Neil MacNeil is rough on the darlings at times, but he'll take good care of them straightaway."

"I thought that's what you and Elizabeth were talking about. When she talked to you about the animals."

"And when was that supposed to be?"

"When she dropped back to speak with you while we were first on the trail. She said that's what she spoke to you about."

"She did no." Donald Fraser stopped a moment. Looking at me like I was daft. I nodded. To affirm that's what Elizabeth told me. He continued walking.

"That was no what she talked about at all," he said. He poked with his bayonet at a bush. To see what kind it was, then moved on.

"What did she talk about then?"

"It was strange indeed. Somehow she knew I was present when Colonel Berry of the Onagonas talked to Lieutenant Stewart, the last time the chief came to the fort. She wanted to know what all they talked about. If I had heard what the chief told the lieutenant."

"I told her that you said you were there, but that I d'no think you told me everything that went on."

"Aye, I was there. The sergeant had me there with him. He was concerned the old man would pull a knife or something on the lieutenant. Try to kill him or harm him. But it was no like that at all. The old man came to warn Lieutenant Stewart."

"You mean warn Lieutenant Stewart about the danger to the Onagona."

"Aye, that too. If Colonel Berry tried to move his village. Like I told you before. The other tribes said they would kill him and all his people. But Colonel Berry came to warn Lieutenant Stewart himself. He said Lieutenant Stewart was marked for vengeance."

I stopped momentarily to look at him. "Are you sure, man?"

"Aye. There was no mistaking it. His exact words: 'marked for vengeance.'" Donald Fraser nodded. Carefully so as not to start another headache. As we continued on. "The old chief said that Lieutenant Stewart had been a friend to the Onagonas, and he d'no want to see harm come to the lieutenant."

We were starting up a dark ravine. Overgrown with bushes and fallen trees from some storm years ago. I looked back down the hill where we had come. To make sure I had my bearings. Through the trees farther down the slope I could see the lightness of the open valley. Glimmers of the stream where we were camped. I walked on. A few steps behind Donald Fraser.

"Did the chief say why Lieutenant Stewart was marked for vengeance? Or who singled him out?"

"That's what the woman, Elizabeth, wanted to know. I was surprised she knew about it at all. She even knew the very words Colonel Berry used. I know I d'no talk about it to anyone, not even you. And I doubt that Robbie Stewart did."

Elizabeth knew already that Lieutenant Stewart was marked for vengeance. Knew even the old chief's turn of phrase. Before any one of us told her. The awareness of it registered somewhere in my thoughts. But there were more urgent concerns pressing for answers.

"Why did you no tell me all this before? When I asked you about why the lieutenant took the men up the river?"

"I d'no know you then, did I? I d'no know that you might get Robbie Stewart in trouble, if you said something to them at Fort Pitt, about why the lieutenant went upriver."

"Do you think there was more to it than trying to protect the Onagona?"

"Aye, if you ask me. I think when he heard he was marked for vengeance he wanted to find out who it was that marked him, and why. Robbie Stewart was no coward. He was a brave man, that he was, and he would no run from a fight. He would no run from someone sworn to vengeance on him either. He would go right to the man and have it out with him. That's why I think he went, if you want the truth of it. I think he wanted to find out who it was that marked him, and he thought it must be the same as them that attacked the Onagona."

"What did you say to Elizabeth when she asked you? Did the old chief say who was sworn against Lieutenant Stewart?"

He turned to speak but I silenced him with an upraised hand. Something moved farther up the ravine. A shadow among the brush. I pointed forward, held my finger to my lips to warn him quiet. We each cocked the hammers of our flintlocks. Then moved slowly ahead. Picking our footsteps among the ferns and dried pine needles. In the overgrown ravine the bushes were nearly black. Impenetrable to our eyes. I thought: The Shades of Death. Directly ahead a fallen tree slanted across our path. A patch of light above it, a glimpse of evening sky. In the bushes beyond the fallen tree was a vague shape. The shape of a head watching us. Glint of eyes. I started to ease my way cautiously to flank the tree. The shadow moved. Ducked down. Then leapt, filled the patch of light. A mountain lion jumped over the fallen tree, landing a few yards in front of Donald Fraser. In reflex he stumbled backward and his musket discharged. Sending the lion scurrying off into the brush. The darkness of the evening. Gone as quickly as it appeared.

"A lion!" Donald Fraser shouted. "A bloody lion! Did you see it, Ensign?"

"Aye, that I did. Are you all right?"

He looked at me incredulously. Near hysterical. But not with fright. It was a kind of joy. "It was a bloody lion! I saw a bloody lion, this close! Oh, Saint Andrew, you d'no suppose my musket shot hit him, do you?"

"Your musket was aimed at the treetops when it fired, Private. I'm sure you did no hit a thing with it, unless maybe an unlucky bird."

"I came to America to be killed by red Indians, and instead I could have been eaten by a lion!"

The idea seemed to please him beyond measure, in keeping with his love of animals I suppose. Though I suspected it was as much a fever brought on by too many months here of butchery and wilderness. He started back down the ravine. Throwing all caution aside. Kicking his way among the brush and twigs, laughing and talking to himself about seeing the animal. I hurried after him, looking around. Afraid that the lion might return with serious intentions. Or that there was something else besides ourselves that had scared the animal. As we emerged from the mouth of the ravine, Sergeant MacKenzie came running up the slope toward us. Running knee-deep in ferns and brambles, basket-hilt sword in his hand. Donald Fraser marched on past him, saying proudly, "It was a lion! A bloody lion!"

"A lion?" the sergeant said. Looking after Donald Fraser. Then turning to me. "A lion?"

I nodded. "A lion." Elizabeth had left the camp and run a little ways toward us. But stopped once she saw Donald Fraser and myself. Saw that we were all right. She stood watching us, her hands folded in her apron.

"Bloody hell." Sergeant MacKenzie looked around. "Now every red man within earshot knows we're here."

"I think Elizabeth would say they knew already. Without the gunshot."

"Aye, and the missy would probably be right. Still, I hoped for a little surprise in our favor. Let's get back."

Elizabeth didn't wait but walked ahead. Back at the campsite, Donald Fraser was sitting on his bedroll. Knees spread wide in his kilt, holding his head. Still muttering to himself about the animal. After we told Duncan Murchie and Elizabeth what had happened, it was decided that we needed to post a guard through the night. Because I was still wound tight from the encounter, I offered to take first watch.

"I'll take the watch after you," Donald Fraser said. Not looking up. "I might as well, I'll never sleep well again in this country."

Elizabeth looked at me as if she had something to tell me. Though in the dusk I could not read her eyes. Her hands rolled into the waist cloth of her skirt. Then she turned away to get ready for the night. I took my musket and plaid to wrap up in against the evening chill and walked off a ways into the woods.

I am not alone in the blockhouse. At latest count there are eighteen spiders of various kinds and sizes in various parts of the structure. Though what they hope to feed on is beyond me. Only rarely does a moth or bumblebee make its way through the musket ports. To circle lazily around my five-sided room. Admittedly there are more flies now. The number growing though I will not think about that. Cannot. Meanwhile the spiders sit among their webs, waiting for what the Fates send them. I've come to feel very spider-like myself. My own recluse. These writings my web. But I know I am the very opposite of a spider. *They* are the spider, the ones who are outside. Waiting for me to make a move. Waiting to pounce. I am the prey. Peering out from the darkness of my funnel-ports.

And I have my own wee beastie. A field mouse has adopted me. Come to my rescue, as it were. Visits several times a day, sitting on the flagstone floor in front of me. Wanting a treat. He could just as easily find the kernels of spilled corn himself. But he has chosen to sit, one paw on my buckled shoe, waiting for me to hand them to him. Poor wee beastie. He must be very lonely, to choose me for his companion. The fact is, before I would have killed this mouse on sight. Vermin. Something to be eradicated. Something to be destroyed. Carrier of filth and disease. Carrier of death. But now he seems no better than myself. No different. No different.

He takes his prize and scurries away across the floor. Across the sheen of morning sunlight on the miniature waves and ridges of the flags. Back to the shadows where he knows he's safe. There were flagstones in the great hall at the university in Edinburgh. The oil lamps on the tables and the sconces on the pillars casting their sheen across the stone floor, red and orange. The sheen from the tall narrow windows. A medieval hall. Hall of stone. The granite pillars of the buttresses and archways like great tree trunks, petrified. Heavy plank tables and benches for the scholars. In the midday darkness of the great hall, the glow of lanterns and lamps like scenes of a village at night. Tableaux of men and women sitting at the tables in the gloom, heads bent at their reading or quiet talks. Glimpses of other lives, somehow tender and close.

I was sitting at one of the tables reading when she first appeared. Vision out of the gloom, stepping into the circle of light from my lamp. A young woman in a short tailored jacket with wide lapels. Tricornered hat. Large brown moist inquiring eyes. The eyes of a hind.

"Excuse me, sir?"

I didn't look up. I was looking up already. Thinking of something, not of her. Not focusing until she spoke. Looking then at the young woman who had entered my life. Who would fill my life.

"Could you tell me where to get oil for my lamp? . . . Why are you staring? Is there something on my cheek?" She set her lamp on my table and lifted her gloved hand to her face. To wipe away some supposed blemish or spot. Imperfection, where there was clearly none.

"I'm sorry, was I staring?" I said. Belatedly jumping to my feet. For a moment totally forgetting my manners. "I certainly did no mean to. What you took for staring was probably my thinking face."

"Your thinking face?" she said, amused by the term. Or perhaps my befuddlement. She cocked her head to the side. Trying to read upside down. "And what are you thinking about so earnestly, to draw such an intense countenance?"

I looked down at the books and papers spread across the table. As if hoping they might provide me with a ready answer. "Hume. David Hume. I was taking a few notes. . . ."

"It appears to be more than a few."

"Yes, well, sometimes Mr. Hume can be rather dense. I d'no suppose you know of him. . . ."

"Surprisingly enough, I am acquainted with the gentleman," she said, a little put off. Taking a sudden interest in her gloves.

"I did no mean to offend. I did no know if you are a student, or. . . ."

"Or what?" She closed her eyes, then opened them slowly. To regard me in her own good time. Leaving me struggling there, like a specimen. A kind of beetle perhaps. Mounted on a pin. "Something else? Such as one of the servant girls who wait upon fine young gentlemen as yourself?"

"Please accept my apology. I had the impression that. . . ."

"Ah, the 'impression,' was it? Thus we have apparently proven Mr. Hume's theory of knowledge anew, haven't we? Mr. Hume would say that the only thing that can be said to exist with any certainty is our perceptions, our impressions and ideas. You had the impression that I am an attractive young woman. And you had the idea that if an attractive young woman were at university, she must be a serving girl. Therefore we have demonstrated once again that there are no causal connections among these perceptions and ideas, in fact there can be no knowledgeable causality anywhere. Your perception being correct that yes, I am an attractive young woman, but the reality being that I am a student like yourself."

I felt miserable. And a bit overwhelmed. It must have showed, for the next moment she took pity on me. She laughed gaily, suddenly. Taking off her gloves. Two quick practiced tugs per fingertip. Never in my life had fingers, a pair of hands, seemed more revealed. Naked.

"I'm being hard on you and I shouldna be," she said, smiling. A little pleased with herself. Her large brown eyes now kind and playful. "It is an easy mistake to make these days. We may be tucked away here in Edinburgh from the great cradles of civilization like London and Paris. But women here have more of an opportunity to better themselves through education. The opportunity to study and even converse with the likes of David Hume. What exactly are you reading, may I ask?"

Her short maroon jacket and blouse underneath were cut low, exposing an expanse of skin below her neck. Isn't she cold? I wondered. As she bent over to see my place in the book, I could not help but peer down her décolletage. The curve and fullness of her breasts. She glanced up at me from under the thin reddish arc of eyebrows. Aware that now I did stare for certainty. She smiled knowingly, but didn't straighten up right away.

"Ah. *An Enquiry Concerning the Principles of Morals*. Somehow appropriate, do you no think? 'Reason is the slave of the passions, and can never pretend any other office but to serve and obey them.' A scandalous proposition, as Mr. Hume is quite aware. For if such a proposition is so, what can be the relation between private vices and public good? It has been the source of quite a bit of notoriety for the poor man. He was saying just the other night at dinner, 'They say I am a skeptic, and perhaps I am. But I would label me a mitigated skeptic. For if I were a true skeptic, I would no believe that each time I come to this table I will receive a most delightful meal, such as the lamb we had this evening.' And with that he lifted his glass to my mother. A most delightful and courteous man."

"You know him personally then?"

"Yes, he is a friend of my father's. He often comes to our house for dinner. A most delightful man, as I said, though with the most unfortunate hair sprouting out of the rims of his ears. Not the ear itself, mind you, like my father and other older gentlemen I have observed, but around the rims. It makes Mr. Hume look quite devilish at times. I wish my father would say something to him about it, but I guess that would be a topic that gentlemen would no discuss with one another. Perhaps you would be interested to join us some evening, to meet Mr. Hume? You would be more than welcome, if, as I say, you promise not to laugh or call attention to the man's unfortunate ears. For myself, I can hardly restrain a giggle every time I see him."

I felt as though I was caught up in a whirlwind. Not only from her wit and quickness of mind and busy speech. But from a storm of emotions of being in her presence. An intensity of feeling of which I was unacquainted. Or had carefully avoided in my life. There was no question that she was showing off a bit in her knowledge and acquaintances. But her nervous affectation held an even stronger measure upon me, because it meant she must be trying to impress me. Me. I was unused to such attentions. Especially from an attractive—no, a beautiful young woman.

I was finally able to regain my wits and accept her offer of dinner at her family's. Which was followed by an even more awkward exchange of names, for it occurred to her that she would not know how to introduce me. She wrote her name—Jean Munroe—upon one of my note pages along with her address and some hasty directions. Invited me to dinner the following Tuesday when Mr. Hume was scheduled to be at her house again. Afterward, I helped her with her lamp. Escorted her across the great hall to the keeper of the oil. Helped her refill it and carried it for her back to her table. Once I had returned to my own table, the rest of the afternoon was spent trying not to peer across the room. To where she sat. Though the few times I did I thought I caught her looking back at me. Then I became engrossed further in my studies. If I were to have dinner with David Hume, I must certainly be prepared to converse knowledgeably with him. When the closing bell sounded and I was pulled from my readings again, I looked up to find that Jean Munroe had left sometime during the afternoon. I stared at the piece of paper with her name and address of her parents' house. Her flowing hand. Letters interlaced with loops and flourishes. Filled with hope. My heart overflowing with promise of the future, the loveliness of this world. The possibilities of love.

I remember now. Last night I dreamt once again of fire. Of torture at the hands of the Indians. Of Lieutenant Gordon at Fort Venango. Roasted alive for days over a low fire. Though in my dream, what I can remember, I was a hart. Roasted on a spit. Still alive as the Indians flayed me. Removed my skin, then impaled me on a long pole. Turned me slowly over the flames. The fat dripping from my exposed muscles. Hissing and spitting on the hot coals below me. Slowly my body becoming encased in a hard crust. Crinkly. Papery. Brittle. Like a carapace. Splitting with the heat along the seams. Suspended in the pain. And I remember Jean was standing there among the Indians as they watched. Jean, or perhaps it was Elizabeth. I can't remember now. Will not.

The light is dimming. The day appears to be clouding over. I leave my writings briefly and go to the musket ports. Survey my domain. The sky above the valley has grown chalky. Graying. Dirtied milk. The quality of light changing slowly. The shadows of the early morning becoming less distinct. As though being swallowed into the ground. Sucked away. The objects of my world—the charred ruins of the outbuildings, the trees along the slopes of the hills, the river—left to their own light. Glowing from within. Perhaps before too long I will have to light a candle to continue at my work. Which I will do if need be. I have been away too long from my story as it is. Have feared I think to tell it. But there is no time for such fears now. No time.

The first evening of our journey up the river. I took up my sentry position 50 yards from our camp. On the gentle rise away from the streambed. Sitting, settling down, my back against a fallen tree trunk. Hidden I hoped from anyone approaching from the hillside. Wrapped in my plaid against the evening cooling. Night growing around me, seeping out of the ground, rising from the ferns and bushes. High above, a sprinkle of stars among the deep leaf cover of the trees. The leaves stirring occasionally with a slight breeze. The sounds of night accepting my silence among them. Crickets. The call of an owl. Small scurryings in the underbrush.

Duncan said that whatever had been trailing us had crossed the stream above us. Which meant it probably watched us still. Listened to our voices. I had chosen my position beyond hearing of the camp to try to outmaneuver whoever or whatever it was.

Spot any movements. But I had seen nothing to indicate another presence, human or otherwise. Perhaps it truly was only one of Black Duncan's visions. Donald Fraser was convinced the watcher was the lion that had leapt out at him. But I was unsure. It occurred to me what Elizabeth had said. That if Indians were following us we would only see them if they wanted us to. There was something in her statement, almost foreknowledge, that troubled me. But as I sat there I could not place it. Order it with what I knew.

My eyes gradually adjusted to the blackness. The faint moonlight sieved through the leaves. Ghostly forms of tree trunks. Purplish hues of the underwood. I sat for an hour or so thus. Then a voice whispered, soft as a breath, "Thomas."

I started to jump to my feet. A strong hand on my shoulder held me in place. Beside me squatted Elizabeth. "I didn't want to startle you."

"It's too late for that," I said in a low voice. "What are you doing out here?" I didn't ask her the other question I thought of. How did she get there without my hearing her? I was afraid I had fallen into a wakeful sleep, a dream of being awake.

She nodded toward the slope, up into the forest. "Come. They may still be able to hear us at the camp."

"We must no. Duncan said whoever was tracking us is still out there. . . ."

A chiding smile grew across her face. She was without her bonnet, her dark curls spilling around her head and shoulders like black coils. Ringlets of night. "It was only one of Duncan's bogles. I've scouted all the area, there is no one about. Come."

Crouched low. Keeping her eye back at the campsite, as if any threat was there, she started off into the brush. Blending again into the night. When I continued to sit there, my mind racing for a hold of what was happening, she reappeared again. Ethereal. The chiding smile back on her lips.

"I'll protect you, Ensign Keating," she whispered. She took my hand and I followed her. Crouching. Farther up the rising slope.

We maintained our vigilance for another 20 yards or so. Then straightened up. Walking side by side among the dark tree trunks until we came to a grove of hemlocks. A darker night among the evergreens hidden from the camp. Elizabeth still holding my hand. Then she turned abruptly. The pressure on my hand almost painful. Kissed me quickly on the lips.

"Don't pull away, Thomas," she said. Her voice above a whisper now. But urgent. "You know that thought had occurred to you."

I was at a loss as to what to say or do. But she changed just as quickly. She dropped my hand and walked a few steps away from me. Came back.

"Aren't you going to ask me?" she said. Matter of fact.

"Ask you what?" My heart racing. Pounding against my tunic. I cradled my musket across my arm. A gate in front of me.

"Why I lied to you. On the march here. You asked me what I was talking to Donald Fraser about, and I told you it was about the animals back at the fort. I'm sure Donald Fraser told you it wasn't that at all."

"He said you asked him about Lieutenant Stewart. About what he might have heard when the lieutenant talked to the sachem of the Onagonas."

"You said you had talked to Donald Fraser about it at the fort, but that he wasn't forthcoming about the subject. I thought perhaps he might tell me. A man will often tell a woman something that he wouldn't tell another man. Not always to a woman's credit, I might add."

"Why did you no tell me that at the time?"

"I didn't want to concern you, if it turned out to be nothing. You have things enough to think about on this travel. But I thought he might have heard something important, something that didn't occur to him at first. That would help give understanding of what you may be facing up the river."

"I asked him about it again, when we were out looking for strawberries. It was one of the reasons I offered to go with him."

"I thought it might be." Despite the darkness she must have caught some shading to my look. She smiled quickly. The coquette. "You see? I know you very well. In such little time."

"So you seem to."

"And does that bother you?"

"No. Quite the contrary."

She laid a hand on my chest. Then took it away. Looked away briefly. Looked back at me. "So what did Donald Fraser tell you?"

"He said Colonel Berry told Lieutenant Stewart that he was marked for vengeance. The exact words, according to Donald Fraser. But we were interrupted before he could say who marked him or why."

"And you think that has something to do with why Robbie Stewart went to aid the Onagonas?"

"I d'no know. None of it makes any sense to me."

"Why should it? Why are you so concerned with Lieutenant Stewart?"

"Because he put his entire command in jeopardy, to go upriver to aid the Onagonas. He left an insufficient garrison at the fort in case of an attack. And even with all his men, he did no have the troops to effect an action if he had encountered a war party of any size. He acted against all his training and experience. Everything he knew he should do. He threw that all aside, and it probably cost him not only his own life but the lives of his men."

She grew quiet a moment. Looking around at the night. The dark branches of the hemlocks. The lighter darkness beyond. I had forgotten her feelings for Lieutenant Stewart. Her love, if that's what it was. Whatever had driven her to follow him from Fort Pitt to this wilderness. I regretted talking about him in such a manner, but she seemed to be thinking along different lines.

"Perhaps what really concerns you," she said in a soft voice, still not looking at me, "is not Lieutenant Stewart at all. But your own fears. Your fears that you will make the wrong decision, despite all your training and experience. Despite what you think is right. That it will cost the lives of your men. Perhaps that's what troubles you so much about Lieutenant Stewart and what he did."

"Why would you be concerned about what might trouble me?" I asked. Perhaps hoping for something else. Something more. As if in anticipation I rested my musket on its stock beside me.

"Does that surprise you? It shouldn't." Then she thought about something. "If nothing else, you are in command here, in case you have forgotten. Though Sergeant MacKenzie thinks he is, even so. And I do not trust your sergeant." She looked down. At the narrow space that separated us as we stood there. Then she stepped into it. Putting the flats of her hands on my chest. A gesture that could have been used to push me away. But instead drew me to her. As though against a counterweight that sent my arms about her. My musket dropping away. I held her close to me as my mouth lowered to hers.

Then we were on our knees. Together, facing each other, joined at the mouth. Locked. My hands searching her body through her clothes. Freeing her breasts from her dress as my mouth broke free of hers to suck her. Her hands beneath my kilt. Taking me in her grasp. I pulled away quickly from her. Out of her hand, but not from repulsion. Because I feared the intensity of my desire. The length of time since I had had a woman. The few times. Afraid I would come too soon. For a brief second she questioned me with her eyes. Then seemed to understand. She turned away on her knees. I thought she was moving away from me. But instead she pulled up her skirts and petticoats. Exposed herself. Her buttocks and thighs. The incredible softness of her skin. The beauty. I mounted and entered her. My kilt draped over her back, my face buried in her black hair. Searching with my lips her neck and shoulders. My arms bracketed over hers supporting my weight. Uncertain whether I drove into her as much as was drawn. Pulled along in my thrusts as if every part of my being would be dragged from me. I reached climax in a few thrusts but she was already ahead of me. Yipping softly into her own shoulder. Murmuring, "O Love O Love" repeatedly as I spent myself. And we grew still again.

I rolled from her. Night and the stars and the branches of the hemlocks spinning around me. Then immediately recovered my senses. Grasped for my musket lying in the ferns. Reaching with my left hand to make sure my sword was still at my side. On my knees again. Looking around wildly. Elizabeth, her head at rest on her forearms, her buttocks still exposed to the night air, looked at me. And grinned.

"And what do you think would be there, Thomas? What do you think might come and get us for such a thing?"

"I never should have done that. I never should have left my post. . . ."

She lowered herself to her side and curled into herself. Pulling her skirt and petticoats down, into place again. Regarded me in the darkness. Her head of black curls resting on her arms. Her weathered face pale as the moon.

"Thomas, Thomas. Nothing happened. I told you I would protect you."

I continued to look around. Unconvinced. Confused. Elizabeth sighed and sat up, her legs folded under her. Put her hand behind my head and drew me to her. Kneaded her strong fingers up into the hair above my neck. As if to bring me back to my senses. Then looked deep into my eyes. Holding my head to look at hers.

"Nothing happened here, Thomas. Nothing and everything. We will speak no more of it on this journey up the river. If we live through this journey, then we will see. We will see. But for now, no more. Yes, we should get back now. It is time. But do not fear, Thomas Keating. In the grand scheme of things on this earth, we did nothing wrong here. For once something happened that was right."

I recovered my bonnet from where it had fallen in the ferns and we got to our feet. Standing like newborns together. Discovering our legs for the first time. Supporting each other. Walked out of the grove together, though not touching now. Into the lighter darkness, the blue-black world of silent standing trees. Back down the hill the way we had come. My mind torn with the beauty and fulfillment and release of the moments just past. The knowledge that my actions were unconscionable. I had placed the lives of the other men in jeopardy. I had committed an offense for which I could be court-martialed. Deserted my post in the time of war. I had criticized Lieutenant Stewart for jeopardizing his command. For taking the majority of his men up the river to aid the Onagonas. Leading them into harm's way, leaving the fort unprotected. But how was I different now than he? Only in degree, not in kind. And for no other motive than to give Elizabeth the green gown, a roll in the grass. What kind of man was I? And yet my heart sang with joy still from the time with her. The beauty of her body. The smell of her dark hair. The touch of her hand in mine. More alive than I had ever felt before.

When we got back to where I had left my plaid in the grass, Elizabeth put a finger to her lips. A sign for silence. Not a word. Then kissed it and blew the kiss my direction. And was gone again. Blended into the darkness. Picking her way silently through the night. I stood for a moment. Gazing at the empty space between the black tree trunks where she had been. Then made my way back to the camp.

She was right. Nothing had happened while we were gone. While I abandoned my post. The world was unchanged, though my world had changed forever. All were asleep. Even Elizabeth, or appeared to be. Already curled into her blanket, close to the creek, her back away from me. For all appearances sound asleep. Sergeant MacKenzie lay on his back, snuffling mightily. No eyes open this time, watching my return. I went to where Donald Fraser lay cradling his musket. Despite his prediction that he'd never sleep well again, dead to the world. I gripped his shoulder and his eyes popped open. Then he grinned.

"How goes the world then, Ensign?" he said softly.

"It goes well, Donald Fraser."

"Aye, as well it should. We're still alive thus far through this night."

"From all appearances."

He got up, stretched. Wincing slightly from the twinge of a headache. Gathered his plaid. His musket and sword. I walked with him to the edge of the clearing.

"Are there bogles a-walk in the forest, Ensign?"

"Nothing I could see."

"The Black Lad will be disappointed. I think he lives for them, the way I do the animals. 'Tis a comfort somehow, to know they are there. Och, I'm away then. You rest well, Ensign."

I watched as he walked off into the woods. The colors of his dark kilt, the plaid draped over his shoulders, the colors of night. Becoming night. I went back and lay down where he had been. Wrapped in my plaid. Listening to the murmur of the creek. The breathing forms around me. Drifting into oblivion.

The man stands up from the table, closes the Orderly Book after putting in a leaf from the sycamore to keep his place, stretches,

rubs his stubby forearms like rolling pins over his thick black hair, yawns, sighs, and looks out over the stream toward the fields. He has been reading since early that morning, as soon as they could get started after they shared the morning chores, breakfast of the remains of the johnnycake and a hunk of bacon, picking up the story on the third day of the journal from where he stopped the night before. She watches him, turned slightly away from her, Sara's face set with her anger.

"I know what you're thinking," she says finally when the man won't look at her.

"Aye? Do you then?"

"You're thinking, like mother, like daughter. You think I'm no better than my mother, lifting her skirts and squatting down for this ensign in the woods. Give me the book, I'm sick of this—"

She reaches for the book but he pins her hand beneath the end of his stub. The two of them leaning across the table toward each other, their faces inches from each other. He looks at her from under his heavy brows—his eyes are as dark as a bear's, she wonders for an instant, Was he the bear on the trail in front of me? Crazy talk—until she begins to relax her effort and he slowly releases her hand. He straightens up slowly, watching her, to make sure she doesn't try to reach for it again. Sara studies the pattern of the grain on the table. Not looking at him.

"I'm sorry to disappoint you, lass," he says after a long moment. "But I was thinking I've got a pregnant ox out in the woods. I'll have to bring her into the barn soon and ask the neighbors to help calve her. That's what I was thinking. And now I'm thinking I'm going down into that field by that tree stump there and take me a good shite. Then I'm thinking of coming back here and spending the rest of the day until it's time for chores reading to you the story in this journal. Will you be here when I return then?"

Sara mutters under her breath, "Yes. I'll be here."

"And will the book be here as well?"

He doesn't wait for a reply. The man steps over the end of the bench and heads down into the field. When he is out of sight, Sara stands, stretches, and thinks for a moment of taking the book, grabbing her things from the cabin and disappearing before he returns. Crazy idea to come here in the first place, to want to know what's in the book, what difference does it make what happened to her mother? Nothing can change it. Nothing that happened to her mother can change her own life for the better. Yet something holds her here. It is as if she has stepped into a place that always existed in her thoughts. A place out of time, and within it too. As if she has always sat here on this bench beside the stream under the sycamore, as if she has always looked down the valley at the diminishing hills, listened to the calls of the whippoorwills and thrushes. Crazy talk. The darkness of the man is getting to her. In the tree above her she notices two crows sitting on a branch watching her. A third crow farther up the branches, watching them.

"Oh, go on with you, you suspicious birds. I said I'd stay, didn't I?"

When the man returns, he sits across from her, takes up the book between his stumps, then leans across the table at her, speaking in a near whisper.

"Your mother did what she had to do in order to survive. To survive in the world as she saw it. You need to be able to forgive her. So you'll be more able to forgive yourself. Now, let us read what happened with this Lost Patrol."

He raises his eyebrows as if to encourage her. The slight smile on the side of his mouth. In the branches of the tree overhead, the two crows, as if satisfied at something, fly off, dipping down over the stream and on across the valley, over the fields in a game of Chase Me. The sentinel crow stays where he is, watching them go. Watching the man and woman at the table.

I woke with Sergeant MacKenzie's hand over my mouth. He was kneeling beside me. Gave a sharp shake of his head for me to keep quiet. When he was certain I was awake and aware of his urgency, he released his hand. Gave a nod for me to follow him. The first light was above the ridgeline of the hills but night was still around us. Elizabeth and Duncan Murchie were each still curled in sleep. I took my musket, holding my sword against my side so it wouldn't clatter, and followed the sergeant. Away from the camp. Up the gentle slope into the forest away from the creek.

Fifty yards or so he stopped. Near the spot where I had posted sentry the night before. He looked at me and I wondered if somehow he had found out what had happened here. Knew something of Elizabeth and myself. He looked away into the ferns. At first I didn't see what he was looking at. Donald Fraser sat against the base of a tree. Close to where I was sitting when Elizabeth came to me. Then I saw it. Donald Fraser's throat had been cut. The blood spilled down the front of his tunic, sitting in a drying pool on his kilt in his lap. His head angled sharply to one side. Resting on his shoulder, as if he were trying to see under something. The savagery of the cut left his head barely dangling on his neck. The top of his skull like a blood-streaked moon where he had been scalped.

My stomach wrenched, but I kept from throwing up. Choked back the bile. Sergeant MacKenzie watching me. Watching my reaction. How I would handle myself. I did not speak, surveyed the scene. Until I was certain my voice would hold.

"You just found him then?"

"Aye. I woke and realized he had no wakened me for my turn at sentry. And came out here and he was thus."

"The others?"

He shook his head. "Still asleep."

I looked around at the forest. The lighter sky dawning among the leaf cover high overhead. The murky shapes of tree trunks and ground cover around us. "Whoever did this could still be out here."

"Is probably still out here. Aye, and is watching us this moment."

I was grateful that I had kept my composure at the sight of the body. Grateful I kept it now. I had seen dead men before. But never from the acts of war. Acts of savagery. And thought, You mustn't be surprised or shocked. Isn't this what you came to see?

"We must wake the others. And continue up the river. There would be no point in turning back now. We are in jeopardy wherever, it would seem."

"We must bury the lad first. Before we go anywhere," Sergeant MacKenzie said. Blue eyes squinting at me. His initial horror fading and his fierceness setting in. Looking for a target. Leveled at me only if I dared provoke him.

"Of course. That goes without saying. He was one of ours."

The sergeant nodded and was mollified. I hadn't thought far enough ahead to realize the need to bury Donald Fraser. But the sergeant was right, it had to be done. The form and rituals had to be maintained. My inclusion of Donald Fraser, as well as myself by inference, in saying "one of ours," seemed to raise me somewhat in the sergeant's eyes.

"Go back and get the others. We'll need Dunnie to help us dig the grave. Och, we have no trenching tools with us. We'll have to make do. I'll stay with the lad here."

It was an order I probably should have given. But it was not the time for the proprieties of command. The sergeant in no state of mind to be questioned. I headed back to the camp. I had gone only a short distance when I happened to stop and look back up the gentle rise. Among the trunks of the trees. Sergeant

MacKenzie stood above Donald Fraser's body. Shaking his head slowly, I couldn't tell if he was crying. Then he turned and faced the expanse of the forest before him. Took out his basket-hilt sword and held it over his head. Not pointing with it. Held it in defiance. A challenge, a threat. To whomever might see it or might be there. Then he must have sensed something. He turned and saw me watching him. For a moment we looked at each other. I drew my own sword and held it thus as well. Briefly feeling some connection with the sergeant. A bond, however viscous. Thick as blood.

I woke Duncan and told him what had happened. What we had to do. Then woke Elizabeth. Knelt on one knee and took her shoulder. Felt the roundness of her body through the muslin of her blouse. Memory of the night before swept over me. A brief surge of desire coursing through me, filling me with shame. She opened her eyes slowly, returning to consciousness. Saw me and smiled. Remembering herself perhaps the night before. But then caught something else in my look.

"What is it, Thomas?"

"Donald Fraser's been killed. On sentry. We're going to bury him and then be on our way. You need to get ready as soon as possible."

"Yes, of course." She rose quickly, instantly awake. Helped Duncan and myself gather up Donald Fraser's and the sergeant's things. Then I led them back to where Sergeant MacKenzie guarded the body. I stopped a few yards away and told Elizabeth to stay there.

"I've seen worse things than what happened to Private Fraser. Whatever they did to him. Believe me."

It hadn't occurred to me that perhaps she had. But I told her, "This is a soldiers' matter."

Without shovels it was difficult digging. Scraping at the earth with our dirks and bayonets. Our hands. Forcing us to leave him in a shallow grave for now. When we returned we would retrieve the body and provide a proper burial at the fort. As we decided thus, each one may have thought, though no one said: If we return. We removed Donald Fraser's sword and waist belt. Wrapped him in his plaid. Laid him carefully to earth. Then dragged the loose soil with the sides of our shoes over him. When he was covered, Elizabeth came forward and took up Donald Fraser's musket and haversack. Draped the sword and waist belts around her.

"What are you about, missy?" Sergeant MacKenzie said.

"I can at least carry them for you," she said. Looking at me before responding to the sergeant. "And I might surprise you, I might be able to make use of them for you as well. It would seem you need every able-bodied person you can get your hands on now. Even if it's a woman."

"You'll mind what you're told, missy, or you'll earn a soldier's discipline as well. Mark me."

"I mark you, Sergeant MacKenzie. Very well indeed."

I reached for Donald Fraser's haversack, hanging from her shoulder. Elizabeth pulled it away. Glared at me.

"I said I'll carry it," she hissed at me. "No one needs to help me, ever."

"I'm no trying to take it from you," I said. Trying to remain calm. "I'm only trying to take something from it."

She eased off a little. Though remained wary as I took the bag again. Opened it and removed Donald Fraser's volume of Hume. Placed it in my own bag.

"It's no to lighten your burden," I said, "but to lighten my own."

She looked apologetic. Her eyes. For snapping at me. But would say nothing. It not being in her nature. Only shifted the weight on her shoulders in preparation.

I fashioned a small cross from twigs tied together with grass. Placed it at the head of the mound. Before covering the mound with brush to try to hide it. As we finished our work, Black Duncan took his fiddle from its case. Sat off a ways among the ferns as he tuned it. I wondered when we were finished if Sergeant MacKenzie or I should offer some words. Prayers for the dead. But as we stood looking down at the brush-covered grave, Duncan Murchie began to play. "The Flowers of the Forest." The song traditionally played by a piper at graveside. The slow lament keening through the morning stillness. The silent witness of the trees. When the music was finished we continued to stand there. Became aware again of the calls of thrushes and warblers. The small winds high above in the leaves. The shifting light. Sergeant MacKenzie looked at each of us in turn. No sadness in his eyes now. Only intent.

"We're away then," he said. Almost under his breath. "And the Lord help us."

"*Nemo me impune lacessit*," I said. To myself only. No one provokes me with impunity. To remind myself. Sergeant MacKenzie looked again at me.

"We will see, laddie. We will see."

Did Sergeant MacKenzie actually say that? Did I say the Latin phrase out loud, loud enough for him to hear me? Or did he read my mind, and answer in response? I don't know now. It seemed real as I wrote it. But imagination has become part of memory now. Dream part of reality. All things one. Captured and created and living within the mind. Within me now as I am here in the blockhouse.

There is a noise from the roof. Someone, something. A scratching, scraping. Like a tree branch dragging across the wood slats in the wind. Though there are no trees close to the blockhouse.

No wind that I can feel through the gunports. A sound like someone trying to pry off the slats.

I grab two of the dozen muskets I keep loaded and primed, leaning up against the wall at intervals around the perimeter. Hurry up the wooden stairs to the second floor. I tell myself it is impossible, I must be imagining things. No one could climb up on the roof. A squirrel or raccoon perhaps. But how would even an animal make it, without something to climb up? I run to the gunports. Looking for a ladder resting against the building, a pole even. But there's nothing I can see. Maybe it's a hawk or eagle. Landing there to eat a catch. But surely not a person. With my clamoring about the noise stops. I wait. Breathing hard in the heat. The hot humid air. The second floor of the blockhouse intolerably close. I feel faint from the sudden exertion. The lack of air. The tension. Fear.

The noise starts again. And the supporting timbers creak. As if under weight. Or seem to. Perhaps only with the heat. It occurs to me it might be possible, for a person to climb there. At a corner of the structure, using the gaps in the mortar for handholds, footholds. I look out the ports again. Looking for I don't know what. Others standing on the ground looking up. Watching. Waiting for their chance. But still there is nothing there. I scurry around from port to port. The noise stops for a moment. Then starts again. In earnest. A scratching, scraping. Prying.

"I'm warning you," I say out loud. "I know you're there. Get down now."

As if I were talking to neighborhood kids who have climbed a tree. Naughty boys. Stealing all the cherries. Get down now.

The sound of my voice slows the activity briefly. But not completely. Not for long.

"I said I'm warning you."

Now it continues unabated. Oblivious to empty threats. I see the first of the cedar shakes jostled and finally lifted. Ripped from place. The crack of sunlight widening in the gloom. As if from within a casket. The lid slowly opened. A second shake ripped away. Another and another. Peeled back. Then the painted face peering in. Peering down. Grinning evilly at my helplessness. In my mind's eye.

I take one of the muskets. Cock the hammer, aim, fire. Though at the last second aim away from where the noise is coming from. Only close to it. I don't know why. The ball crashing through the slats. Splintering through the roof. Itself opening a crack of sunlight, a glimpse of milky sky above the gloom. In the close confines of the room my ears are ringing. I cough at the cloud of smoke that engulfs me. Taste the bitter metallic powder on my lips. My cheeks crusted. For a moment I can't hear anything. See anything. Was there a thud? Something scrambling away? A body struck and rolling down the slanted roof. A thump as it hit the ground. A cry. I can't tell.

I run to the ports. Looking for someone running away. Indians running to help their fallen comrade. But there is nothing. The grounds of the settlement are still. The smoldering ruins of the outbuildings. Nothing. No one. Only the wind now blowing the trees on the hills. Shifting, undulating waves of the leaves as a storm comes up. The hills of the valley alive. Like the rippling muscles of a great beast stirred. The breeze through the open ports caressing my face. Clearing the smoke from the room, the smell of gunpowder, flint. The noise from the roof stilled. Quiet again.

I wanted desperately to speak with Elizabeth, after all that had happened. To reassure her, if such reassurance were possible. To comfort her after Donald Fraser's death. There was no question now that the Black Lad was right. Something was out there, something was stalking us. No animal this, nor bogle—something all too human. With human savagery. And I wanted to ask her about what had happened between us in the night. I wondered if she had second thoughts about it. If she regretted it. I suppose, most of all, I wondered if it was real, that emotion. For her. Perhaps for me as well. But there was no time, no chance to be with her alone. We were already late starting. It was close to mid-morning by the time we had paid our respects to Donald Fraser, had something to eat, and loaded up to continue our journey. Once, while we readied our muskets for the day, as I reprimed the pan of Donald Fraser's weapon for Elizabeth, our eyes met briefly as she held the musket for me. Our hands brushed against each other. But her eyes gave no special message to me. Our hands like the touch of strangers. If there was emotion there within her, she kept it hidden. I steeled myself with memories of her. Of her telling me that she would act thus until we returned from up the river. Tried to concentrate on the matters of my small and threatened command.

We set off through the ferns and underbrush, to pick up the trail again. Duncan Murchie once more in the lead, though not far ahead now, only a half dozen yards. Sergeant MacKenzie next, with Elizabeth behind him. Myself now bringing up the rear. I deferred my spot behind Duncan, more in the lead, because I assumed the sergeant was familiar with where we were going. Having patrolled this river trail in the past. And I felt more sure of myself behind Elizabeth. More able to defend her if we should be attacked. As I now strongly expected we would be. Now that first blood was drawn from Donald Fraser.

Beyond the confluence of the creek with the Allehela, the trail followed close to the river for several miles. The valley becoming increasingly narrow. The tree-covered bluffs across the river rising sharply above us. The hills on this side more gradual, a gentle slope away from the bank. Before rising sharply, narrowing the sky. Filling the valley with shadow at all but midday. Which came quickly after our late start. The trail followed along the edge of the forest. A world of half light, half darkness. The sun blocked until it gained the zenith, then glowering down at us. Making us grateful for when it finally slipped beyond the ridge across the river. Baptizing us into full shadow again.

Why had Stewart come here? What drove him to come upriver this far, into hostile and dangerous country? To rescue the Onagona? It seemed improbable at best. He must have known that if the Onagona were under attack, he could do nothing to help them. Both because it would be too late by the time he got there, and because of the meagerness of his command. And still he went. What would make a person do that? My eyes searched the dark forest to our right. The standing columns of the trees. The impenetrable underbrush. To our left, the peaceful water of the Allehela. Crystal blue, a flowing mirror of the chasm of sky overhead. The wall of the valley opposite. The river bending one direction, then back again. Serpentine. The aspect opening in front of us. Then closing again as we gained the next bend. The green and shale cliffs stacked above us. Each step taking me further into the question. And other questions. There is too much time on a long march. Too much time to think. Step after step.

Too much time for other questions to bubble to the surface. Questions considered long dead. Why did I accept Jean's invitation to that first evening? Why did I go to meet the famous man as the guest of a young woman I barely knew? To have dinner with a family I had never met? I guess equally the question was: Why did she invite me to meet him?

She lived with her parents not far from the university. Near James Court, in the shadow of the castle high on the hill. Among the narrow cobbled wynds and closes off Lawn Market, the beginnings of the High Street. A district known for its writers and men of letters, and lawyers like her father. Through one passageway after another, following her hastily scribbled directions.

Down some granite steps and into the courtyard. Her parents' house a beacon of light across the way—a number of beacons from its many windows—in the gloom of a foggy and chill Edinburgh evening. Auld Reekie, as the city is known. Affectionately. From the terrible smell of the place. From the coal smoke, caught in the fog and lack of prevailing winds. A forest of chimneys burning coal at the rate of 500 tons a day. Which actually helps mask the other stench. Of excrement running in the gutters, from the chamberpots emptied there, sometimes simply dumped from windows high above. This stone courtyard no exception. As I walked across the open space, I kept my eyes skyward, fearful of windows above. Ready to cry "Hoad yare hoand" in the custom of the city—Hold your hand till I am past. Auld Reekie. Testament to the questionable capacity of people not only to get used to something unpleasant, such as a city that smells of coal smoke and sewage. But to actually embrace it. Be proud of it. Take it as one's own, a badge of identity.

The house was an architectural mystery. An engineer's marvel. One of the jumble of squeezed-together six- and seven-story buildings that had grown upward as Edinburgh had grown larger. A hodgepodge of additions, like a child's set of building blocks, teetered and balanced on one another. One level stuck out here, another piled on there. Its brick chimney extending several stories above the gabled roof, ready for future additions, supporting its complement of chimney pots. A rooftop monolith, as if to mark the structure. The home's many windows glowing in the darkling. Both inviting and intimidating, glimpses of a multitiered world, self-contained. Flared and muted in the fog.

A maid answered the door, took my longcoat, and led me up the oak-paneled stairway. Up the several dark lower levels, past corridors of closed doors, the servants' world. Climbing to the upper regions of the house. Sounds of conversation, laughter, tinkling glassware drifting down as I ascended. Jean descending to the landing of the last flight as I emerged as from a well into the light. Hurrying to meet me.

"Welcome, Thomas. I'm so glad you're here!" Her face all smiles. Eyes twinkling.

I was surprised at the ardor of her greeting. As if we were old friends, rather than mere acquaintances, one time at the library. I was uncertain beforehand that she would even remember she had invited me. Or what I looked like. For my own part, her image had vanished from my memory from the time I met her. Until only a glow remained, a presence. Burned into my consciousness nonetheless, though I could not remember the particulars of her face or hair. I feared I might walk right by her without recognizing her. But I needn't have worried. Once she was before me, she filled a void within me exactly her size and shape. And with it, an attending feeling of completeness. She took my arm and escorted me proudly up the remaining steps. As if a prize. Along the hallway and into the sitting room that dominated this level of the house.

At the library she had been dressed like a country lass. Short jacket, plain skirt, her tricorn hat. Now she was all the young lady. A young lady of prominent background. Gray brocade dress, with a band of silver spangles to outline her décolletage. Around her shoulders a matching gray net shawl. A black velvet ribbon around her neck, like a collar for a lead; in her hair a small silver tiara. Her skirts were puffed out with crinolines and hoops, accenting her narrow waist. Her hips. Giving a flounce to her walk. Enveloping my legs as I walked beside her as if kicking through clouds. Made worse, as she led me along a corridor, toward the sitting room, by snuggling close against me. My heart overflowing at her touch. The implications.

"Mr. Hume is already here. Everyone is anxious to meet you," she whispered. A confidence as if between lovers.

"I don't know why. . . ."

She leaned away, with a look as if I had said an empty-headed thing. "It's no every day I bring a young gentleman into the house. That in itself is an occasion."

It was a large room, the front of the house overlooking the courtyard. One of the welter of additions I had viewed from below. A somber heavy room, for all the gaiety of the conversation under way. Oak wainscoting, exposed timbers above, with red velvet drapes. Sconces flickering against the last gray light. Chairs placed around the perimeter of the room, in the French fashion. With Mr. Hume in the most prominent chair as one entered the door. As if to make sure no one missed his presence. As if anyone could. He was an oversized man, and not of a proportion. I had heard he presented a rather ungenteel appearance, but I was not prepared for the specimen before me. Grossly overweight. Tall and ungainly of movement. A red bloated face, as if from overindulgence, in either food or drink. Or both. His bob-and-curl wig, out of place for such an occasion, unpowdered and slightly askew. The brocade trim on his coat tattered, the lace at his sleeves torn. And of course the fringe of hair around his ears, as Jean had said. Glowing now from the backlight of the fireplace. As if the side of his head were on fire. Jean glanced at me sharply. As if to admonish the thoughts I might have. But her eyes were merry and mischievous. A secret between us.

There were others invited for the evening. Two or three older couples, friends of Hume and of Jean's parents. I barely caught their names then, a fault of mine, and I barely recall them now. Hume was holding forth, in the midst of a story, something to do with salons he had known in France. Listened to eagerly by the assembled guests, though directed in the telling to Jean's mother. A small, birdlike woman in a bustled lavender gown and gigantic wig. Flitting around, nodding and cooing in the appropriate places, as she directed the servants for more cakes and claret. Jean's father, a tall severe man with prominent cheekbones like bastions for his eyes, sat at an angle to Hume. Listening with cocked head and squinting eye. His hands folded in front of his mouth, fingertips touching, like a gesture of prayer blown open. When Hume was finished and all had laughed as expected, Jean presented me to the room. Making the rounds of introductions— I learned I was a tutor of Jean's at university, *student* I suppose sounding too young for her tastes. Flattering at the moment but I should have wondered.

As Jean and I got settled on a small sofa half a room away from Hume, Jean said, "David has been regaling us with tales of his life in France. He has just returned from Paris. He was Embassy Secretary there, you know."

"Regaling you with tales, as you regale me with food and drink. A fair exchange, I would say," Hume laughed. Resettling his bulk in the straight-backed chair.

Jean's mother cooed and tittered, directing more cakes in Hume's direction.

"You find the French agreeable then?" said one of the gentlemen. "Though they signed the Treaty of Paris, I should think their experiences in the colonies would leave a bitter taste in their mouths."

"One they may yet spit out in our direction," said another. To general appreciation of his wit.

"The French love me, nonetheless," Hume said. Helping himself to a handful of cakes from the offered tray. "Perhaps it is no more than I am a Scot, and their bitterness is to the English. Amusing, wouldn't you say? The very quality that makes me anathema to the Anglo-Saxon makes me acceptable to the Gaul."

"You are too modest, David," Jean said. "You were a favorite of the great salons. You told us so yourself."

"It is true," Hume admitted.

"And a favorite with the ladies," Jean's father said.

"Oh the petite mademoiselles." Hume smiled.

"And with the madams, from what we hear," Jean's father added. With a look in Jean's direction.

"Their adulation was gratifying, if unexpected," Hume said. A flurry of crumbs cascading down the front of his jacket from the cake he was eating. The man neither aware nor caring. "It is enough to make one wonder if the translations they read of my work adequately carry my ideas."

There was general agreement that Hume was again being too modest. I ventured to finally say something.

"And are you writing anything at the moment, sir?

"At the moment, sir, I am eating a cake." There was general laughter at the witticism. I hoped my face hadn't colored. Feeling much the dolt. Hume apparently sensed that his amusement at my expense had embarrassed me, and attempted to make amends.

"I apologize for my facetiousness, young sir. That is one feature of the great Paris salons that I shall have to unlearn, if I wish to ever return to polite Edinburgh society. To answer your question: no, I am no writing at the moment. Though I hope to again soon. As soon as I can determine where I wish to settle now that my position at the embassy is drawing to an end, whether to return here to Edinburgh or to remain in Paris."

At that the conversation turned away from me again. And soon Jean's mother hustled us all to our feet, for the climb to the next level of the house for dinner. The event is a blur now, a cacophony of sights and sounds. Tureens of soup and silver serving dishes. Racks of lamb, roasted duck, a piglet. Mounds of vegetables, lakes of creamed dishes. Tinkling glasses, silverware. Attempts at conversation with the lady on my left. And through it all, across from me, Jean. The axis of my swirl of sensations. Her rich auburn hair piled high on her head catching the highlights from the candles. Her tiara winking. Her doe eyes wide and brimming with excitement. Sitting tall and erect, as if to keep me in her view. Or her in mine. Though there was a triangulation in her attentions through the meal. Her gaze traveling from Hume at the head of the table, talking to her mother. To me, then back to Hume.

When dinner was finished, Jean's father called for the table to be cleared. For the ladies to depart to another floor and drawing room for cards and entertainments. While the gentlemen should remain for brandy and pipes and conversation. But Jean announced that she would not leave. That she would remain with the gentlemen, and have at least a brandy and conversation, if not the pipe.

"Why should I have to leave, I should like to know? I would like to hear what is said when ladies leave the room. Is it possible that it is that much different than when we are present? Or is it because it is so distasteful, perhaps even indecent, that it would be improper for a young woman to hear?"

Jean's father sputtered, not knowing what to say. Her mother flittered about in circles as if she had lost her tail feathers. A social catastrophe was averted by Hume's good spirit. Laughter.

"Let her stay then, by all means, if she desires our company so ardently. Perhaps we should take a lesson from the French, who look to the women not only for pleasure to the eye but for stimulation to the wit."

"Thank you, David, for recognizing my value," Jean said. Her face flushed from triumph. And perhaps too much wine. Her net shawl had slipped down on one side. The side toward Hume. Exposing one fine bare if somewhat boyish shoulder. The expanse of skin seemingly all the more daring, forbidden, by the velvet collar around her lovely neck. "And do you find me a stimulation to your wit?"

"My dear," Hume said. Sitting up straighter in his chair. Taking a glass of brandy from a proffered tray and raising it in her direction. "If no for the presence of your father, and of your friend

Mr. Keating, I might tell you that I find you as well a stimulation to my pleasure."

He looked around slyly at the other gentlemen. Who all leaned back in laughter and appreciation. Casting meaningful glances to one another. Jean's father apparently trying to reason out that Hume had indeed said what he announced he wasn't going to. Though Jean was not to be undone.

"And you, sir. Because of the very presence of my father, and of my tutor, I will tell you that I take pleasure in your wit, as well as find you a stimulation to my eye, there being so much to admire in such a . . . great . . . man."

There was a nearly audible gasp around the table. From the daring of the double entendre. Jean's mother dropped the glass she was about to put on a servant's tray. The collective concern at how Hume would take the obvious reference to his size. Whether Jean had gone too far. But Hume roared his laughter, thumping the table in approval, and everyone joined in the laughter.

"That's what I've missed most these past years," Hume said. Taking a lace handkerchief, a dirty one, from his coat sleeve. Dabbing at his eyes, tears of enjoyment. "The . . . cheek . . . of a bonnie Scottish lass." He placed his hands together and rested them against his own cheek. Rubbing slightly as if to indicate sleep. And what it might imply.

There were more sniggers at Hume's cleverness. And the conversation moved on. To the news of the day, the word from the colonies. The latest trends of thought coming from the continent and London. But the exchange between Jean and Hume had depressed me, I wasn't sure why. I felt closed off. A watcher at an amusement, not among the players. I said little while the others carried forth. Though I noticed Jean too now took a listener's role. Looking at me occasionally. To see, I thought, if I had anything to add to what was being said. Or if I was enjoying myself.

For a time Hume held back in the exchanges. Offering only an occasional sagely "Yes, yes," "Very true," "Well said." Then grew impatient I sensed with talk not centered upon himself. Not to his level. With a commanding "Harrumph!" and much throat clearing, he once again held forth.

"Say what you will about the French, it is still very tempting to remain there in Paris, now that my work at the embassy is nearly done. Ah, as Adam Smith says, I am completely light-headed about the subject of my future abode. I confess I have no these four months risen and gone to bed in the same mind. When I meet with proofs of regard and affection from those I esteem here in Edinburgh, such as all of you this evening, I swear to myself that I shall never quit this place. But regardless, I must needs return to France before I make my final decision as to where to settle. There is still some unfinished business at the embassy I must attend to. And I will be mounting a rescue for the unfortunate Jean-Jacques Rousseau."

"Is he still in trouble with the authorities?" a gentleman named Willoughby said.

"More so than ever, I'm afraid."

"And are they still going on about that book?" Willoughby said.

"*Émile*," Hume said. "Yes, the French clerics have no taken kindly to his views on education. Of course as the Great Infidel, I'm used to such dilemmas. After my own unpleasant dealings with our own Edinburgh clerics."

"So you have been in contact with Rousseau?"

"Indeed. I have corresponded with him for a number of years, though I have never had the pleasure of meeting him in person. He even calls himself my 'pupil,' of all things. My friend the countess, Madame de Boufflers, has asked me if I could escort the nice little man to London for his protection, and I have agreed to do what I can."

"I have read Rousseau's notions of the Noble Savage, that society is artificial and corrupts the natural man," I put in. Quite before I realized I was going to.

Hume cocked one bushy eyebrow. As if a new plant form had just broken ground. He took a sip of his brandy and shifted his bulk my direction. The better to address me. "Have you, Mr. Keating?"

"I have. And I would add that such ideas seem quite in contrast to the reports from the colonies. From everything I've heard, the savages there are simply that: savages. To the extreme. They indulge themselves in the most heinous atrocities, torturing even women and children. There does no seem to be anything noble at all about such savages."

"In defense of the nice little man," Hume said, "I would reply that Rousseau has changed his thinking considerably since his early works. You must no be familiar with *The Social Contract*, it appeared a few years ago. Not widely read as yet, I'll admit, even in his home country, but I predict it will be. There he says that nature is a brutish condition without law or morality, and that there are good men only because men band together into society. It is the presence of society that makes men good."

He looked around at the group of gentlemen sitting at the table. At Jean. The light from the candles on the sideboard behind him haloing the tufts of hair around his ears. I wondered if Jean saw it, if she was having trouble not to laugh. As she had mentioned at the library when we first talked. But the expression on her face seemed anything but derisive. She met his gaze, sitting taller, regal. Like a cat does, rising to meet the hand that would stroke its head.

"On the other hand," I said, turning back to Hume, "it is said that the French were instrumental in turning loose the savages of America. That in the early days of their colonization, they were the ones who encouraged the Indians to display their savagery and atrocities. That in fact some of the worst atrocities, the torturing of captives, were committed by French soldiers themselves."

"I have heard that," Hume said. Taking new interest in me. "I have also heard, during the time I was in France, of equal tortures and atrocities committed by good English lads."

"See here, Hume," Willoughby said. Fairly sputtering. "I appreciate your love for the French and all. But to say that an Englishman, or even a Scot, would conduct himself in such an inhuman manner goes too far."

"I am only repeating what I have heard. In the same way that Mr. Keating is only repeating what he has heard about the French."

"Let us say for the sake of the argument that both reports are true," I said. Unwilling to let go, now that I had the great man engaged. Hoping in some way that Jean was following my logic. Admiring my reasoning. My ability to conduct at all such a discussion with Hume. "Then how does one find morality in such a world? You have said that morality exists because of the sympathy one man has for another. But surely, the savage in burning his captive at the stake or cutting chunks from his flesh has no sympathy in him."

"His morality would exist in the eyes of his fellows. They would share the rightness of the act, in sympathy for why he performed it, and thus would find what he did in torturing his victim, as we would call it, moral."

"But what of the Absolute? What of the morality that encompasses all? That reflects in all of us?"

"You are referring to God and some immutable laws. Some Greater Good, as it were. But that is what I've said elsewhere. You cannot know that such laws, or even God, exists. You have only your impressions, what you experience."

"But then how do you know what is right?" My voice, even to my own ears, becoming higher pitched. Strident.

"I would ask you," Hume purred. "What is this 'right' that you talk about?"

Hume looked around at the others. Who nodded and smiled and purred back their admiration for the turn of his argument. I felt suddenly, increasingly desperate. If what he said were true, how could he simply sit there calmly talking about it? The world was chaos, void. Incomprehensible. I knew the words on the page from reading him. But now I suddenly saw them. Grasped the world to which he referred. Horrific and terrifying. And he could sit there and discuss it placidly as if referring to a cribbage score. I wanted to try to pursue it further, but Jean interrupted.

"I think we have talked enough about tortures and dreadful things," she said. Looking at me sternly. Smiling only when she turned back to Hume. "This is supposed to be an evening's entertainment, you know. I would say you need a woman's touch after all, to keep your spirits and conversations from such darkness."

Hume raised his near empty glass in her honor. "You are intelligent, my dear, in the same degree that you are lovely. Speaking of tortures, eh gentlemen?"

Everyone laughed and raised their glasses in salute. Jean looked around happily. Her eyes traveling the table. To finally come to rest on mine. Happy again, this time sharing it with me. Almost anxious somehow, as if she were the one now who was seeking approbation. Appreciation of another's appreciation. My approval of her. I felt lost in my attempts to understand her, her twists of mood. But at the same time, found. In the radiance of her smile. Filled with the idea that she came to me to fill her.

He came out of the forest, running. Breaking through the brush. From 30 yards or so up the slope beside us. Fast. Screaming as he came. An Indian, naked except for loincloth, moccasins and thigh-high leather leggings. His body painted ashen, his face half-black, half-red. His war club raised. And a second. A few yards behind and to the left of the first. Running. Screaming. In total rage. Tomahawk in hand. The instant thought, terror: Are there more? And then: Does it all end here? But no, there were only the two. At first the sight taking us totally by surprise. I stood transfixed. Figures of a terrible beauty. Both of them angling down the hill. Each on a course. Converging. Toward Sergeant MacKenzie.

The sergeant was not as spellbound as I. At first sight of the Indians, he turned to face them. Cocked his musket. Aimed. Fired when the first attacker was only a few yards from him. The Indian slammed to the ground. Like a dropped stone. But the second Indian was now almost upon him. Elizabeth fired Donald Fraser's musket but the ball went high. The kick of the musket hurling her backward, knocking her off her feet. MacKenzie braced for the charge. The events unfolding in front of me as if in a dream, slowed in time. The sergeant, infinitely slow, reaching for his sword. The savage, in increments, racing down the slope forever. And in a dream I fired. The ball hitting the charging Indian in the shoulder. Spinning him like a child's toy, a rag doll. Flinging him into the bushes.

The explosions of the muskets rang in my ears. Smoke drifted over us, the sergeant and myself, as we stood there. Looking around. Waiting for the next wave. Duncan, wakened from his own dream, hurrying toward us. The stillness of the place, of the afternoon, gradually returning. Settling over us again. The awareness that at least for now it was over. The granules of gunpowder bitter on my lips. The smoke from the muskets drifting off, through the brush, among the trees. Like shades returning to the forest. Ghosts returning from where they came.

"Load again, Ensign," Sergeant MacKenzie said calmly, almost under his breath. Already biting the end off a cartridge and priming the pan. "Quickly. And then fix your bayonet. The savages may no be done with this business."

I fumbled with my cartridge case. My fingers all at once not working. Shaking, trembling violently of a sudden, a life of their own. The sergeant, an eye still on the brush up the slope, moved sideways to where Elizabeth, dazed, sat on the ground in the ferns. Duncan coming over to help too.

"Aye, missy, 'tis no the time for sitting around playing the wee shepherd lass," MacKenzie said wryly. Trying to ease our tension. Trying to relieve his own.

He reached down, placed his free hand under her arm. Lifted her to her feet. She tried to pull away from him and gave a yip. Slumped in pain.

"It's her shoulder," Duncan said, reaching for her. Trying to steady her on her feet.

"Brown Bess can deliver quite a kick," the sergeant said. Not without sympathy.

He turned and looked at me. "And you, Ensign? Are you all right then?"

"Yes, yes, I'm fine," I stammered out. "I'll be fine. What do we do now, Sergeant? Will they come again?"

"I think they're through for now. These two must have been a test. To try our resolve, I suppose."

"They were coming for you, Sergeant."

"Aye, they were now, weren't they? But it was a futile thing, as it turned out. I thank you for your quick wit and good aim. Now I think we must finish this business here."

He was watching the second Indian. Wounded, moaning softly. Trying to drag himself off. Into the brush. A trail of blood over the liverwort and Queen Anne's lace. MacKenzie handed me his musket. Started to unsheathe his basket-hilt sword. Then looked at me from under his sand-colored brows.

"Unless this hunting is yours?"

I could only shake my head. He nodded, drew his sword, and went to the fallen Indian.

"Sergeant," Duncan said. "Perhaps if it was only a test, we should let him return to his fellows. Perhaps it would help give us passage up the river."

The sergeant paused. Looked at Duncan a moment. Almost as if disappointed.

"A few miles behind us, Donald Fraser breathes dirt through the wound in his throat. Looks for the sky but sees only the earth that covers him. I would no pay for safe passage with that memory."

He went and stood over the crawling Indian. Rolled him over so they could see each other. The Indian, his mouth full of blood, trying to speak.

"*Cuidich' n' righ,*" MacKenzie said. Almost in an undertone. Almost like a prayer. Lifting his basket-hilt sword two-handed, blade pointing down. The hilt raised above him like the host at mass. Then plunging it straight down into the Indian's heart. A sickening crunch of bone. Gurgle of blood. The man's brief cry. The sergeant pulling it out again just as quickly. Looking down at him. "*Luceo non uro.*" Then looked at us. As if to punctuate a discussion.

Elizabeth ducked her head into Duncan's chest. I could only stare at Sergeant MacKenzie's eyes. Two chinks of uncaring sky.

"How is she?" the sergeant asked Duncan.

"I don't know. The shoulder may be broken."

"We have to go on."

"Don't concern yourself with me, Sergeant MacKenzie," Elizabeth said. Moving away from Duncan. "I will match you step for step on this journey. Broken shoulder or not."

She reached down to pick up the fallen musket and yipped again. Nearly fell. Duncan grabbed her. Held her until she was steady again. Bent down and picked up the musket.

"You can't. . . ," she started to say.

"Aye, I can," Duncan said. "I'll take the belts and bags as well. 'Twould be off-balance without them."

He helped Elizabeth slip out of Donald Fraser's sword and cartridge belts, the haversack, which she had draped about her. Picked up her cloth bundle where it had fallen and rolled into a bush.

"You can't take everything," she said. Taking the bundle. Tucked it gingerly under her good arm. To show that she was able to manage it. I wanted to go to her. Be the one to help her. But knew I couldn't. Shouldn't.

The sergeant studied her a moment, then looked at me. As if to cue the command.

"Duncan will lead again," I said. Fighting to keep my voice steady. The voice of an officer. "The same formation as before. Let's away."

Duncan and the sergeant turned and continued along the trail. As Elizabeth started to take her place we looked at each other.

"Are you sure you can make it?" I asked.

"Don't worry about me, Ensign." She started to turn away then stopped. Softened a bit. "We still have much to talk about between us. When this is over."

I think I colored slightly.

She smiled, though in obvious pain. "The sergeant owes you his life, you know."

Before this is over, we will probably both owe him ours.

"I think it will be another way, Thomas. But we will see." She touched my arm. Ahead on the trail, Duncan and MacKenzie had stopped. Looking back at us. I motioned with my head to

Elizabeth and we fell in single file behind the others. Continuing along the river.

Above the cut of the valley, tall clouds mounted in the strip of sky. Building higher, roll on roll. Sliding eastward quickly. Blown by winds that couldn't touch us along the river. Darkening with the possibility of storms. We had been on the trail again less than an hour when Sergeant MacKenzie pulled up. Stepped aside into the brush, letting Elizabeth pass him. Watching her as she went by. She watching him defiantly as she passed as well. The sergeant waiting for me to come along. Joined beside me. The two of us lagging back a few paces.

"How d'you think she fares then?" he asked.

I watched Elizabeth on the trail ahead of us. Aware that her pace had slowed since the attack. Her body canted slightly. Favoring her right shoulder. "I think she's struggling a bit. But would rather die than admit to it. To either one of us."

"Aye. 'Tis probably so." He shook his head ruefully. We walked on for a minute or two. Our muskets, bayonets attached, at the ready in front of us. Before he got to what was on his mind.

"May I ask what she said to you back there when we were starting off again, Ensign?"

"You may no, Sergeant. 'Twas a private matter."

"Aye, I have no doubt. But in our situation, I fear there can be no private matters. I would no ask you if I did no think it important. If I did no think she might say something to help us know the way of things."

"How would she know more the way of things than you or I?"

"I d'no know. But I would feel the easier if I could know she dinna."

"Why do you no trust her, Sergeant? Perhaps you're the one who knows more and should be telling me. Or is this like the

missing sheep when the dog was killed back at the outpost? You
lied to me about that. And I know you told the men to no talk
to me. It would seem if anyone is keeping information about the
way of things, 'tis you."

We walked together in silence several minutes. I wanted to
turn to see the expression on the sergeant's face. But now that I
had raised the attack, I didn't want to give anything away on my
own.

"I d'no know much about our situation then, Ensign. And
what I did know. . . . Well, I d'no want to bother you, I d'no
think it concerned you."

"Yet I was the ranking officer."

"Aye. A very new ranking officer."

"In other words, you d'no think I'd know what to do."

"There was no knowing about it. There was no anything to
do, at that time. But aye, you're right. I suppose I was trying to
forestall as much as safeguard you."

"And has that changed?"

"Aye. I know you better now. You've shown you are a fighting
man."

"No just an engineer."

"Aye. No just an engineer."

"No a Highlander, though," I said. Unable to resist the jibe.

"Well, a part of one, it seems," he said. I turned and caught
the slight smile on the man's face as he added, "The better part."

Something seemed to have lifted from between us. Something
had passed. I felt for the first time as though I might have a
companion here in the wilderness. Someone who might stand beside me. Joined. I felt for the first time a true soldier of the Black
Watch. Though I still had questions of the man.

"You still have no told me, Sergeant. Why do you distrust the
woman so?"

Sergeant MacKenzie sighed. As if he hoped I had forgotten.

"There is something no right there, Ensign, as I told you back at the post," he said after a moment. Choosing carefully his words. His thoughts to express. "And I am no alone in the feeling. Black Duncan shares it, but he is a better man than I. He can show kindness. I am more chary."

I was torn. On the one hand to know more of his suspicions. On the other to defend this woman with whom I had shared intimacy. Who had entered my feelings.

"Is it because of why she came to the outpost? Because she followed Lieutenant Stewart there from Fort Pitt? Or because she follows him now up the river? When he felt so strongly that she should no that he had you tie her to a post? It would seem that he was trying to stay a distance from her. Did he share your suspicions of her?"

"I d'no know why Robbie Stewart did no wish her to follow him. It may have been simply from the danger, which was surely reason enough. Yet I agree it would seem he was trying to stay a distance from her. And that was no the case before."

"What happened before?"

"Och, I have said too much of Robbie Stewart as it is."

Perhaps she heard the mention of Lieutenant Stewart. Or perhaps she had other reasons for wondering what the sergeant and I discussed. Perhaps, I wondered, she just wanted to see that I was there. Hoped. Whatever the reason, Elizabeth looked back over her shoulder. At the sergeant and me. I met her eyes, nodded, and she turned back to the trail. I did not look at the sergeant. To see if he was watching me. But by unspoken consent, we slowed our pace. To drop back farther, so as not to be overheard again.

"I appreciate your loyalty to the man, Sergeant. I hope someday to earn that degree of loyalty and trust from the men who serve in my command. And I understand why you've tried to keep me from knowing too much of what went on with him. You were concerned that I might carry such tales back to Fort Pitt. That Lieutenant Stewart could risk court-martial if they learned in Philadelphia or London that he risked his command on a questionable rescue mission of an obscure Indian village. I admit a few days ago I probably would have made sure such tales were heard at Fort Pitt. But I have learned quickly that there are too many unknowns in this wilderness to judge quickly a man for the decisions he makes here. And I remind you of your own words: our circumstances here dictate that there can be no private matters. I need to know as much as I can about Lieutenant Stewart. And about Elizabeth."

MacKenzie looked ahead. At the back of the woman walking before us. "Aye, Thomas. That you do, to be sure."

The sergeant told me that after Lieutenant Stewart came to the outpost, he returned occasionally to Fort Pitt. Accompanying the details he sent there for supplies. To oversee the procurement from the quartermaster's stores, as well as to make his reports to the commandant. Then one day last winter, the lieutenant went to the fort alone. Told Sergeant MacKenzie that he had been ordered there, that he would only be gone a few days. The sergeant was not aware of a courier who could have carried such a message, but he did not question it. Thought it odd but had no reason or inclination to doubt. He was more concerned with the thought of the lieutenant traveling through the forest without a guide or escort. In winter when a storm could come up at any time. But when he mentioned his concerns to Stewart before he left, the lieutenant for once was curt with his replies. Gave the sergeant his duty orders while he would be gone, and told him, in effect, to tend to his own business.

Which the sergeant did. Until, two days after Lieutenant Stewart had left, a dispatch arrived for him from Fort Pitt. The sergeant questioned the courier, learned there had been no other recent dispatches for the lieutenant. No special orders of which the courier was aware. MacKenzie had the presence of mind to tell the courier that Lieutenant Stewart's reply to the dispatch he had brought would follow in a few days. Giving himself some time to try to find out what was going on. It was obvious, though, that Lieutenant Stewart was not at Fort Pitt. Had never intended to be. At least not at the fort itself, which didn't rule out the town around it. MacKenzie's first concern was that, wherever the lieutenant was headed, he had made it there safely. He was ready to organize a search party. Called in a couple of Mohawk scouts to help. When Lieutenant Stewart returned on his own. Sergeant MacKenzie wanted to either kiss him or hit him. Threat of the cat-o'-nine-tails forestalled the latter, his anger the former. Instead he presented the lieutenant with the dispatch.

"What did he say?" I asked.

"He just looked at it a moment. Asked if I had read it. I told him I had no, that it was no my place. So he opened it. Turned out to be some general order, an unimportant thing. He asked what I had said to the courier and I told him. He looked relieved and thanked me."

We walked in silence for several moments. Falling naturally into step, our buckled shoes in measured tread. Crunch of fallen twigs along the trail. Dried leaves, pebbles, dust. Above the valley the sun was playing games among the clouds. Hiding behind the gathering thunderheads. The world plunged momentarily into the strange half-light of an eclipse. Then bursting forth again. Golden beams radiating through the breaks. Glinting off the edges of darkling clouds swollen with rain. The trees around us still motionless. Holding their breath that the storms would pass. While on the ridgelines of the hills, the trees were caught in the higher winds. Branches, treetops swaying like supplicants to the air. All praise.

MacKenzie had been forthcoming in his story of the lieutenant. I didn't want to push him, drive him away. I wanted to continue to build, to earn his confidence. In a few minutes, as I had hoped, he continued.

"I reminded the lieutenant that I had put myself in jeopardy. That my lie could lead to a court-martial, if it should come to that. He said he would make sure it did no."

"You did no ask him anything more about where he was? Or why?"

"I could no. No more than I can ask you now about your relationship with the woman."

I hoped my embarrassment didn't show upon my face and went on. "But you think his being away had something to do with Elizabeth?"

"Aye, but d'no ask me how. A feeling, a sense, that was all of it. And then she turned up at Fort Bouquet a few months later. Just at the time smoke was seen from the Onagona village."

"You think there was a connection?"

He shrugged. "How would I know?"

"Do you think Lieutenant Stewart thought there was a connection? Do you think that's why he went up the country, and wanted to keep the woman here? What kind of connection could there be?"

"I dinna know, Ensign. And I d'no know what was on Robbie Stewart's mind when he left. I only know he did so, at a time and for a reason he should no. And he left the woman with me. Och, he left me with orders to tie her hands, but it was mine he tied. . . ."

"Sergeant! Ensign!"

Ahead Duncan Murchie came running back along the trail. Pushed Elizabeth to the ground and knelt in front of her. Facing the forest. Motioning us down as well. Sergeant MacKenzie and I turned to where he was looking. At the dozen Indians up the hillside. Standing motionless among the trees.

There is a blinding flash. Illuminating for seconds the room around me. Beyond the midday, my blockhouse has grown increasingly dark. Gray as wash water. Now the flash of light is followed by the crash of an explosion. Dark rumblings. For the briefest moment I think: They have come. They attack. Cannon. But I know already such is not true. It is lightning from outside, a fierce summer storm. A flash again, repeated. For the moment I leave my writing and go to stand at the musket ports. Knowing I may never see the like again.

Air presses through the westward portals with the winds. As yet the rain only splatterings. Single heavy isolated drops. I hurry up the stairs to the second floor for a better view. Now the drops are more frequent. Like musket balls at the far limits of a fusillade, though I have never experienced such a thing. Drumming on the wood slats. I watch across the distant Ohio. The hills beyond the wider valley to the west. Obliterated. A dark veil of gray drawn over them, approaching. Obscuring everything before it. As the main front of the storm reaches, engulfs me.

Then all is water, darkness. The curtains of rain sweep over the ramparts and the blockhouse. Peppering, plashing the roof above my head. My face close to the musket port is dampened, washed fresh. I press my face to the opening, open my mouth and feel the fresh fresh water over my tongue and lips, anointing my cheeks. I am immersed in the joy of being alive. I can no longer tell if the moisture on my face is from the rain or tears.

I cross the five-sided room. Under the holes I put in the roof earlier with the musket shot when I thought someone climbed there. The rain in several streams, creating puddles on the floor. To the gunports with their view of the remains of the outbuildings. The slope down to the Allehela River and the hills on the opposite side of the narrow valley. Though now all is rain, rain. Sheets of rain rippling down the hill, curtain after curtain, gray upon gray. Broken with flashes of lightning, deep thunder. As I watch, a bolt cracks the sky. Jabs and jabs the bluff of the hill across the river. I stand in wonder at the scene unfolding, for me alone.

In the flash of light, are those figures moving among the ruined buildings? Hunched, stealthy. Ghosts of men. Looking for who knows what. Using the rain to approach the blockhouse. I cannot tell. I have learned, though not soon enough, to trust nothing that I see. Impressions, that is all. Hume's words, though now I live them. The world a shadow. Phantom of itself. Even when most real. Most deadly.

What did Elizabeth think when Sergeant MacKenzie dropped back to talk to me? When the sergeant and I walked together behind her, keeping out of earshot. Talked together like conspirators. Her brief reminder to me, as we started on the trail again, stirred my emotions all over again. That there was still much for us to talk about. Once this journey was complete. That small crumb of interest had made me hungrier than ever to talk to her. To reaffirm the events that had happened between us. To assure myself that what had happened was real. That her feelings for me were real. Wondering even as I talked to the sergeant, seeking information on my suspicions of her.

I wanted to know the depth of her affections for Lieutenant Stewart. If by some chance we did find Stewart and his detail alive, if reunited with the lieutenant, would she forget all thoughts and feelings for me? I feared, could only believe it would be so. She had followed Stewart from Fort Pitt. Alone, through a dangerous forest. Having no idea what she would find when she arrived. What else would drive a woman so except a deep and abiding love? The thought made me cringe inside. Then, as the memory of it does now. Didn't it mean that, to her, I was only close at hand, available? Nothing more? I shared Sergeant Mac-Kenzie's suspicions of her, but for different reasons. I needed to know more of her in the past, to determine the course she had in mind for the future. I longed to go to her, to walk with her, be with her. Even at the moment I was questioning the sergeant about her. But the new threat we encountered up the valley drove all such questions out of mind.

Sergeant MacKenzie and I ducked. At the sight of the Indians up the hillside among the trees. Knelt on one knee, then scrambled forward, beside Black Duncan. Elizabeth lying behind us, closer to the river among some rocks. Wincing with fresh pain from her shoulder, from Duncan pushing her.

"How long have they been there?" MacKenzie asked, checking his musket.

"I d'no know," Duncan said. "I just noticed them."

"What are they doing?" I asked. My heart about to burst through the belts across my chest. My bowels cramping, watery.

"Nothing from the looks of it," the sergeant said. "Watching the wee Highland laddies play groundhog."

We knelt in silence several minutes. Waiting. The Indians on the hillside apparently waiting too.

"If they were going to attack, they would have," Elizabeth said behind us. Sitting up, sidesaddle on a low rock.

"Are they Huron?" I asked.

She nodded. Rubbing her shoulder inside her blouse.

"'Tis the same war party that came to the fort," Sergeant MacKenzie said. "I recognize the lad there, the one with his face painted black with the red stripes. It appears your friend, the one you spoke to, has followed you, Ensign Keating."

My heart sank. Was I the reason the Indians were there? Had they come for me? Thoughts raced through my mind. That I should sacrifice myself for the others. For Elizabeth. If I offered myself, would they allow the others safe passage? Was I brave enough to do that? But Elizabeth spoke behind us.

"It is not the ensign they come for."

We looked at her. But she kept her head lowered. Working her right shoulder with her opposite hand. As if it were her only concern.

"Aye missy, who is it they come for then?" Sergeant MacKenzie said softly.

Elizabeth ignored him. Rubbing her shoulder.

"If they did no come for me, perhaps they did no come for any of us," I offered. Feeling as I said it that such a thought was only wishful thinking.

"Aye, I'm sure of it," the sergeant said. Sarcastic. Turning back to the hillside. "'Tis only a wee stroll in the woods the Indian lads are after. Afraid the petticoat warriors might be feeling lonesome."

The Indians continued to stand motionless among the trees. Not talking among themselves. Watching. Waiting for something. After another minute, Duncan lay down Donald Fraser's musket, undid the case for his fiddle from his back. Took out the instrument and bow.

"And what do you think you're about, Black Duncan?" MacKenzie said. "Play the lads a tune, then? Charm the savages with a reel or strathspey?"

"It would appear, Adam, this may be my last day on this earth. And I c'no stand the thought of never playing my fiddle again. It would seem it will have no bearing on the outcome here. And that's the way of it."

"Och, why no?" MacKenzie looked back at the hillside. Shaking his head. "The Indians love the crazy ones. Maybe they'll take pity on you. Pity on us all."

Duncan finished his tuning. Sat on the edge of the trail. Close to Elizabeth. Facing the river. The expanse of the slow-moving water through the sycamores along the bank. The steep rise of the opposite wall of the valley. And began to play. "I Would Search a Long Way." "Red Angus' Wife." "The Kaimes Lasses."

The sound of the lone fiddle winding among the murmur of the river. The touch of wind in the tall trees. The calls of blue jays. A thrush. Crows.

On the hillside the Indians didn't move. Blank-faced. Unreadable. Almost as if they expected the music. Were waiting for it. Had come to hear it, though such was not the case. After several minutes, while Duncan still played, the leader took several steps forward. Raised his war club above his head. Stood motionless.

"What the bloody hell is the bugger up to now?" the sergeant said.

The Indian continued to stand there. War club raised.

"Maybe he salutes us. Or Duncan," I said. "The way you raised your sword to the woods, after you found Donald Fraser."

"I d'no know. But if the red devil does no do something soon, I say we continue on."

"We might as well try it," I said. Getting slowly to my feet. The sergeant standing up beside me. "Are you still with us, Elizabeth?"

"I am still with you, Ensign."

I went over to help her to her feet. Our eyes meeting briefly. Before each looked quickly away.

"Duncan, will you continue to play as we go?"

He nodded, rising to his feet. Elizabeth took up her bundle again. I picked up Donald Fraser's musket, slung it over my shoulder.

"'Tis a wee humble parade we make, my darlings," Sergeant MacKenzie said. "Let us see where the long path takes us. And may the Lord of All Things Holy walk with us."

"Amen," I said. Forgetting for the moment Mr. Hume's skepticism. Keeping my eye on the line of sullen Indians within the dark edges of the forest.

"The Brown-Haired Maiden." "Over the Water to Charlie." "Johnnie Cope." Duncan led us in single file along the trail. The line of Indians keeping pace with us, shadowing us along the low slope of the hill. Among the trees. The Black Lad played for a mile or so. Then rested a ways, plucking the instrument for his own hearing as he walked, before taking up a tune again. The day had continued to darken. Layers of clouds, gray upon gray, streaming above the hills. Following the course of the river. Like a curtain drawn over the length of the valley. A net. On the distant hills before us rain drifted through the slopes of the forest. Obliterating the world in patches, smudged beyond recognition. Though always ahead of us, the rain holding off around us. By midafternoon rain would have been a relief. The air heavy, humid. The heat oppressive. The wool of our tunics and waistcoats damp to the touch. Sweat soaking our bodies. Our pace slowed noticeably from our exhaustion. The awareness of Elizabeth's difficulties, her sore shoulder. The tension from the presence of our Indian familiars. Then Duncan would begin to play again. Our spirits, if not our pace, lifting a little. "The Forty-Twa." "The Black Bear." "Highland Laddie."

Late afternoon. The rain had stopped on the distant hills. But the air around us was heavier than ever. Damp. Dank. The shades of gray seen earlier in the sky over the valley now the color of the valley. A world of gray. Ahead the valley steepened even further. The sandstone bluffs on this side rising abruptly from the river. Cutting off passage. The path turned toward the river. Shallow now after the spring runoff. Receding with the advent of summer. Shrunken to the middle of the channel. The dry banks sloping down to 10 yards or so of exposed riverbed. The path visible again on the other side of the ford. At the top of the opposite exposed riverbank, climbing up into the forest. We stood clustered together on this side's stony bank. Watching the shallow rapids. Elizabeth rested, sitting in the crook of a low tree above where the water normally was.

"How far is it from here to the Onagona village?" I asked the sergeant. He in turn looked to Duncan.

"'Tis only a mile or thereabouts from the other side of the crossing," Black Duncan said.

I was surprised the sergeant deferred to Duncan. But there were other concerns at the moment to pursue. "I d'no think we should go forward this night. For the same reason you had when we left the fort, Sergeant. We are too tired now to confront whatever it is we shall find with the Onagonas. We need to rest and attempt it in the morning."

"And what of our Indian lads out there in the woods? D'you think they'll be content to sit on their haunches till we're ready to move again?"

"It would seem to be no matter. If they're going to attack us, they will do so whenever it suits them, either here or at the village. Or wherever. We can do little more than wait regardless. For my thinking, we take our chances and try to get some rest."

"Och, I suppose you are right. It pains me to be this close to finding out what happened to Robbie and the others. But we are in no shape to help anyone in our current state. We must post guard, though. If the savages attack in the night, I would take some with me to help greet our Maker."

"What do you say, Elizabeth?" I asked her.

She looked at me from her low perch. As if to read the motive for my inquiry. Though I was unsure myself why I asked it.

"The sergeant can get his rest," Elizabeth said finally. "The Indians will not attack tonight."

"And would you know as well why they keep us company on our unhappy jaunt?" MacKenzie asked.

She looked away. As if too tired, too weary to try to explain. Herself or the Indians.

"Maybe I can catch us a fish or two," Black Duncan said.

"Aye, that's a good idea," I said. "Our food is running low."

Black Duncan set about. Full of new enthusiasm for his project. Taking a hook and line from his leather pouch. Digging grubs from the soft soil under the crust of the riverbed. Trailing several lines in the shallow stream. As the sergeant and Elizabeth and I made camp and got settled in the grass along the top of the bank. In a short time Duncan had a row of bass and catfish lying on the bank beside us. He sorted them carefully into two groups, one with a few more fish than the other. Then looked around till he found a bough with the branches attached. Stripped it of leaves and pruned the small branches till it looked like a crude candelabrum. Stuck the openmouthed fish from the larger pile on the remaining branches, a splay of fish. Then holding it in front of him like a shield, a reliquary, he took it a ways up the hillside into the woods. Near to where we last saw the Indians. Planted it in the ground and came back down the hill to camp. Gathering sticks of firewood as he came.

"I d'no think my wee gift will stop them from whatever it is they have in mind for us," Duncan said. Digging in his haversack for his flint and steel to start a fire. "But maybe it will confuse them a bit."

"Aye, I guess we may as well have a fire," Sergeant MacKenzie said. "'Tis certain enough they know we're here."

As Duncan built his fire, the sergeant prepared the fish and mounted them on long sticks. The four of us at the four points of the compass. Holding our fish over the fire. Like swordsmen pledging our loyalties to each other. The oil and water hissing and spitting as they dropped into the flames. The gray light emptied quickly from the valley. As though sucked into the dark forests on the hills. Fog rising from the water in wisps. Like genies, hovering. The world muffled. As the darkling turned to dark, we could see the Indians' fire farther up the slope among the trees. Mirror of our own.

When we were finished eating, we wiped our fingers in the grass. Tossed the bones and fish heads into the river so as not to attract bears or vermin. Sergeant MacKenzie wrapped his plaid loosely about himself. Lying beside a log.

"What think you, Ensign?" he said. Closing his eyes. Appearing close to sleep. "Do we trust our missy when she tells us that the Indians will no attack this night?"

I looked at Elizabeth. For assurance or a sign. But she was already curled into her blanket. Asleep, or trying to be.

"I will trust her, Sergeant. She has given us no cause to think otherwise."

If Elizabeth was awake I hoped she heard my support of her. My faith in her. And in the doing, was there also the wish to make it so? Whatever, Sergeant MacKenzie did not reply. Already succumbed to his exhaustion.

For a time I sat there, my back against a boulder. Watched the flames diminish into ashes. An occasional spark popping free, tiny skyrocket. Rising to oblivion. The smoke from our fire hung in the heavy air, mixing with the fog. Settling in layers through the darkness around us. Duncan was also awake. Sitting at an angle to me, my west to his north.

"Even on a warm evening," I said, an introduction to conversation, "there is something of comfort in a fire."

"Aye. I was thinking the same. And wondering of the others. Up the hill there. Do they feel the same comfort as we? Or do they no have the need? By being the pursuer, no the pursued?"

"I would think they do. They are men, after all. Like you and me."

"Do you think so then?" Duncan said. Considering the matter for a moment. Eyes downcast under his dark brow. "There are many who think no. But I agree with you. Though they are different beings, for all that. The Onagona, to be sure."

"What do you know about the Onagonas? They seem a mystery to everyone."

"They are that to be sure, a mystery." Duncan removed his bonnet, ran his hand through his shaggy hair. Staring into the fire. As though remembering something. Reflecting. "But aye, I probably know more of them than most. I was with Lieutenant Stewart when he went to the Onagona village."

"I d'no know he had been there before."

"Last winter it was. Colonel Berry, the chief, invited Lieutenant Stewart to visit the village."

"You mean when the chief came to warn Stewart? Donald Fraser told me that was in the spring. Just a few weeks before the scouts saw the smoke from up the valley."

Black Duncan was shaking his head. "No, it was earlier. Like I say, 'twas the winter. The month of February, though I could no tell you the date. Colonel Berry came to the outpost to trade. Some bear and beaver skins for salt. The only reason the old chief came later to warn him was because Robbie Stewart had showed he was a friend of the Onagona."

"How did he do that?"

"By trading for the skins when he did no need them. Because he knew the Onagona needed salt. And because he made the trip to the village, when the old chief invited him. For his kindness Berry told him the Onagona would let him see the gods who dance under the earth. The gods from the Underworld."

"And he invited you too? Did anyone else go to the village? The sergeant?"

"No. 'Twas only me and the lieutenant. The chief told the lieutenant to bring me along. Berry said I was the only one at the outpost who already saw what the lieutenant would see."

"Was it true? What you saw at the village—had you seen it before?"

"Och, no. I d'no know what the old man was blathering about. I never saw anything like it in my life."

Light snow had begun to fall soon after Duncan and Lieutenant Stewart started their journey up the valley. On the day appointed by Colonel Berry for their visit. By the time they neared the Onagona village, crossing over the frozen river, an inch or so of snow covered the ground. It was dusk, evening coming early with winter. The gray day—gray the sky, gray the color of the hills and forests—deepening quickly into darkness. Broken by the glow of fires ahead through the trees. Coming from the doorways of the forty or so dwellings. The collection of oblong huts, made of woven branches plastered with mud. The glow from dozens of outdoor ovens shaped like beehives. The air thick with wood smoke. The smell of burning pine. Fresh-made bread, meat, unfamiliar food and spices. Light snow still falling.

The village was bustling with activity in the darkness. Groups of women gathered around the outdoor ovens. Men wrapped in blankets and layers of robes bustling about. As if in preparation for a feast or festival. After the long hike, the trail slippery and difficult with the skiff of snow, Duncan and Lieutenant Stewart were famished. Their stomachs rumbling with anticipation at the host of delicious smells. When the two tired soldiers finally located the chief, Colonel Berry greeted them warmly. The old man skittering about them with delight that they had come. But rather than taking them to one of the houses and offering them something to eat or drink, he hustled them over to a raised platform in the center of the village. Which turned out to be the roof of an underground structure. An opening in the roof with the parallel poles of a ladder pointed to the sky. Berry told them they needed to hurry if they were to get good seats and led the way down the ladder. Duncan and the lieutenant looked at each other.

Having no idea what the old man was talking about. But they followed him down the hole. Into the earth.

They found themselves in a large chamber. Large enough to seat everyone in the village around the perimeter, if they sat close. Colonel Berry led Duncan and the lieutenant to a raised area at one end. Finding them seats among the elders already seated there. The Scottish soldiers apparently guests of honor. The villagers continued to climb down the ladder. Talking in hushed, excited voices, a feeling of expectation in the air. The four sides filling up quickly. Leaving a long empty space in the middle of the floor around the base of the ladder. When everyone was settled, wooden bowls were passed around and cauldrons of food appeared. A kind of stew made with venison and vegetables. And loaves of fresh bread. Everyone eating with their fingers, slurping noisily and sopping up the liquid.

Duncan and Lieutenant Stewart began to wonder if the meal was what they were invited for. Because after they ate, everyone continued to sit where they were. Talking quietly among themselves. When they looked at Colonel Berry for guidance, the old Indian just grinned at them. As if telling them to be patient and chiding them for not being so. Then in the distance, from above-ground, they heard something. Growing louder, coming closer. A many, measured tread. Rattles of some kind, alternating with sleigh bells. *Clack-jingle-clack-jingle.* And low voices. Chanting. A song. As the figures walked on the roof, circling the opening. Then descending. Slowly, with great dignity. Twenty figures or more. Identical. Their bodies painted white. Eyes enlarged with black circles. Mouths like black slits. With a ruff made of pine boughs around the neck. Dressed in a kind of kilt, white, woven of rough cloth, with the ends of a long sash dangling down. Each with a rattle made from a turtle shell tied to the back of one leg. A sleigh bell tied behind the other. In the right hand another rattle. In the left a small bow and arrow, like a child's toy, decorated with feathers and pine.

The figures drew up in a line, extending from one end of the chamber to the other. Accompanied by an old man, whose job it seemed was to keep them in order, shout encouragement. When they were arranged, the figures began to chant. Keeping time with the rattles in their hands. Stomping with the right foot in the dust on the floor. A low rolling chant, as if sung from some great distance. The song weaving in and out among the onlookers. As they sang, the figures turning slowly. Starting at the head of the line, one after the other, until all were facing the new direction. Then turning again, one after the other, working their way down the line. Until all were facing the original direction.

The song. The stomping. The rhythmic clack of the rattles, jingle of the bells. Reaching inside Duncan and the lieutenant. Right through them. As if grabbing them within their beings. In their bellies, in their bowels. The two Scots mesmerized by the chanting figures, the closeness of the room, those sitting around them.

At one point, Colonel Berry leaned over to Duncan. Whispered in his ear. "You see, Scottish soldier. We have petticoat warriors too." He leaned away and grinned widely to Duncan. As if it were a great joke. Though his eyes glistened, bore into Duncan. As if it were the most serious thing in the world.

After an hour or so, the figures stopped their singing and dancing. Climbed back up the ladder and went away, their muffled chant, the sound of the rattles and bells, growing distant. But no one in the chamber moved. A few spoke in hushed voices. Made comments about the figures, the song. Then after a period of time came the distant *clack-jingle-clack-jingle* again, the chant growing louder as the figures returned. Descended into the chamber to repeat their dance. The cycle repeated through the night. Until dawn. The first gray light of day illuminating the hole in the roof.

Though this time when the figures climbed the ladder, the Indians in the chamber rose and followed them, Colonel Berry directing Duncan and Lieutenant Stewart to follow as well. After the heat and stuffiness of the chamber, the cold hit them at the top of the ladder like a wall. The snow had stopped during the night. Only a few flurries drifting in the predawn air. The Indians followed the dancers through the village. Duncan and the lieutenant trailing behind. Everyone in total silence. Only the sound of the rattles and bells, the crunch of footsteps in the crust of snow. The Indians following to the edge of the village then stopped. Standing in silence as they watched the line of dancers disappear into the dark woods. Duncan and Lieutenant Stewart with an overwhelming sadness and feeling of loss.

"What happened then?" I asked.

Duncan was lost in reverie a moment. A dark squat figure, shoulders rolled. Sitting crosslegged before the last of our cook fire. The remains of logs turned to embers, glowing from within.

"Berry took us to one of the huts. They had more food for us there, and bearskin blankets. We slept most of the day. We both hoped there would be more dancing the second night, but if there was, we were no invited. The next day we came back to the post."

"It made an impression then, what you saw at the village?"

"Aye," Duncan smiled to himself. "An impression indeed." But he wouldn't say more than that.

"And Lieutenant Stewart?"

Duncan thought a moment. Wanting to get it right before he spoke. "I think what the lieutenant saw changed him. But you'd have to ask him to be sure."

"I hope I have the chance. That's one of several questions I have for him. But I think we both know I may no have that chance. Tell me why you think it changed him."

"I think it changed the way he thought about the Indians. Before I think he saw them as savages only. I know the Onagonas are different than other tribes. That they d'no really belong here, they're just passing through on some kind of migration. But I think seeing the dances opened his thinking to all Indians. It made him aware there might be more to them than he thought."

"What makes you think that?"

"Before he used to wonder why white people had any sympathy for the Indians. Why some white people even went to live with them. He talked to me about it, when we were with Colonel Bouquet bringing the captives back from the Ohio."

We both looked at Elizabeth. Curled into herself next to a rock. Her back to us. Asleep. Or pretending to be. I didn't dare ask if she was the reason the lieutenant had such questions. But Duncan realized something of my wondering.

"Aye. That too."

I tried to think what else I might ask him. That wouldn't raise more questions if Elizabeth were to hear. Surprised at myself, to find I had such reluctance.

"So he had more respect for the Indians, after visiting the village?"

"Aye, at least for the Onagona. He felt he had some kind of bond with them I think. Particularly after Berry came to the post a while after that and told him the Onagona were leaving and that the old chief feared the other tribes might harm them."

I nodded at Elizabeth's sleeping form. "She said he was a man of conscience."

"Aye, he was that, certainly. A moral man. Probably too much so for his own good. It got him into trouble, do you know."

"How did it get him into trouble?'

"His conscience and his morals would tell him one thing. And what he'd been taught would tell him something else. When a man's divided like that, it can tear him in half. And he can end up making his decisions with the wrong half, to spite the other."

"Did you know the old chief supposedly told the lieutenant he was marked for vengeance?"

"What does that mean then? 'Marked for vengeance'?"

"Evidently the lieutenant wasn't sure himself. At least according to Donald Fraser. Donald thought that was why the lieutenant was so quick to go up the river to the village, after he saw the smoke coming from that direction. Even to the point of jeopardizing the rest of his command. He wanted to know who attacked the Onagona, because he thought it might be the same ones who had sworn vengeance on him. He wanted to find out who it was that had singled him out, who wanted revenge and why."

"Och, I d'no know anything about that," Duncan said, shaking his dark shaggy head. "The lieutenant did no speak to me before he went, and why should he then? So I d'no know for certain why he was so quick to go up the river. But if the old chief said the lieutenant was marked for vengeance, I would no think it meant what you said."

"What do you think it meant?"

"When you said it, I thought it meant that Colonel Berry said he was marked to commit vengeance, not that he had it marked upon him. So that going up the river to aid the Onagona was a self-fulfilling prophecy. He saw the smoke and thought the Onagona must be under attack, and he went to avenge them. Robbie Stewart was that kind of man. He would no think of the consequences, if he thought a friend in trouble. He would go to help them, and the devil be dammed."

It was a different view of "marked for vengeance." One that hadn't occurred to me before. But one that seemed to make sense. More sense than Donald Fraser's view, of the man hurrying to the village to find out who had singled him out. Such selfishness on the part of Lieutenant Stewart did not seem in keeping. With the picture of the man I was getting from the men who served with him. Loved him.

And I realized as I sat there. Staring into the ashes of the fire on this warm evening. Thinking of the man I was chasing. And of the man I wanted to be. Realized that I was tired of being afraid. Not of the Indians attacking. Nor of what we might encounter at the Onagona village on the morrow. Those were realistic fears. Concerns. Those were threats that needed to be dealt with. The fear I carried was related to those fears. But it was something beyond them too. It was a general all-encompassing fear. With no face, no name. And needed none. It could assume the face and name of anything. Hook on to whatever situation I might be wary of. And absorb it. Absorb me with it. So much unlike the men with whom I served here. The lieutenant I had followed into this dark wilderness.

Sitting there as night closed about us. I vowed to fight to overcome that fear wherever I might find it. Drive it from me. Destroy it. I knew it would not be easy. I had been afraid so long it seemed normal to me. My way of living. My way to confront the world. Without question the threats of this wilderness and of our situation in it were all too real. All too demanding their due. But I felt I had the chance to lighten myself of that essential burden and weight. To free myself of that fear that had always been part of me. Been my constant companion. I would accept instead a new companion. One that was strong enough to drive away the other, petty fears. One who would sit with me and walk with me and talk with me. One for whom, in the face of which, everything else would pale. And that new companion would be Death. It would be my confidant. My friend. My adviser. And the knowledge of Death's new companionship lightened me. Freed me. Gave me new strength for what was ahead.

There were many questions I yet wanted to ask Duncan. More

of Robbie Stewart. More of what the lieutenant had done to win such respect from his men. And questions of Duncan himself. What he had seen in the woods to make him say he would never fight again. What else he saw, that we didn't. But it was getting late, we needed rest for the morrow. One additional question, however, seemed pressing for an answer. Though I did not want to ask it in Elizabeth's hearing. I waited until Duncan and I walked a few yards from the camp. Stood together on the dry bank of the river. Lifting our kilts to relieve ourselves.

"Around the time you went to the village," I said, keeping my voice low, "were you aware Lieutenant Stewart made a trip to Fort Pitt?"

"Aye, I was. I remember because Sergeant MacKenzie found out the lieutenant was no there at Fort Pitt at all."

"How do you know such a thing?"

"Sergeant MacKenzie told me, he did. We are kinsmen, Adam MacKenzie and I. He can tell me things he might not tell another man."

The connection between MacKenzie and Duncan raised several new questions. But it did not seem the time to pursue them.

"Do you know where Lieutenant Stewart was then, by chance?"

"Aye, I do. He was there to see the woman. Elizabeth."

"And how do you know that?"

"Because he told me."

"Is Robbie Stewart a kinsman of yours too?"

"Och, no." Duncan laughed. Dropping his kilt into place again. Standing looking out at the night. The remains of the river. A sliver of current in the quarter moon. The dark outline of the dark hills of the valley. "Lieutenant Stewart and I are no kinsmen. But he thought he could talk to me like one. I would no tell you anything about it now except I can see you need to know in order to help us."

"How do you know that?"

Duncan shrugged. "A wee birdie told me. That's all. A crow." Then he turned to look at me in the darkness. "What is the rest of your question then?"

"When Lieutenant Stewart went to Pittsburgh. To see Elizabeth. Was it before or after the two of you went to the Onagona village?"

"After. Right after, and that's the truth of it. It was as if what we saw there made him want to see her all the more. But I d'no know for sure. He never told me that. Now I'm going to bed, Ensign Keating. May you rest well the night."

I told him the same. Still thinking of what he told me. And what it might mean. Up the black slope of the valley, the dull glow of the Indians' fire. Like a reminder. A memory. I followed Duncan back to our camp and lay in the grass. Not needing my plaid on the warm evening. Lying among my companions. My brothers-in-arms. Falling into a quick and deep sleep. Without dreams.

My little friend has returned. The mouse. Gray wisp of dust. Smaller than my thumb. Large black button eyes. The undersides of his paws flesh-colored. Like tiny palms, miniature misshapen fingers. He's grown bold again, after the storm. Lightning and thunder. Spent tucked away most likely in some dark nook. Trusting the strength of this man-made world in which he finds himself. Protection for his mouse-world. And this time he's brought a friend. A second mouse. Who holds back, and rightfully so, not so sure. His ladylove perhaps. Though curious I would assume the first one was a male. The effects I suppose of the man-world in which I find myself. When in fact the first mouse might be female. Probably is female, as I think of it. More driven, as I have learned of late. More fearless in the pursuit of her goals. Curious too that I would welcome them so. That their presence fills me. Approbation of a kind. That there is perhaps kindness in me still. Goodness even. After all that has happened. That a creature on this earth would find me worthy.

The wee mouse climbs upon my upturned hand resting on the floor. To take the kernel I have offered. Claws tickling my palm. Tail stiff as wire. Eyes all pupil. Takes the proffered corn in minuscule teeth and drags it a few feet away. Its companion still holding back. Watchful. I make the mistake of tossing a kernel to it. Both mice gone in a blink of an eye. Unaware it was a gift. Frightened by what they didn't know. And for a moment nothing seems more human than a mouse.

I leave my writing implements. Go to the row of gunports—I almost called them windows, I have thought of them thus for so long. Brightened now after the rain. Late afternoon sunlight flooding the valley. Washing down the slope from behind me. Stretching the shadows of the ruins of the outbuildings. The blockhouse itself. Trees on the hill. Other forms I don't recognize. Is someone standing there? Out of my line of sight, only his shadow visible? Two men. I hurry to another wall. Taking up one of the loaded muskets I had leaned there in readiness. But there is no one. Only the western sun. Yellow orb. Golden pendant. Tingeing the carpet of the distant tree-covered hills. I return the musket to its place. Return to the other port. Preferring for a time the world of shadows. Remembering a time with Jean. What the silhouettist told me regarding the truth of outlines, the world of shades. Remembering one of our days.

"I dinna know why you always attack David at every opportunity," Jean said.

"What do you mean, attack him?" I said.

"Every time the subject of David comes up. You attack him. And that night you came to dinner at my parents' house. You attacked him then too, his ideas. To his person that time. Though I must say he defended himself quite ably against your assaults."

"Please hold still, miss," the silhouettist said. "I need you to hold still, if I am to take your likeness correctly."

Behind the screen, Jean gave a quick nod of her head. Either to acknowledge the artist's direction, or to punctuate her statement to me. Resumed her quiet pose again. Her shadow on this side of the screen still again. Fixed.

It was a few weeks after the dinner at her parents' house. We had met regularly since then. Each day after her classes at university. Walking together in the chill gray afternoons. Along the broad High Street, the Royal Mile. Or exploring the narrow passageways and closes of Edinburgh. The courtyards tucked away, the unfamiliar markets and humble shops. It was mid- December. The holiday season. A festive air about the city. The shops and entranceways decorated for Christmas, if they celebrated the English holiday, or Hogmanay, the eve of the New Year. Wreaths and pine boughs hanging from the doors. Garlands tracing the doorways, decorated with ribbons and berries. Candles aglow. The lights from the shop windows spilling across the fog-glistened pavement.

It had been a sudden whim of hers. Through the narrow passageway of Advocate's Close and down several flights of stone steps. A tiny shop in a row of tiny shops. A sign, ARTISTE DE LA SILHOUETTE, jutting out above the door. With the profile of a man, cut from thin black metal. Tall and gangly, rail thin, with tousled hair, protruding Adam's apple. The sign swinging, creaking. Stirred by a winter breeze I couldn't feel.

"Come, Thomas," she said. Her hand emerging from her muff to take mine. Pulling me toward the door of the shop. Her eyes excited and happy despite the late afternoon gloom. Mischievous almost. Aglow with a sudden plan. "I have a gift that needs purchasing."

"But what is this place? What is a silhouette?"

"Let's take a look and see."

The shop was long and narrow, the rear disappearing into shadow. A curious odor of straw and manure, as if it had once housed horses. It put me in mind of my grandparents' stable in Perth. Not an unpleasant odor to me, though I was unsure how Jean would find it. I shouldn't have worried. She was too busy looking around, enchanted. The walls displayed examples of the artist's work. Profiles of prominent citizens of Edinburgh. Cut from black paper. Some life-sized, some smaller. Plus intricate scenes of everyday, all in outline. Children following a cart. Men conversing on a street corner, under a tipsy lamp. A woman filling her bucket from a well.

"These are what I know as *shades*," I said.

"Many people call them that," a voice said. The proprietor, emerging from the shadows at the rear. "The French call them *silhouettes*, after one of their ministers, Étienne de Silhouette, who cut them out as a hobby and made them popular there. Do you like them?"

"Oh very much," Jean said.

He was the tall rail-thin gangly man, with the protruding Adam's apple, from the sign over the door. The same unruly hair, hooked nose, a study of protuberances. Dressed in layers of jackets and sleeveless waistcoats, the palms of his hands wrapped in strips of cloth for warmth in the chill, damp shop. What the silhouette above the door didn't show was the dead leg that dragged when he walked.

"And did you learn your art in France?" I asked.

"From a Frenchman, but no in France," the silhouettist said. He told us he had been wounded in battle, a saber cut to the thigh, at Minden during the Seven Years' War. In hospital back in England, he had convalesced next to a French officer who whiled away the hours cutting out profiles of the other patients.

"One day I asked if I could try. It seemed my hands came easy to the art."

"And to your heart as well, I might add," Jean said. "They are quite evocative."

"You are very kind. Sometimes it seems the outline can tell us more about a thing than its color. Maybe color is too distracting. It has an interest all of its own, it gives too much to comprehend. Particularly of a person. The shadow tells more of the essence."

"Whatever you call them—Shades? Silhouettes? Shadows?—you have convinced me of your art," Jean said. Looking around at the walls. "But these are all too large. I would like one smaller. A miniature. A Hogmanay gift for a learned friend."

"Ah, well. These large ones are taken directly from life. But I can make you one as small as you like. Come."

He led the way deeper into the shop. Lit a candle lamp on a pedestal and placed Jean in a chair next to a screen. A wood framework holding a large pane of milk glass. I watched on the other side as he positioned her so the side of her face was an inch or so from the glass. Her profile emerging amid the white glow.

The silhouettist came around the screen and stood beside me. One arm supporting the other. A finger arched across his upper lip, as if to help support the weight of his nose. Studying the figure on the glass.

"If you like, miss, you could remove your hat." Referring to her tricorn.

"I could but I will no," Jean said. In mock indignation. "It is a part of me. How else would people know it is I?"

The silhouettist looked at me. A slight shrug to his shoulders. A knowing smile. "I think they will know you, miss. With or without your beloved hat. But as you wish. I was concerned that it makes you sit a bit farther from the glass. So that your image is less distinct than it could be."

"I will trust your art to capture me as I am. Besides, all you can know of me is your impression of what you see. And I am certain you must already have that impression firmly in place in your mind. Isn't that what David would say, Thomas?"

"Ah yes. Le Bon David." I wondered, but didn't say out loud, when he would join us this day.

The reference to Hume made me sad. I guessed that the portrait was a gift for David, her "learned friend," as she'd said to the silhouettist. And mention of him now indicated he was never far from her thoughts. I wondered anew what their relationship was. Beyond the furtive glances I had noticed the night at dinner. The few times I had seen them together since. When we happened to encounter him along the sidewalk, or at a coffeehouse. The passionate exchange of ideas when they engaged in conversation. The almost hidden smiles. These flashes of memory revealed more of my feelings than I would have liked. An intonation in my voice, when I said Le Bon David, the name Hume told us he was known by in Paris. Giving rise to Jean's remark of my verbal attacks on the Great Man.

"I d'no know why you put it in such terms," I tried to counter. "You make it sound as though I'm out to assail Hume."

"I didna say it. David said it himself."

"So you've seen him again recently?"

"I see him nearly every day, Thomas." Her chin in silhouette assumed a set that wasn't there before. "David has a home there in James Court, you know. Even though he hasn't occupied it for the past few years because he was living in France. He's been seeing my father a lot recently to help him straighten out some of his business affairs."

The silhouettist interrupted. "My impression is, miss—if, as you say, an impression is all I can know of you—that you will make a more pleasing image if you relax your mouth. And refrain from talking further."

The black image on the glass gained a smile. Then, adjusting her shoulders, settled into herself again. The Jean I knew and admired most. A studious and thoughtful Jean. With just a hint that at any moment she might burst into laughter. I watched in wonder as the silhouettist began his work. Holding a 4-inch square of black paper in his hand. His scissors ready. Studying carefully Jean's profile on the glass. Then the scissors entering the plane of the paper. A cut. Slit. The artist quickly turning the paper this way and that. The incision growing. Taking shape. Continuous. The silhouettist glancing up occasionally at her image but not stopping. As if following a tracing only he could see. Jean's profile beginning to appear from the center of the paper. Unwinding in the wake of the angling blades. Her determined chin. Turned-up nose. Intelligent forehead. When her outline was complete, the square of paper, hollowed of her silhouette, twisted away. Fell to the floor.

"You can come from behind the screen now, miss," the silhouettist said. Holding up the small black image between finger and thumb. Studying his handiwork. Then held it for me to see. As she stepped around the frame, Jean stopped and posed in profile. Beside the silhouettist's outstretched hand, holding the image. For me to compare. Life and Art.

"It is indeed your likeness," I said. "Remarkable."

The silhouettist turned it Jean's direction. For her to view it. But she shied away. Demurred. Laughed at herself but held up her hand to ward it off.

"It is too frightening. To think I might be captured so swiftly," she said. Quickly changing the subject. "Do you have a frame I might put it in? Something so it might be carried easily?"

"I do indeed, miss," the silhouettist said. Taking a small silver case from a shelf. "Though I'm afraid it is quite dear."

"Price is no matter," Jean said. "If I or my likeness is destined to be captive, I might as well be prisoner in a fine prison. Do you no think?"

She smiled brightly to the artist, then turned to me. The silhouettist bowed slightly, a nod. Gave me a look as well. And carried the case and image to the rear of his shop.

On the floor was the discarded square of paper, the remains of the silhouette. I picked it up, joined the two cut ends. The paper itself holding a perfect likeness of Jean. Though now opposite, in negative rather than positive. Not a shadow but a window. Exactly in her shape. I held the small opening close to my eye, scanning around the shop. At the other silhouettes on the wall. At the silhouettist at the rear, bent to his task. At Jean. The cutout a frame around her. Form and substance the same. She smiled at me patiently as I spied her through the mold. As if tolerating my foolishness.

"You know that David is in love with me, I assume."

I lowered the paper frame. Played with the two loose ends, watching my hands. Not wanting to look at her. Or reveal too much of my thoughts. "I was no sure. But there were intimations."

"Oh yes. Quite head over heels." She walked a few steps away. Gazing at the silhouettes on the wall. A slight swing to her step, as if on an outing to an exhibition. Carrying her gloves in one hand, slapping them occasionally into the other. A flimsy cat-o'-nine-tails. Her muff pushed up on one arm, burl-like. Turned and came back toward me again. "I believe he wants me to be his Muse."

I looked at her then. Questioning.

"To help him get away from the influence of that dreadful countess he always speaks of. When he leaves Paris for good."

"How do you know?"

"A woman can always tell." She nodded. As if a matter of course.

"I wonder if that's true," I said. Thinking that she had been unable to see my own feelings for her. Though she took it to mean I doubted what she was telling me.

"And David told me so himself."

At the rear of the shop, the silhouettist looked up from his workbench. Where he stood mounting the image of Jean, fitting it to the silver case. Looked at me. Across the depths of the room, from out of the shadows. Evidently able to hear what was being said, whether he wanted to or not. Much like myself. Looked back at his work. When I didn't say anything, Jean prattled on.

"One evening David arrived when my parents weren't about. Poor man, after he pulled himself up all those stairs, I didna have the heart to send him away. I was afraid he was going to collapse on the spot, he was panting and mopping his brow with a handkerchief. So I sat with him for a while in the sitting room while he rested. We were simply chatting about one thing or another. And then the next thing I know he's down on one knee in front of me, pouring out his heart. Declaring he loves me and needs me. That he desires me to be his inspiration, to be with him always and guide him. He claims I would be the determining factor for him, as to where he would settle after leaving the embassy, because he would take me wherever I choose to be."

"What did you tell him?"

"It was quite sad, really. To see a great man like that humble himself before the likes of me. When I was slow to respond, he started weeping and suffering and carrying on, he was really quite a wreck. After he calmed down a bit I told the poor darling that I was very flattered and that I would consider his offer, but that he could no let my parents or the servants see him in that condition. He agreed and tried to collect himself. And then found he could no get himself to his feet again. I had to place a straight chair beside him, so he could brace himself to lift himself up. Poor David, he's such a sweet man. While he was struggling to his feet, he said that one of his lady friends in Paris called him her 'fat wag,' laughing at himself. He said he would like it if I called him that as well."

"And do you then? Call him your 'fat wag'?" I found it difficult to look at her. And yet was drawn to. To try to read her intentions. Why was she telling me this? The braggadocio of a young woman? Light-headed with the power of her charms? Or was she purposefully trying to wound me? And if so, why? What could she gain by impaling my heart so? Turning it slowly over the flames of jealousy?

"I couldna call him such a thing, d'no be foolish." She flicked the gloves in her hand at me. A bouquet of wilted fingers. Though more amused than petulant. "I have too much respect for the man. For his ideas. All the things you and I have talked about. . . ."

She turned her head quickly. Her face bright and welcoming again. As the silhouettist came from the rear of the shop. Handed her the small silver case.

"Here you are, miss. Though you may want to keep it closed, if you do no want to look at yourself as you said."

"No, I would like to see. I was just being a silly goose."

She opened it carefully, expectantly. Peering inside, as if opening the lid of a small flat coffin. A receptacle that if she weren't careful might release something dreadful. Then relaxed. Her face expanding into delight as she opened it further. Held it for me to see. Jean in perfect miniature.

"It's wonderful," she said. Touching the silhouettist's arm. "I feel as though for the first time I truly see myself as others see me."

"I'm glad you're pleased, miss."

I was still holding the black square of paper. With Jean's cut-out profile. As Jean reached for her purse to pay the silhouettist, I asked him, "Might I purchase this as well?"

Before he could answer, Jean spoke up. "Why would you want that, Thomas?"

The silhouettist smiled. "Actually, some people prefer the paper to the silhouette. It's called hollow cutting. Though usually I cut the image from white paper and mount the black behind it. But I suppose, if you really prefer it the way it is, I could mount a square of white behind it. A white shadow, as it were. . . ."

"You d'no need that, Thomas," Jean said. I did not like her bossy tone.

"Perhaps I want it," I said. Deciding to take a stand.

Jean softened. Trying to smooth the moment. "You misunderstand me. You d'no need it. Because this image is for you." She held up the silver frame in her hand.

I didn't understand. Unable to grasp her intention. The consternation on my face amusing her.

"Who did you think I was getting it for?" she asked. Leaning forward, head canted. As if trying to see me under a ledge.

"I didna know. Your family perhaps . . . or David."

"Dear silly man." I didn't know whom she referred to. But I was willing to take it as an endearment to me.

"Perhaps then I should get a silhouette of me for you." Taken up in the spirit of the giving and the promise of what her gift implied.

But she looked sad briefly. Before turning away. Reaching in her muff for her purse to pay the silhouettist. "No, that's no necessary. It is you I fear who will need to keep a memory of me. I already have your profile cut from my heart."

She handed the silhouettist the coins from her purse and thanked him. Smiled quickly, almost furtively. Then hurried out of the shop. As if suddenly fleeing something. The silhouettist and I looked at each other. An expression on his face as if he knew the answer to a question I had yet to ask. I returned to him the square of black paper. The hollow image of Jean. Said a hasty thank you and followed after her.

I fell asleep. Sitting here at my barrel desk. After writing the story of Jean and the silhouettist. In the last glow of day. The musket ports like a rope of pearls around me. Too weary to go on. Either from the demands of my current situation. Or from the efforts to remember. And not remember. The pain of might have been. Regardless, having finished my reflections, I fell asleep. My head on my folded arms. Overcome. Oblivious. Though I remember now a dream. Someone reaching out to me. Though I couldn't see, can't discern now, if it was Elizabeth. Or Jean. Or some nameless woman I have yet to encounter. Have searched for all my life. I only know her touch. In the dream. Soft as a whisper. Which turned suddenly sharp and spiky.

I woke startled. In total darkness. Something on my hand. Flicked it away in fright. And heard then the soft thud across the room. Knew in an instant what had occurred. I groped hurriedly for my flint and stone. Tinderbox. A candle. Finally had a light. And there it was. At the base of the wall. The lifeless body of my little friend. The mouse. Come for another treat. Another kernel. Having learned to trust. The hand that fed it. Its friend. Only to be hurled away. Its life broken against the bricks.

I would like to cry. I would like to scream and rail. Against the monstrous injustices of this uncaring uncertain world. But I find I can't. Not because the spent life of a field mouse is an insignificant thing. But precisely because it isn't. Because it is as significant as any other. As my own. Precisely because all life is precious. No, sacred. And because of that there is no time for mourning. For a field mouse. For Donald Fraser or Neil MacNeil or Black Duncan. Or any of the multitude of crumpled lives paid out every day. Replaced by new life every day. There can be no time for tears, because all would be tears. We have to go on. The mourning in our hearts. As if it did not exist. It's all we can do.

I take the little body in a pinch of fingers. Bless it. Ask forgiveness from its spirit. Ask the powers of the world to welcome it. Realizing that, in doing thus, I have become like the Indians. Seeking forgiveness of their kills. Recognizing the sameness of all life. All death. Take the lifeless body to the gunports. Reach down the narrow opening. Drop it into the night. Gone. Staring into the blackness for several minutes afterwards. I have no idea the time. After midnight? Most likely, or close to it. Unconcerned now, I go across the room to the supply boxes. Take a dozen or so tapers from their packing. Set them around the room and light them. The interior of the blockhouse ablaze with light. Aware that the Indians may come and shoot in now. The world reversed. Where during the day I could shoot from darkness out, at night they could shoot from darkness in. But it is not a worry now. There is only one thing that impels me. To complete the tale I have started. Our journey up the valley. And our return. Because if all life is sacred, then tales of life are sacred. Stories the only way that life continues on. With a new sense of spirit and resolve, I return to my story. A new journal entry. In the middle of this dark night. Irrespective of the growing odor of decay. The stench so familiar now it is part of me. Surrounded by these flickering candles. A new day.

The man closes the book, rubs the knobs at the ends of his arms into his eye sockets, then looks at Sara. In the darkness and the slight breeze on the night air, the light from the betty lamp dances over his face. A landscape of highlights and dark spaces.

"My mother's not there," Sara says.

The man looked puzzled.

Richard Snodgrass

"She's not there in the blockhouse with him. As he's writing this."

He waits a moment. Considering what to say. "Did you know him then, this Robbie Stewart? Did you ever see him when he went to Fort Pitt to see your mother?"

"I think so. I don't remember for sure, I was only eight. And there were a lot of men." She looks at the man, to see his reaction, but finds none. "But I think I remember him, somebody at least. My mother looked forward to seeing him, more than anyone else. And whoever it was, I remember he was kind to me."

"Aye, that would be the lieutenant, kind to a child. From what we read of him here," he adds.

She remembers for an instant lying in bed in the dark as a child, buried under a stack of old wool blankets against the cold of their shack below the ramparts of Fort Pitt, listening as a drunken soldier or drover humped away at her mother. And remembers in the same instant the times her mother and a Scottish soldier sat together on the edge of the bed talking the night away as one candle after another burned down and out. But she doesn't want to think of those things now. She looks out into the darkness that surrounds them sitting across from each other at the table under the sycamore. In the distance, lightning flickers beyond the black silhouette of the valley's hills, the sky above the far horizon alive, crackling with light. As if the sky is crumbling to reveal a glowing vision behind it. At any moment she wouldn't be surprised to see ghosts or fairies dancing in the dark fields, angels descending on golden ladders or a giant glowing silver crow filling the night sky, a talking bear appearing from the woods to join them at the table.

"This is a magic place," she says.

"D'you think so then?"

"I'm so at peace here."

"I d'no know about what you call magic. It would seem there's always such magic around us, wherever we are, we just d'no see it. The magic is only what you let yourself be open to, and that's the way of it. It's like the good ensign in his blockhouse in the book, peering out at the world through his peepholes. He thinks there's something out there but he does no know for sure. And he c'no learn for sure, for better or ill, without taking the risk to go out and see for himself. For all its magic, the world is still a dangerous place, and that's the way of it."

The man turns away, looking into the night, the flickering sky. His face pained as if for the briefest moment he can see what happened here, the brutality that happened here. Before she can say anything, he cups the flame of the lamp with the snuffer, plunging them into darkness.

"I'm going to sleep now, lass. I would you to do the same."

On her way to the cabin, Sara happens to look back. The man stands beside the table, looking off into the darkness, the flickering sky behind him, as if addressing something or someone. And for the briefest moment, perhaps from the dark clouds or the branches of the sycamore, she thinks she sees extending from his back a pair of enormous black wings, the feathers ruffling in the night air.

Day the Fourth

We broke camp at dawn. Though there was no first light this day. Only a gradual exchange of black to gray. The valley, after the rains of the day before, filled with fog. The air thick and damp. An all-pervasive gray. Sight limited to a few feet. The closest trees only indistinct forms, vague shapes of trees. Like memories. Dreams. Sounds muffled. In fact no sounds at all from the endless forest around us. Only the dampened whisper of our movements as we made ready for the day. Gathered our packs.

Ate our rations of hardtack and salt beef. Reloaded our muskets, adjusted fresh flints in the locks. Trying to prepare for what we thought the day would bring. At last the four of us standing together. In a rough circle. Looking one to the other. Asking each other without words if all were ready. I looked at Sergeant Mac-Kenzie. His blue eyes narrowed with purpose. Though a rueful smile passed quickly at one corner of his mouth. As if to say, Aye, laddie, this is it. Whether we like it or no. I nodded. He motioned with his head toward the river. And we set out.

We kept the same order as before. Duncan in the lead. Though only a few feet ahead of Sergeant MacKenzie now, lest we lose each other in the fog. Elizabeth in front of me. Her shoulder aggravated by the dampness. Walking stiffly, trying to hold her right side immobile. Though refusing help as before. Insisting on carrying her bundle, Donald Fraser's haversack. We made our way down the riverbank, across the dry riverbed, the edge of the channel exposed by the summer drought. Our footsteps breaking through the surface, the dried crust. Leaving tracks. Oozing with mud, glistening with water. Fog in wisps lifted from the water running in the center of the channel. Though the blanket of fog that filled the rest of the valley had lifted here. Hovered above the channel. The riverbed clear. As if the wisps of fog lifting from the water's surface were columns, supporting the mass of fog above us. I looked back across the clear channel under the fog ceiling. Standing on the bank where we had been was the band of Indians who had shadowed us the day before. But they gave no indication of trying to follow us further. Or to attack us. Standing there in a line under the fog. Satisfied that we were moving on. As if that had been their purpose all along. Witnesses to our progress.

The rains elsewhere the day before had swollen the water running in the center of the channel, deepening it closer to the level before the drought, speeding its flow. Water plashing against the rocks of the shallow rapids where yesterday it only slipped by. New eddies and currents, the water as we entered it nearly up to our waists. Our muskets held shoulder-high as we crossed. My kilt petaled about me on the surface of the water, as were the sergeant's and Duncan's. Three dark flowers, tartan water lilies. Ahead of me in the mist and fog, Elizabeth struggled to keep her balance. Against the swiftness of the current, the pull of her long skirt, the weight of her bundles lifted above the surface. At one point she stumbled and started to fall. I reached and grabbed her by the arm. Steadied her until she could go on.

"Stay close to me this day, Thomas," she said. Looking at me intently. Green eyes burning into mine. Her hair across her face like a partial veil.

"I am right here, milady."

"Milady? As if I were a gentlewoman?" she said above the sound of the current. The water lapping about her. Disbelief on her face. Almost a smile, as if at a mistake.

"This way," Sergeant MacKenzie called. Enshrouded in a wisp of fog, barely visible.

Elizabeth continued to gaze at me. Part mocking, part questioning. As I supported her, my hand on her waist, guided her to surer footing. The sergeant reached to help her as we approached. I expected her to pull away from him, as she had in the past. But she accepted his help. Let him take her arm, direct her toward the shallows. Following Duncan.

"I d'no know what you said to the missy in your wee tête-à-têtes," the sergeant said to me. His voice raised above the murmur and plash of the water around us. "But it seems to have made the lass almost friendly. 'Tis good for us all."

Elizabeth said nothing to the comment. But her face betrayed a slight smile, as if she shared a secret with herself.

I didn't know what I had said either. Or she to me. But I felt closer to her. Stronger than before. As if plaited. A bond between us. The reservations, questions I had of her motives. Her feelings for Lieutenant Stewart. The reasons for her coming to Fort Bouquet. For accompanying us now. Allayed with the warmth of her smile. The look that came into her eyes. Meant for me alone. I was set with new resolve. To find out what had happened to Stewart's command. To get us all back safely to the post.

When we gained the dry stream bed on the other side, we stopped to wring the water from our clothes. I looked back across the river. The wisps of fog continued to lift from the surface. A forest of ghosts. Muffling the sounds of the current. Or the sounds of pursuers. Obscuring my view. Whether the Indians were still on the bank on the other side. Obliterating everything behind us, the way we had come. Without speaking, we continued on across the dry-cracked bed and up the bank.

Among the rocks along the top of the bank were a number of upturned canoes. Their hulls slit like open wounds. While the sergeant and I examined them, Duncan found several dozen more canoes inside the treeline. Partially hidden among the brush. Their hulls intact.

"Whose are they, do you think?" Duncan said.

"I wager the ones destroyed along the bank belonged to the Onagona," MacKenzie said.

"And these must belong to whomever came to attack them," I said.

"The lads who came to the fort and were shadowing us?"

I looked at Elizabeth. She had been watching us as we looked at the canoes. Standing back several feet. Now she came forward and looked more closely. Walking among the brush-covered hulls.

"Some of the designs are Huron," she said. Coming back to us again. "But others could be Shawnee or Delaware. Even Seneca. I don't know."

"Aye, 'tis a large war party," the sergeant said, looking at the rows of hulls.

"And if their canoes are still here," Duncan said, "it means the Indians are still here too."

Instinctively we all looked around. At the fog-shrouded forest before us. The gray shapes of tree trunks diminishing to nothing within a few yards. The branches overhead lost in the mist. Gray, only gray.

"I'm sure by this time whoever is here knows all about us," I said.

"Let's get on with it then," the sergeant said.

I nodded to Duncan. He looked quickly at Adam MacKenzie, as if to make sure. Blessed himself. Hefted Donald Fraser's musket in his hands as if taking its measure. And started off through the ferns. Finding the trail from the river. The sergeant, Elizabeth, and myself falling in behind. Keeping close. Four silhouettes, starting into the fog and the forest.

"Would you like more water?"

"Yes. Please."

I held the dipper to her lips. Held the back of her head as she took a few more swallows. My hand entangled in her thick black curls. Helped her to lay back again. Arranged the blanket over her again. Against the chills that periodically coursed through her.

"What are you thinking, Thomas?"

"Nothing, really."

"Of course you are. I can see it in your face." She added weakly, "I've known you long enough to recognize that in your countenance."

I smiled. "I was remembering, actually. When we were crossing the river. Before we got to the village. You told me to stay close to you. I was wondering how you meant that."

"How do you think I meant it?" Elizabeth said. Lying on the straw-filled mattress on the floor of the blockhouse. Her eyes closed. Talking as if she were already listening to something else. Already far away.

"At the time, I thought you meant that you wanted me to stay close to you for your protection or guidance. I thought it meant you were unsure. Afraid."

"You think I wasn't afraid?"

"I'm no sure now. The more I've thought about it, it's occurred to me that it sounded more like an admonition."

"An admonition of what?"

"You could have meant that I should stay close to you . . . for my protection. That you knew something of what we'd find at the village. And you were afraid . . . for me."

"You think too much, Thomas."

"I've been accused of that before."

"By the girl you left in Edinburgh? What was her name?"

"Jean. Yes, she said that of me. In so many words. . . ."

I remembered in a flash. Standing on the tower wall in the late afternoon. The gray day, clouds in layers overhead. And below us. Rain drifting across the plains toward the Firth of Forth. I had told her what I planned to do. To join the Black Watch. To go to America. Her brown eyes liquid. The eyes of a young hind, watchful. The animal within her ready to bolt. "Aye, Thomas," she said, "And will you find yourself in the dark kilt of *Am Freiceadan Dubh* then?"

Elizabeth had opened her eyes again. Head turned so she could see me. "No, I didn't know what we would find at the village. But I was afraid who we might find there."

"The Indians we saw at the outpost? The Indians who followed us?"

She ignored what I said. "And yes, I was afraid for you. More for you than for myself."

She waited a moment. Watching me. Before she said, "Do you believe me?"

"Yes, I believe you," I said. After a moment.

"You hesitated. Did you have to think about that too?"

"No. I was thinking about how much I do believe you. Trust you."

"And you're surprised at that?"

"I suppose in a way I am. I'm surprised that I seem to have no control over it. Over my feelings. I just do. Feel that way about you."

"It's understandable that you might question. Question me. Considering what all has happened. What all you've seen of me. I guess I'm surprised as well. That you can trust me after what happened. Surprised I'm that fortunate."

"You should rest now." I reached over. Took her hand. She smiled. Closed her eyes again. Took a deep breath. Against the pain and tiredness. Before going on.

"We are very similar, you and I, Thomas. Do you know that?"

"D'you think so?"

"I know so."

"What makes you think that?"

"For one thing, because neither of us belongs here. In this wilderness. Barricaded in this outpost. We were brought here to this frontier by forces totally outside of ourselves. That had nothing to do with us. You in service to your king. Me because my family looked for a new life. Have you ever thought how different things might be for us, if we had met in a different place and time?"

I could understand why she might think so. That there were similarities in the factors that brought us here. But my circumstances were much different than hers. Having asked to come to America. To this wilderness. To discover . . . what? Myself, I thought. A self I thought existed. Only to find a very different me. And I was yet to discover how different. But such thoughts were for my reflection only. Would only trouble her. In her present state. I only smiled. Said nothing. Let her thoughts follow their own conclusions.

"Do you also remember when we crossed the river? You called me 'milady.'"

"Yes. I remember."

"It slipped out. I don't think you even knew you were going to say it. As if I were a gentlewoman. Your lady."

"You must try to rest now."

"I have been called many things in my life. But never that before. Milady."

She was starting to drift again. Further. Back into someplace deep within her.

"Save your strength. Do no try to talk."

"What else is there now but talk, Thomas? Words. . . ."

A slight turn of her head. Her eyes opened partially to view me. Then she fell into her sleep again. Away. Her breath easier though short, like small bursts.

I adjusted the blanket about her. Against the chills that racked her. Even though the heat in the blockhouse was intolerable. Took the opportunity to check the cloths we had wedged beneath her skirts and petticoats. The flower of blood still growing slowly. Oozing again despite the attempts to stop it. I went to the bundle she had taken with her up the river. Undid the knot. Looking for more clothes, petticoats I might use to try to stop the flow. As I sorted through her things, something fell to the flagstones at my feet.

Something unthinkable. Dried blood and hair. I recognized Donald Fraser's scalp.

The trail climbed gradually from the river. Up the slope of the valley. Deeper into the forest. The fog growing thicker. Duncan barely visible though he was only a few feet ahead. The fog like smoke around us. Eventually the trail leveled off but I had no sense of how far we'd come. Or if we were even still on the trail. My consciousness focused on the back of Elizabeth in front of me. Trusting that she was keeping in view the others in front of her. The only sounds the drip of moisture from the branches. The swish of our footsteps along the path. Brushing through the damp ferns. Over tufts of grass and lichen. Elizabeth's petticoats.

Fog. A world of gray. Nothingness. Suddenly there was the sound of wings. Everywhere in front of us. A great uplifting, flapping. But we still couldn't see anything. We stopped, fixed.

"What was it?" Duncan said. Musket leveled. Scanning the fog.

"Birds of some kind," I said. "Hundreds of them. But why would they be here?"

"Maybe pheasants or such?" the sergeant offered. "Nesting on the—"

Elizabeth screamed. We looked where she was looking. The fog had a face. Directly before us on the trail. Hovering, part of the fog. The color of fog. Deathly white. Ghostly. Was it one of Duncan's visions? But we all saw it too. Then there was a second face beside it. A third and then a fourth. All the color of the mist, fog. With staring eyes. More, seven or eight. A line of faces. All dead.

MacKenzie, Duncan, and I approached slowly. Muskets leveled. Elizabeth behind us, hand clutched to her mouth not to scream again. There were perhaps a dozen in all. Across our path. Their bodies painted white, with white kilts. Pine boughs tied to their upper arms. Their hands holding more boughs, miniature bows and arrows. Their lidless eyes staring at whatever came along the trail toward them. Bodies impaled on stakes to stand them upright.

I motioned Elizabeth to stay where she was. The three of us moving cautiously through the line of figures. Eyes straining to see what else the fog might hold. Circled the figures. In amazement. Horror. Seeking signs of life. On their faces, blood had trickled down like tears, dried on their cheeks. From the cuts to remove their eyelids.

"Were they dead, do you think, before they were. . . ?" Duncan said softly.

"If they were lucky," MacKenzie said. None of us at the moment believing in luck.

"Are these the dancers you saw at the village?" I asked Duncan.

"Aye. I recognize a few of them. Poor sods."

"Why would anyone do such a thing?" What I meant was: How could anyone?

Adam MacKenzie sighed. Shaking his head. "A sign, or warning. An example, maybe. Och, I d'no know. The other question is: Who was it meant for?"

We looked at each other. Each reluctant to voice the obvious. For us?

Back along the trail, Elizabeth was barely visible in the fog. As if disintegrating into atoms. Her arms wrapped tightly about her. I went to her, took her by the hand. Led her through the line of figures. To where Duncan and MacKenzie waited.

"Go ahead, ask your questions," Elizabeth said. Defiantly, looking at each of us.

"No, missy," the sergeant said softly. "No questions."

"I don't know who did it," she said. "I don't know if it was Huron or not."

"We did no think you would," the sergeant said.

"So that was the sound of wings we heard," Black Duncan said.

At the figures farthest from us, stretched off into the fog, half a dozen crows had returned. Alighting on the figures. Pecking at the eyes, Tearing pieces of flesh. More crows descended from the fog. Dozens. Silently.

"We should go on," I said.

Adam MacKenzie nodded. Duncan started forward, to take his place in the lead. But I laid my hand on his arm.

"No. No this time. You stay close to her," I nodded toward Elizabeth. "I'll take point."

"Aye, 'tis a fine and noble thing you're thinking," MacKenzie said. "But I would no have you get lonely out there. And two muskets are always better than one."

I nodded and the two of us set out. First attaching our bayonets. Continuing along the trail. Side by side, elbows occasionally brushing against each other. Muskets leveled.

"Fire only if you have a clear target," he said under his breath. "Make it count, give them something to think about. Then be ready with your bayonet. There will probably be no time to reload. Remember you've got your pistol, and that sword on your hip is no just for picking your teeth."

We glanced at each other briefly. An understanding. Then turned our attention again to the fog. Waiting for shapes to appear from among the darker gray of the trees.

Then the trees were gone. We entered a clearing. The trail climbing over a slight rise. Down a gentle slope.

"We're coming into the village," Black Duncan said quietly behind us. Elizabeth a step behind him.

"Should I halloo?" I whispered to the sergeant.

"Who would you want to answer?"

We moved on. Watching as the dim shapes came into view. What might have been a village once. But now was only a wasteland. Charred remains of huts. Broken shells of beehive ovens. Personal items strewn about. A water bucket crushed. A child's pull toy split in half. A doll in the shape of the dancers we had seen fixed upon a pole and burned. No one was about. Nothing moved. Silence.

As we continued slowly through the village, the fog lifted somewhat. Becoming cloudlike drifting about us. Drifting among the scorched ruins of the huts. Ahead was the raised platform Duncan had described in recounting his earlier visit to the village. The roof of the underground chamber. Ladder poles from the entrance aimed at the sky. And some other things Duncan hadn't described. That obviously weren't there before. A row of what appeared to be misshapen balls. Lined up as if for some sort of game. What turned out to be, as we got closer, a row of human heads. Twenty or more. Lined up facing something that had once been human sitting tied to a stake.

"Stay here with Elizabeth," I said to Duncan. Without turning from the scene in front of us.

"And keep watch," the sergeant said beside me. Also without turning away. "Whoever did this might still be close."

The sergeant and I stepped slowly onto the roof. Fanning out. Approaching carefully. The row of heads facing away from us. When he noticed us, the figure slumped against the stake moaned. We stepped carefully between the heads. Hurried to him. Squatting down on either side.

"He's still alive."

"I would no call it that," the sergeant said. "'Tis the old chief. Colonel Berry. What's left of him."

The sachem was tied with a cord around his chest. But it was only to keep him upright. Not to restrain him. It being impossible for him to move anywhere on his own. Every bone in his arms and legs had been broken. Fingers, hands, feet. Methodically. His limbs like sacks of bones, useless. With open wounds, where the flesh had been torn away. From animals, dogs or raccoons or foxes, or rats. Clouds of flies lifted from him when we first approached. Settled again.

While Sergeant MacKenzie supported him, I cut the rope tying the old man to the stake. Carefully we tried to lay him down.

But the old man feebly shook his head. Wanted to remain where he was.

"Easier to breathe . . . sitting up . . . I don't have long. . . ."

The sergeant poured some water from his canteen into the palm of his hand. Cupped it into the old man's parched lips. Most of it running down his chin. His tongue working uselessly. While the sergeant tried to help the old chief, I looked at the row of heads in front of him. Some of them were Indians. Several old women, children. A baby. And there were other heads too.

"Sergeant, is that Stewart? His men?"

MacKenzie looked briefly. "Aye," he said quietly. Turning back to the old man.

"They wanted me to watch," the old man whispered. "They wanted me to see. What my decision had brought . . ."

"Save your strength, old man," Sergeant MacKenzie said.

"You have to know. . . ," the old man said. "The rest of my people. Ran into the forest. Those were the only ones left."

"So the rest of your village got away. That's good at least. Did the other Indians go after them?"

The old man nodded weakly. Had trouble swallowing. The sergeant gave him another palmful of water. But it set the old man to coughing.

"Some of them wanted to wait," he said. When he could speak again.

"Who wanted to wait?" I asked. "What would they wait for?"

The old man managed to look at me. Eyes from the depths of pain and sorrow I had never seen before. Then he turned his head slowly. To watch Elizabeth.

She had moved closer, onto the roof platform. Duncan tried to stop her. Reached for her arm but she pulled away. She walked slowly along the row of heads. Until she came to one and stopped. Fair-haired. What had been a handsome young man in his thirties. The head at a slight angle. Trying to turn away from something. His chin and cheeks speckled with sand and dirt. As if someone had kicked them in his face.

"Who did they want to wait for, old man?" the sergeant said. With a new kind of urgency. The answer seeming to take on sudden importance.

"Death," the old man managed to whisper. His eyes on Elizabeth. Watching her. She turned as if she felt them burrowing into her. Met his gaze.

"We have to do something," I said to MacKenzie. As we both stood. Moving a few steps away so the old man wouldn't hear. "We can no just leave him like this. . . ."

Elizabeth glanced at me. Having heard. Her eyes wild. With grief I thought. Or something else I couldn't know. Didn't recognize. She went over to the old man. Knelt on one knee in front of him. The old man's eyes fixed on hers. Watching her every move. Elizabeth reached out and touched his cheek.

"I d'no know how we could take him with us," MacKenzie was saying. Looking around. He seemed dazed. Thinking of something else. Eyes focused on something far away. "There's no way we could carry him. . . ."

Duncan seemed dazed as well, though of a different sort. He had put down the musket. Laid it in the sand and dust of the low roof. Stood in front of the row of heads. Visiting each face. Spellbound. Elizabeth and the old man staring into each other's eyes.

"I know you," the old man said to her. "What you bring. . . ."

"Rest now, old man," she said. Caressed his forehead with her left hand, the top of his head. Then held him firmly as she took from the folds of her skirt a hunting knife. Slit his throat with one quick motion. "It is over now."

The old man's mouth gaped. Worked but no words came out. Only a gurgle. Blood pumping from his throat. Down his chest. Elizabeth stepped away quickly. Faced us.

"What have you done!?" the sergeant cried. Rushed to the old man. But there was nothing to be done. The old man's mouth continuing to work. Bubbles of blood. Elizabeth backed away a few steps farther. Uncertain what anyone would do.

Duncan groaned at the scene in front of him. Sat down in the dust where he was. As if unable to bear his own weight further. The sergeant stood over the old man. Dead now. Head bent, chin resting in a bib of blood. Rivulets of blood curling in the dirt beside him.

"What have you done, missy?" the sergeant repeated. Quieter now. His eyes had regained their focus. Intense again. Growing fierce. At Elizabeth.

"I did what had to be done," she said. Holding the knife behind her.

"Aye, that you did. But for whose sake?"

I had been watching, unable to move, function. The horror so complete that it seemed beyond me. But I was wakening now, to a nightmare gone real.

"Hold on, sergeant—"

"No, you hold on," MacKenzie said. His burr growing stronger as his anger mounted. The rage within him taking on a life of its own. "The old man there was trying to tell us something. About the whoor. That's why she killed him."

"Get a grip of yourself, Sergeant—"

"Aye, do you no see, man? She has you fooled, she had everyone fooled. But I knew there was something else. That's what the old man was telling us. That's who the Indians were waiting for, after they massacred the village. After they killed Robbie and the others. They were waiting for her. She was part of it all along."

"You're talking nonsense. Maybe they were waiting for us. They must have known we would be coming to find out what happened to the others. She loved Stewart. . . ."

The sergeant was shaking his head. His eyes never moving from Elizabeth. Who met his gaze unflinchingly. As if waiting to hear what he would say.

"No, that was no it at all, was it missy? They were waiting for you, whether we were with her or no. Because she is what this was all about, isn't that it? That's who was leading the band who did this. That's who was leading the band we saw at the fort. I thought I recognized him but I never got a good look at him before, and now he had all that war paint and his hair in a top-knot. He was with the Indian who followed her back from Ohio. He was with her Indian husband—"

"You're a fool, Sergeant MacKenzie," Elizabeth said. Then she staggered. Turned away. Holding her stomach.

"Where are you going?" MacKenzie demanded. Totally captured in his rage now.

"I have to . . . sit down. . . ," Elizabeth said.

"It's another trick of hers. Stop her, do no let her get away. . . ."

As Elizabeth stumbled toward the edge of the low roof, Sergeant MacKenzie caught up to her. Grabbed her by the elbow and tried to pull her around. Twisting her wounded shoulder. Elizabeth cried out and seemed to collapse. Falling on one knee. MacKenzie bent over her to lift her up.

"Get up, whoor. You c'no fool me. . . ."

I hurried toward them. "Stop—"

He tried to lift her to her feet again. Pulling again on her wounded arm. Then he brushed her bonnet aside, grabbed her by the hair. Pulling her upright. Elizabeth tried to fight free. Reaching for her hair. Then jammed the knife up into the man's stomach. Tearing upward into his heart. Yanked the knife free. MacKenzie clutched at the wound, crying out. Spun away from her, losing his footing. Fell to the ground. His body arched once and shuddered and grew still.

I stood rooted where I was. Unable to move or think. Duncan sat on the ground clutching himself, moaning. Rocking back and forth. Elizabeth stood over the body of the sergeant. After a moment I came to myself. Went and knelt beside MacKenzie. Lifted his head, felt his neck for a pulse, looking for signs of life in his eyes. But he was dead. Elizabeth had stepped back, watching me, what I would do. I looked up at her. Trying to comprehend.

"Whatever you think of me at this moment, Thomas Keating. We have to leave here. Now."

"But how could you—"

"And don't talk to me of love, Thomas Keating," she hissed. Her bonnet gone, her black hair wild about her face. The knife still in her hand. Blood dripping from the blade. "Of my love for Lieutenant Stewart. Or for anyone else. You know nothing of it. Nothing."

Suddenly she screamed, doubled over. Fell to her knees.

I hesitated as to what to do. But only a moment. I went to her, knelt beside her, my arm around her shoulders. She was bent double, gasping for air. There was blood on the front of her skirt. A rosette the size of a hand. Growing larger. Had she been shot? I looked around. The fog had lifted more. We were exposed on the low roof. My only thought was to get her to someplace safe. Where she could lie down.

I helped her to her feet. My arm around her, supporting her. Blood was soaking through her skirt, she was crying with pain.

"Help me, Duncan," I said.

"They're coming," Duncan said. Sitting on the ground. Holding himself in a wrap of arms.

"Who's coming? The war party?" I looked around wildly. To see what he was looking at. But he was looking somewhere far away.

"You c'no stop them, you know?" he said, looking at me. Almost tenderly. "The crows are everywhere."

I couldn't tell if he was talking about Indians or birds. But I knew we had to get out of there as quickly as we could.

"Come, Duncan. Hurry."

He was calmly taking out his fiddle. He looked at me as he held the base of it against his chest. Plucked the strings, listening for the pitch.

"I can no. I tried for you, Ensign. For you and the others. Against what I knew to be true. I carried a musket again. But I'm going nowhere now. I'm staying here. With Adam and the lieutenant and the others. But you must go. Hurry. They are coming. On black wings."

There wasn't time to try to persuade him. The blood soaking Elizabeth's skirt had stopped but she was close to deadweight against me. As we started back across the low roof, Duncan called.

"Take one of their canoes. You can make it then. But destroy the others before you leave. Then you'll be safe. I can see it. The crows will sing you home."

As we hurried on, Duncan began to play behind us. The plaint of a lament following us as I helped Elizabeth back through the remains of the village. Back toward the trail. The fog was continuing to lift, the sun starting to burn through the mist. A silver disk above the dark shapes of the valley. The sound of Duncan's playing following us as we found the entrance to the trail among the trees. Stumbling on. Expecting any moment to hear the sound of war cries behind us. The crack of long rifles. Ahead the crows had returned to the carcasses of the impaled dancers. Hundreds at the feast. As we approached they stopped. Turned their heads toward us. But didn't fly, remained where they were. Watching as we continued on through the line of upright corpses. The sound of Duncan's playing like a call in the distance behind us. Then the playing abruptly stopped. In midfigure. Cut off. Elizabeth and I looked at each other. Overhead a crow on a tree limb flapped its wings. As if aware that something had happened. Began to caw. Filling the sudden silence. In response. The other crows joining in. Hundreds of rough singers. A dark chorus. My arm around Elizabeth's waist to keep her from falling, we went on. Through the forest toward the river. Back the way we had come.

"Wait," Sara says. Interrupting the man's reading. "Wait."

He looks up at her from under his heavy brows. His eyes full of sympathy for her, concern even; she knows what he is thinking, knows that he thinks it is the horror of what he just read to her, but that isn't it, or at least not all of it.

"He doesn't say what happened to Duncan, does he? He doesn't say the Indians killed him. Only that the music stopped."

"Aye, 'tis true enough. Keating only talks afterwards in the journal about what happened to himself, and to the woman, Elizabeth. Trying to get away from the village and back to the outpost."

"So the Indians might not have killed Duncan."

"I d'no see. . . ."

"Maybe they showed mercy on him. After all, he gave them food, the fish he caught in the river."

"We d'no even know that the Indians who attacked the village were the same who shadowed them up the river."

"But all the Indians seemed spellbound with his playing the fiddle. Maybe they wouldn't kill him because of that."

"Or maybe the music was the thing that frightened the Indians about him. That he had the power to make such melodies come from the wee woman-shaped box. The sweet melodies unlike anything they'd ever heard before. Maybe they did no want to kill him like you say, but maybe they wanted to take the power from him. Otherwise the power of the music might come back and take

its vengeance on them. The savages only knowing savagery—where are you going?"

She gets up from the table and goes into the blockhouse. From a far corner she takes a bundle, the size of a baby's coffin, wrapped in an Indian blanket, and carries it back outside to the table. When the man sees what she is carrying he lowers his head, braces his forehead on his upraised stumps. She places the bundle on the table between them, opens the blanket to reveal the wooden fiddle case.

"When I saw this hidden away in the corner I thought you must have found it in the blockhouse when you settled here, or maybe you found it in the woods. But you brought it with you. You're the Duncan in the story. Duncan Murchie. Black Duncan."

"You should no go poking around when someone opens their place to you, takes you in."

"You don't need to read the story in this book. You've known all along what happened to the outpost here, to my mother and the others."

He shakes his head. "I knew my story. I knew my version of what happened. I d'no know the ensign's. Or your mother's. Until I read it thus."

"The ensign must have thought they killed you."

"For many years I wished they had. Which I think is what the savages wanted me to feel. When they found me there at the Onagona village, they must have thought I tried to enchant them with the music, that the music had a special power and that I must have a special power. So they had a more elegant torture for me. They took my hands because they knew it would be a hell for me, to go through life without being able to play again, to make the music again. The buggers were right."

"How did you survive?"

"The last thing they wanted was for me to die. As soon as they cut off my hands they gave me over to an old woman to nurse me. She plunged my bleeding stumps into jars of some kind of mud and tied leather bands on my upper arms to stop the bleeding. I d'no remember much for the next few weeks, she gave me some kind of tea for the pain that made everything hazy. They kept me with them for months until I recovered my strength. Then they took me close to the settlements across the river from Fort Pitt and left me. As they strapped the fiddle case on me, they laughed. I guess it amused them to think of the struggles I'd have the rest of my life. But I d'no wish to return to the settlements, to the world of people. I returned to the forest, and then the crows came and led me here, to this deserted place, and brought the Indian boy to help me get started. I could no farm with stumps like this, but I knew cattle back in the Highlands and some of the outpost's oxen were still alive in the woods. My wee herd thrived, I d'no know why, and people come to buy their teams. But otherwise people stay away. As it should be. There is nothing I want from people now."

Sara opens the case, lifts the neck of the instrument from its resting place inside, cradling the scroll like the head of a sleeping child.

"Poor darling," Duncan says. "She has no been played since that sad day. She dies a slow death herself from lack of attention."

"Maybe I could learn—"

"No," he says abruptly. Then softer, "No. That's foolish talk, talk of the moment. You will no be here long enough. It takes a lifetime to learn to play. Now, put it away. Put it back where you found it. We will talk no more of the fiddle. What's past is past and that's the way of it."

He motions her with his head to take it away. When she comes back to the table, he begins the reading again. But she can feel that there is something different now between them, a difference in his attitude toward her. He is reading to finish the story so she can be on her way. So he can be rid of her. She is amazed at the depth of the emptiness she feels at that prospect.

"When are you going to ask me?"

"Ask you what?"

"About what you found in my bundle."

I couldn't see her. See if her eyes were open. Or if she was looking my direction. She lay in the darkness of the blockhouse. Night. Earlier I had chanced a candle. While I checked on her. To see if she was asleep. Arrange the blanket about her on the pallet. To see if the bleeding had stopped again. Then I sat in the dark. Across the room from her. Sifting through my thoughts.

"Yes. I found it."

"I think I dreamed that you did. Or I saw you through the fever. I don't know which now. Somehow I was aware of what you were doing."

When I didn't say anything right away, she went on. Though her voice was weak. Almost dreamy.

"After I took the scalp, I knew I should get rid of it. Not take it with me. But I didn't feel I could just throw it away. Toss it into the bushes. It didn't seem right. If you can believe I could feel such a thing."

"So you did no take it as a trophy?"

"No. Of course not. I only took it so you'd think it was the Indians who were following us."

"Did you know who they were? Sergeant MacKenzie thought you did. He seemed to think you were with them in some way. That you communicated with them."

"I knew who they were. But I wasn't part of them. The leader's name is Attigbro."

"The one with the blackened face and red stripes."

"He was the brother of my husband."

She gasped. Moaned softly. I heard her moving in the dark. Shifting her weight on the straw pallet. Rustle of her clothes.

"Can I get you something? Do you want me to light the candle?"

It was a moment before she could answer. "No. I will be all right. For a little while at least. The pain seems to come in waves."

"Do you want some more water?"

"Go ahead, Thomas. Ask me what you need to ask me."

It seemed cruel to pursue such questions now. But she was right in her knowledge of me. As she so often was. I needed to ask her.

"Why was the brother of your husband seeking revenge?"

"Because I carried Robbie Stewart's baby. Does that shock you then?"

"No. I guessed it must be Stewart's. When I realized you were with child. I had no idea you were pregnant until I was helping you back to the river. Your clothes. . . ."

"I tried to keep it hidden. For a number of reasons. . . ."

"But why was your husband's brother seeking revenge? Why was it no your husband? Was no he the one who followed you back to Fort Pitt, when Bouquet took you from the Indian camps?"

"They both accompanied the column when Bouquet brought me back. Attigbro to keep my husband company. But my husband was killed when he tried to return from Fort Pitt. Attacked by settlers, who had their own reasons for revenge. Attigbro escaped."

"Did Attigbro blame Stewart for the attack. . . ?"

"No. But it hardened his heart against the whites, to be sure. What he sought from Robbie Stewart was more personal. With the death of my husband, Attigbro claimed me for himself. He was ready to sneak me out of Fort Pitt, to take me back to his village. But I told him I was pregnant to Robbie Stewart. And his thoughts turned to revenge."

"If you were no pregnant to Stewart. Would you have gone with Attigbro?"

"You are asking me something else, Thomas. You are asking me my feelings for Robbie Stewart. And you are asking my feelings for you. But I can't talk longer now. I need to sleep . . . forgive me. . . ."

Her voice trailed away in the black room. I continued to sit where I was. Listening to her breathe. More labored than before. An occasional whimper from deep within her dreams. Forgive her. It was a mystery to me then. She had killed two of my comrades. Sergeant MacKenzie and Donald Fraser. As well as the old chief at the village. Yet I seemed to have no choice but to forgive her. A foregone conclusion. Already granted. My feelings for her stronger, apparently, than my feelings for anything she had done. Could do. What kind of man felt that way? It seemed I was the one to ask forgiveness. Of the stars. The wind. The night.

Somewhere beyond the walls came the chirr of a cricket. Hoot of an owl. A dark stirring in the grass. The startled call of a robin. As if suddenly wakened from its sleep. Crying out fitfully. Frightened. Then quieted again. Waiting for the dawn. Though I continued to sit within the darkness of the blockhouse. Content with the darkness.

Glint of sunlight on the water. The haze lifting from the valley. Ahead the parting of the hills as the river wound its way. Murmur of the water against the prow. Slipping along the sides of the birch canoe. A whisper of water. The river, though swifter, deeper, from the rains the day before, still only in the middle of the channel. Dry streamed on either side, extending to the banks. Within the valley and yet removed from it. The steep green tree-covered slopes. Sandstone bluffs like battlements. Slipping past as in a reverie.

In my haste to help Elizabeth get situated, I ended up sitting in the front. The canoe from that position difficult to maneuver. But there was no time or opportunity now to correct it. We were fortunate the current carried us along with little effort on my part. Behind me, Elizabeth lay on the floor of the craft. Her head resting on the rear seat. Her body stretched out under the cross braces. The front of her dress covered in blood. Or soaked through, from the hemorrhaging between her legs. Talking as if trying to keep the pain away. Her voice drifting to me as if from another time. A murmur like the water.

"My father brought me to this country when I was eight years old. Before that, we had a farm outside of Philadelphia. We were well-to-do. Aristocrats, really. The farm we had was part of a grant from the King, handed down to the family for past services rendered. Loyal subjects I suppose. But it wasn't enough for my father. He wanted something more. Something of his own. Because he had inherited his position, he felt he hadn't earned it. He didn't feel it was his. So he brought us here. To hack out his own land from the forest, his own farm from this wilderness. This wildness, he called it. Eventually, of course, this wildness, in the presence of a band of Indians, killed him and destroyed all that he tried to accomplish. I've often thought about that. Wondered if he realized that in the moment before he died. Or thought about it afterwards, wherever his soul resides. But for me, when I came here, it was an enchanted place. All the hills and valleys. Land of rivers and streams and brooks. A place where you never knew what was beyond the next hill. What was hidden in the next valley. With the snow drifting through the black columns of the trees in winter. The fogs and the rains drifting through the tall leaf cover overhead in summer. I thought of it like a magic forest in the time of King Arthur. Surely someday a knight in armor would ride out of the trees. Or a skiff pulled by sea horses would come to take me away. Of course what came eventually was a band of half-naked savages. Who took me to their long-houses and made me a wife."

She giggled to herself. Hand flopped over the side. Trailing in the water. Delirious or close to it. A voice full of fever. Like a child's in a sickbed. Then her voice changed again. Back to Elizabeth's.

"You won't leave me, will you Thomas?"

I turned to look at her. "We are almost there now. Less than a mile." I didn't say what I thought. Evidently I can't leave you.

The river made its S-curves. Meandering toward the end of the valley. The first of the two falls before the confluence with the Ohio. The channel widening, the upper falls here barely flowing. I waded in the water. Guided the canoe between the hump of rocks close to the bank. Elizabeth with her eyes closed now. Locked in pain. Once we were in the lower channel I climbed in again. Paddling with little skill to get us there quicker. Ahead the outbuildings of the post came into view. The blockhouse on the rise above it. The orchards and the gardens and the pens for animals. But no one seemed about. I hallooed for Neil MacNeil as we nosed toward the bank. Grounded the prow in the soft mud to hold it steady. Hallooed again as we sat there. Ready to gather up Elizabeth. Help her up the hill to the blockhouse.

He came from between the buildings. Running fast. The Indian who led the band that followed us upriver. Blackened face, with finger-streaks of red. Blackened body. A knife now between his teeth, war club in his hand. Behind him, coming from the treeline, down the slope, the rest of his band. Running, whooping. A dozen of them. I dropped the paddle, took up my musket. The first Indian hurdled a fallen log without breaking stride. Charged down the bank, across the dry riverbed. I fired when he was less than 20 feet from me. He swerved and dodged and kept coming. Before I could reload or take my pistol from off my belt. He splashed through the shallow water, swung at me with his war club. I blocked the blow with the musket. The stock hitting his hand, the club falling in the water. Behind me Elizabeth screamed as the Indian leapt at me, nearly overturning the canoe. Elizabeth's screams increasing as the Indian and I grappled, the canoe rocking back and forth. My hands locked on the Indian's wrist as he tried to raise the knife to strike me. Pulling me from my seated position and into the water. Elizabeth's screams filling my ears. The other Indians almost upon us. My strength starting to fail as the leader and I struggled in the water. His eyes just beginning to take on the glint of victory. His face inches from mine.

Then I saw his eyes dart away. Lock onto something behind me. Elizabeth's screams had stopped. The other Indians stopped as well. Frozen in place just yards from us. The leader suddenly pushing me away. Breaking off my grasp as he stepped back. Still looking at something behind me. Backtracking through the edge of the water and the mud and back up onto the riverbed. I looked behind me. Elizabeth was sitting up in the canoe. In her right hand was the knife from the folds of her skirt. In her other hand dangled something small and slimy with blood. Sickly white. A tiny figure. A fetus. The umbilical cord dangling where she had cut it. Holding up the fetus by its tiny hand. Its miniature arm. For all to see.

The Indians didn't move. As if the thing in Elizabeth's hand were a dreadful totem. A ghastly talisman. Inspiring terror, awe. Then they turned and began walking away. Across the riverbed and up the bank, back up the slope. I looked at Elizabeth. She was holding the fetus now as if intended only for me. Her face, drawn, ashen, set in defiance. Then her eyes rolled back in her head. She fainted, collapsing against the side of the canoe, rolling it toward me. I caught her but not before she let go of the fetus.

Dropping it into the water. The current taking it swiftly away from the shore, circling in an eddy. I feared that when the Indians saw her they would come back. But they were nowhere to be seen. Already melded into the forest. I lifted Elizabeth from her position, half-spilled from the canoe. Lifted her in my arms and carried her up the bank. Up the slope toward the blockhouse. In the trees close to the river a crow was calling. Laughing or crying. I looked back as it set wing. The bird swooped down over the water and plucked the fetus from the water's surface with its beak. Flew on with it toward the trees on the other side of the river. I climbed on with Elizabeth. In my arms. Like a lover to a wedding bed. Drinking in the musky smell of the blood on her skirt. As if a sacrament. Something holy.

I had fallen asleep sometime in the night. Sitting on the small raised platform under the gunports. Across the room from her, my back against the wall. Keeping my vigil in case she needed something. Listening to her labored breathing in the dark. Waking with a start. The room in daylight. Bars of sunlight slanting down from the eastward-facing ports. Rectangles of sunlight on the floor. Elizabeth lay on the pallet watching me. Her face waxen. As if all blood, all energy were drained from her. Her once thick black hair limp and ratty. The petticoats and clothing wedged between her legs to try to stop the bleeding a large lump under the blanket over her.

"You must have been dreaming," she said feebly.

I shook my head. Trying to force wakefulness. "Was I talking in my sleep?"

"No. But you were smiling. Your lips moving as if conversing with someone. Someone you are fond of."

I tried to remember the dream. Thinking that Elizabeth must hope it was of her. But to no avail. "Whatever it was, 'tis gone now."

"Gone with the light of day," she said. Reflective, looking up at the ceiling momentarily. Then back at me again. Watching me as I stood, stretched, tried to work the stiffness out of my joints. I took a drink from the bucket of water. Ladled some water into my hand and rubbed it over my face, back through my hair. Then went to the gunports facing down the slope toward the outbuildings. From the barns came the lowing of the cows, needing milked. But I didn't dare. Not until I knew for certain that the Indians were no longer here. I hadn't heard the cows the day before when we arrived back. Which meant Neil MacNeil must have milked them sometime yesterday. But he was not here now. I could see the sheep and hogs in their pens. But nothing else stirred. I went back and sat beside Elizabeth. Offered her a ladle of water. She shook her head.

"We have barrels of salt pork and beef and hardtack. And water from the spring. So we're in good shape as far as that goes. We can hole up here for days until we make sure the Indians are gone. Weeks even. When Fort Pitt does no hear from us, they're sure to send a patrol to find out what's happened. . . ."

She shook her head again weakly. "We must talk now. While there's still time. . . ."

"But I'm sure we can hold out for as long—"

"Listen to me. Because I want you to know. You asked me if I would have gone back to the Indians. If I would have gone with Attigbro. The answer is no. I wouldn't have gone back. I couldn't go back. Perhaps at one time I might have, if I had had the chance. But I no longer belonged with the Indians. Any more than I belonged with the whites. I ended up not belonging anywhere. With anyone."

"You must have felt you belonged with Stewart. You came here to this outpost to see him—"

"I came to kill him. . . ." A new wave of pain coursed through her. Twisted her on the pallet, bent her double. Her hands clutching at the wad of bloody clothing between her legs. At her lower abdomen. More than a moan, screaming now. As if in childbirth when nothing would come. Or as if everything might. I ran my hand over her forehead. Through her hair, to try to comfort her. Unable to bear seeing her in pain. Unable to think about what she had just said. In a few moments the wave had passed. But she continued to lie on her side. Knees curled into herself. Talking to me, though her face was turned into the rough covering of the straw. Her voice muffled.

"I wanted to kill him. Because he wouldn't marry me, he wouldn't help me with the baby. . . ."

"Hush. D'no try to talk now," I said. Clearing a dark curl from her cheek. But she went on as if she didn't hear me.

"What else was left for me? I didn't belong anywhere. There was no one to help me. When Attigbro heard I was pregnant to Stewart, he said he would take the child if I went back with him. But I couldn't trust how he'd treat the child afterwards. I couldn't trust how he'd treat me."

"So when the old chief told Stewart he was marked for revenge. . . ."

"He probably meant Attigbro. He probably heard of it from other Indians. But Attigbro wasn't the only one who wanted revenge. I had my own reasons. I think the old man recognized it when he looked at me at the village. I could see it in his eyes. He said he knew what I brought him. . . ."

"But why did Attigbro attack the Onagona village? Why did he do those terrible atrocities. . . ?"

"He didn't. Those were other war parties. Delaware and Iroquois, maybe Seneca. The canoes indicated a number of tribes. All with their own reasons against the Onagonas. Maybe Attigbro and his men picked through the bodies afterwards for trophies, I don't know. But Attigbro would try to stay out of the way of the others. That's why they followed us on our trip up the valley without attacking. They must have figured whoever attacked the Onagona would take care of you as well. If Attigbro attacked, it would call attention to themselves. He probably wasn't sure how the others would react to them being in the area."

She had worn herself out talking. She lay there, facing into the straw. Breathing heavily. A wheeze as if her lungs gulped air. Then she turned again on her back. So she could see me again. Watch me as she talked.

"I thought one of you would kill me. If we found Robbie Stewart alive and I killed him. But I didn't care. I didn't care about anything. It would all be over then."

"When you saw Stewart had been killed . . . his head there on the ground with the others . . . you did no seem to have much reaction. . . ."

"You must think I'm a monster. The things you've seen of me. . . ."

"No, I d'no. Maybe I should. But I d'no."

She studied me a moment. As if to see if she believed me. Or if I would believe her. Before going on.

"My feelings toward him changed. Or I realized my true feelings about him. He had taken advantage of me. He was no better than the Indians who took me in the first place. I guess it was understandable, if I cared to think about it. He was lonely here in this wilderness. Maybe it drove him a little crazy. I know his contact with the old chief and the Onagona got him more interested in Indians. And more interested in me. That's why he came to see me in the lower town that time, when he disappeared from the outpost for several days. He wanted to talk about what he had seen at the Onagonas. He wanted to learn more. And one thing led to another. He probably thought he loved me, until he learned I was pregnant. Until he thought about what that could mean. That he might be expected to marry me. A woman no better than a squaw in most people's eyes. He couldn't have that for his career. He was ambitious. He wanted advancement, a major command. And he talked about going home to Scotland. His father was a laird, Robbie had a big house and lands and a position in the Highlands waiting for him. He couldn't have an Indian whore with a baby trailing after him. For a while I cursed him, I cursed all of you. When I turned up here at the outpost, he didn't know if I was the one who had sworn revenge on him, or if it was someone connected to me. But he sensed something and was afraid of me. I wondered at the time if that was why he was so anxious to go upriver when he heard about the smoke from the Onagona village. Maybe he was less afraid of what he'd find there, than what he might find out about me, and about himself, if he stayed here at the outpost. . . ."

The pain appeared on her face briefly. A wild swimmer bobbing to the surface in her eyes. Before sounding to the depths within her again. Her face slowly coming back to itself. I took a piece of muslin, tore it into a strip. Dipped it in the water bucket, wrung it and placed it on her forehead. She took my hand and held it against her cheek. Smiled.

"And then you came along, Thomas. You treated me like I was somebody. First there at Fort Pitt, when you fought off those men who were going to attack me. Fought for me when it was obvious that yours was not a fighting nature. And then here when you found Sergeant MacKenzie had me tied in the compound. Championed me. How is it that two people know that they could love each other?"

"I d'no know. . . ."

"When did you first know you had feelings for me? No, don't tell me. I don't want to know. I don't want to know that maybe you don't. But let me tell you. I knew I was grateful to you for the way you treated me. But I found I had stronger feelings for you when you and Donald Fraser went off in the woods to look for berries. I was worried for your safety, of course, because I knew Attigbro and his band were out there someplace. But I was also afraid of what Donald Fraser would tell you. About me. I was afraid of what he might know. I had been taken and used for so long, handed from one to another, I had forgotten that I could actually have feelings for someone. Of my own will and desire. And I recognized them in you. It made me crazy. It made me do something that I should never have done. All I could think of was that I had to make sure Donald Fraser wouldn't say anything to poison you against me. Then once I had killed him, there was nothing I could do to change it. And when it came time, I found I could kill the old man, and Sergeant MacKenzie too. I can tell you this now because it doesn't matter now. . . ."

When did I know I had feelings for her? I wasn't sure. Nor was I sure the feelings I had for her were the same she felt for me. I had been attracted to her the first time I saw her. This woman who, when I first saw her at Fort Pitt, had just knifed a man. Was ready to fight off others on her own. Later, if I had thought about it, I would have realized she could have been the one to kill Donald Fraser. Could have come to the outpost to kill the man who had been her lover. But I never considered it at the time. Seemed able to disregard it now. Because of what I felt for her. I had been aware of her anytime she was near. Could not keep my eyes from her. The way she'd brush a wayward curl away from her face with the back of her wrist. The shift of her body within her clothes. Was this love? Or desire? And what was the difference between the two? I didn't know. But I couldn't stand the thought of something happening to her. Of not being with her.

She watched me. As if knowing my thoughts. She closed her eyes for a moment. Smiled before opening them again.

"Tell me this, Thomas. The girl in Edinburgh. Jean. Why did you ever leave her?"

"At the time I told her it was to gain experience of the world. To know more of the world so I could be more for her. But as I've thought about it, I've wondered if it wasn't something else entirely. I had discovered that she was using me. To test her feelings for another man. An older, famous man who was a friend of her family's. I've wondered if that dinna have more to do with my leaving than anything else."

"There were undoubtedly pressures from her family, whether she realized them or not, in regards to that other man. She was probably using him as much to test her feelings for you."

"Strange you should say that. I talked to him once about it, and he said much the same thing."

"She was young, Thomas. Just a girl. Trying to engage and find the limits of her power. Her attraction to you. I would wager she cares very much for you to this day. From what you've said, the softness that comes into your tone when you speak of her, you still care for her as well."

"She did no want me to come here to America. She wanted me to stay and help build the new Edinburgh. She said I was a builder, not a destroyer."

"She knew you better than you knew yourself. You should return to her."

"I'm here with you now. I love you. . . ."

"You are a fool, Thomas Keating," she said. Not angry. Almost a lament. "You are an engineer, but you don't know how the world is made. You can add the figures, but you cannot see the sum."

She reached out and touched my cheek. Her hand moving through a shaft of sunlight. Dark to light to dark. I brought her hand to my lips. Kissed the back of her fingers. She turned her face away toward the wall. Tears on her cheek. I wiped them away with my fingertips. Then suddenly became aware of the smell of smoke. Crackling of flames from somewhere outside. I hurried to the musket ports. Below on the slope, the outbuildings of the post were on fire. Barns, barracks, storage sheds, the sawmill. Columns of smoke lifting into a single cloud. Drifting toward the river, filling the valley. But I could see no one. As if the buildings were victims of spontaneous combustion. Silent lightning. I ran to the other sides of the structure. Checking the ports. No one. No signs that anyone had ever been there. Behind me Elizabeth whimpered. I turned to find her tangled in her bedding. Knees to her chest, twisting with the pain. I knelt beside her again.

"What is it . . . the smoke?" she asked. When the pain had backed off.

"They've fired the buildings. But I c'no see anyone out there."

"You won't. You won't know if they're still out there or not."

"We'll fight them. We'll hold them off as long as we need to until help comes. Then we'll get you to Fort Pitt. There are doctors there who can help you. Then we'll leave this wilderness and go someplace where we can be together."

"What a lovely dream, Thomas. . . ." Her voice sounded increasingly far away. Drifting.

"It does no have to be a dream. We can make it real. . . ."

I got up from beside her. Looked out the gunports above where she lay, at the fires consuming the buildings on the slope. Smoke thickening around them, swirling, each one caught in its own vortex. A scene from hell. I went to the ports across the room. Studies in contrast. All was calm here. The view of the Ohio River in the distance. The farther hills, covered with their incalculable forests. High above a hawk on outstretched wings rode a current of air. Keeping watch on the senseless activities of the humans below. To encourage Elizabeth I maintained a steady monologue. To keep her from drifting further from me. As I checked the gunports. The readiness of the muskets I had placed leaning against the walls.

"Still no sign of anyone out there. You're right, there is no way to know if they are still here or not. But no matter. As I said, we've got the provisions and a fresh supply of water. We can wait them out as long as we need to. Then we'll get you well again and. . . ."

As long as I was checking weapons, I reached for my pistol hanging on my belt. It was gone. I looked around. Dumbfounded. Then heard the spring of a flintlock being pulled back. Clicked into position. I turned. Already screaming, "No!" In that brief instant seeing Elizabeth as she lay on the bed. Holding the pistol with two hands, aimed at me. Then disappearing in a cloud of smoke. The flash. The incredible roar from the barrel. As I was spun off my feet, slammed against the wall and to the floor. Clutching my left side.

I sat stunned. Staring at her. The kick of the pistol, even lying where she was, had jerked her back against the wall. Her face spent of all color or beauty.

"Why?" was all I could say.

"You're worse than a fool, Thomas. You're a blind man." She struggled to raise herself to one elbow. Barely able to breathe with the pain and the exertion. Gray as death. In the gunports above her, I could see the billows of smoke from the burning buildings. Reflection of the flames. Pulsing orange and red.

I felt for the wound in my side. Tore my shirt away. A red weld traced my skin where the bullet had passed. But there was no torn flesh, no blood. Though it burned, burned. I looked back at her.

"And what will you do with me now, Thomas? What would you believe of me now? Ah, don't worry, my love. I will save you the trouble. I would do it regardless."

She took the knife she had kept with her. Hidden in the bedclothes. Took a deep breath. And with a look of neither regret nor sadness, only grim determination, plunged it into her chest.

We had encountered Hume several times on our walks. Jean and I. After she was through with her classes for the day at university. After I had finished my studies at the library. So when I went in search of him I thought I knew where I'd find him. The lamps were lit as I made my way along the High Street. Each one hooded in the night air. The fog that drifted ghost-like through the wynds and passageways. Clung to the wreaths and garlands for Hogmanay. Muffled the ring of horses' hooves on the cobbles. The creak and clatter of carriage wheels moving along the streets. Murmur of the festive crowds along the sidewalks. At Stephenssohn's Coffee House I rubbed clear a pane of glass. Peered inside.

The steam and moisture remained on the other side of the glass. But through the murk I saw him. Seated at a table with a half dozen other men. His great bulk stuffed into the limits of a captain's chair. The Great Man holding forth to the Literati. Or the Eaterati as they called themselves. Hand resting on the knob of a walking stick. King and his court. I entered and stood off to one side. In the shadows beside a wooden column. Inconspicuous I thought as I considered how to proceed. The talk from what I could hear more general than learned. Gossipy even. No different than men anywhere. Who was bedding whom. Who would like to. In his laughter at one point Hume raised his eyes and noticed me. A brief smile of recognition passing across his face. I remained where I was. After several moments, Hume glanced again to see if I was still there. Then announced to his companions:

"Gentlemen, this is pleasant beyond measure. But I ask you now to leave me for a time. I see a young friend who has some urgent business to attend with me. I will catch up with you later at the Jolly Judge."

Hume having spoken, the assembly promptly finished their drinks. Popped a last piece of scone or cheese in their mouths.

Got to their feet. Inquisitive glances my direction. Dispersed into the room, into the night. When they were gone and I still hadn't moved, Hume motioned to me.

"Come, Mr. Keating. The coast is clear, as it were. You can approach now. I would come to you, but movement for a man my size presents a number of problems. I think you can understand." He smiled. Amused with himself.

I emerged from the shadows. Keeping my greatcoat wrapped around me as if I was cold. Took a seat among the circle of empty chairs. At an angle to him across the table. The table cluttered with empty glasses, dirty plates. I realized I was hungry. Not having eaten all day. Several days, if I thought about it. Thinking of this moment. What I would say to him. But now I had turned glum and recalcitrant. Pouty even. Angry at myself for acting so, but unable to break out of it. I slumped in the chair. Legs spread, the picture of gawky youth. Not at all the challenger I had envisioned for myself. Cowed in the presence of the man. Whom I knew to be a man of genius.

For several moments, while I floundered in sulkiness, Hume busied himself with a clay pipe. Loading and tamping the tiny bowl. A tiny crucible at the end of a wand. Tilting it to catch the flame from one of the candle lamps on the table. Sucking on the stem as he held it at midlength, not to burn his fingers. Then finally putting it down in disgust.

"I d'no know why I bother with the stupid things. Other men seem to light them with ease and enjoy them. And I like the smell of it about a man, d'no you? It is the very air we breathe in these coffeehouses and clubs. Though I never have much luck at keeping them lit. All I end up doing is sucking on dry tobacco. But I'm sure you dinna come here this evening to hear a diatribe on my difficulties of smoking a pipe."

I remained sullen. Unable to think of anything to say. Hume looked at me for a moment. Offering me the opportunity to begin. Then he shrugged. Shifted his bulk in the chair.

"Nor do I think you came to challenge me to a duel. At least I hope I am correct in that regard. Though I may change my mind, if you continue to stare at me with such a grim visage."

"Why would I wish to challenge you to a duel?" I said. The absurdity of the idea breaking my silence.

"You know. The wronged suitor. The aggrieved lover. Defending the honor of your beloved against the intentions of a lecherous older man. And by one standard, I suppose, the judgment of the world would say you're justified. Throwing down the gauntlet to the old wag who would deign to have intentions to the woman he loves. . . ."

"What on earth are you talking about?" I said.

"You've won it, sir. The young lady is yours. You've achieved your goal in the matter of her affections." Then he regarded me a moment. As if a curious specimen. "Do you mean to say that you were unaware of your success?"

"I was no aware that you and I were in a contest." Not quite the truth.

"But you were aware that I held Jean in the highest regard."

"Yes, certainly. But in terms to a contest for her affections, I assumed you had already conquered the field."

"Ah, the unawareness of youth. It is as Jean says."

"And what does Jean say?"

"She says she admires your naïveté the way other women admire wildness."

Perhaps he meant no malice in the telling. Meant it only as an observation, or a trifle. But I was embarrassed. That I had been the subject of a conversation between them. An intimacy that excluded me. In response I wished to wound. To embarrass in return.

"And she has told me of how you poured out your heart to her on bended knee. And your struggles to right yourself from such endeavors."

"Right myself?"

"You know, regain your stance. Get to your feet again, after such exertions."

He looked at me with new interest. I thought that I must have him. Gained the upper hand.

"I would like to hear more. All that she told you."

"I really d'no think that it would be to your liking. . . ."

"No no, I insist, young sir. I very much want to hear what she told you about me. And in return, as incentive, I will tell all of what she told me of you."

He leveled his gaze at me. Knowingly. As if indeed he were aiming a weapon my direction. Whatever advantage I thought I had quickly dispersed in this new turn. That he knew something equally compromising or unpleasant about me. I proceeded to tell the story Jean had told me. Of the night Hume appeared at her family's door when her parents weren't at home. How she sat with him making conversation while he rested from the climb up the stairs. How he suddenly threw himself on one knee in front of her, pouring out his heart to her. That he wished her to be his Muse, and would take her anywhere she wished to live. And then, when she was slow to respond, how he broke down. Crying and suffering and carrying on. To the point that she had to ask him to collect himself. Afraid her parents or the servants would see him in such a state. Discovering that, now that he was on bended knee, he couldn't get to his feet. Jean having to get a straight chair for him. To brace against so he could rise again. Hume listened the while. A polite smile on his face. That grew progressively sadder.

"Interesting," he said at last. When I was finished. "The things a young girl perceives. Or thinks she perceives. What she imagines. Or perhaps wants to happen."

"Are you saying that the incident she described did no happen?"

"Oh no. It happened, most certainly. Except no with our young Jean. It was a number of years ago, when I first went to France and was a very different man. A story I sometimes tell on myself to show the perfidy of youthful attractions. Though I wonder where she heard me tell it. Perhaps her father told her, after some time I told him. Or she eavesdropped when I told someone else, when I was there at her house. Regardless. Fascinating. That she would picture herself in the role of such a woman. And picture me, in relation to herself. Charming. The part about the chair and of me no being able to rise on my own is new, however. Shows a touch of imagination."

"You did no need a chair to help get to your feet?"

"Sir. Yes, I am a large man. And undoubtedly not as spry as I once was. But I am certainly able to kneel and get to my feet again, if I were so disposed. If you need proof I suppose I could get down on one knee, right here if you like, and show you that, like the phoenix, I can rise anew. . . ."

I waved my hand. Brushed aside the idea. The thought of Hume engaged in such a demonstration was ludicrous. But I had more disturbing concerns. "But why would Jean make such a fabrication?"

"Ah, you wish me to explain the mysteries of a woman's heart. A young woman's heart at that." He laughed. Shook his head. "Speak of the Unknowable. . . ."

I looked away. Smoke hung in layers in the room. From the lamps, pipes. When a serving girl walked by, the layers swirled and eddied in her wake. Gradually settled into place again. I realized I had sunk even further into my chair. Straightened up. Studied my hands.

Hume sighed. "I do no mean to make light of your plight. To answer your question: Why would she make such a fabrication? I'm afraid our Jean has used you. Much as she has used me. Not maliciously, I think. But to her own purposes. She is still very young."

"How has she used me?"

"I'm afraid, Mr. Keating, you are the victim of an attempt to make me jealous. In a similar way that I am victim of her attempt to make you jealous of me."

"I d'no understand."

"It would seem the reason she invited you to that dinner a few weeks ago was to prick my intent. To make me wonder. In brief, to make me jealous of you. It is the same for our encounters in the street. She knows my schedule from my conversations with her family, where I might be at any given time. So it stretches credibility that the two of you just happened to show up. I'm only surprised at myself for no recognizing it sooner."

"But why would she do such a thing?"

"As I said, our Jean is young. Only eighteen. She is just beginning to experience the power of her charms. To test her wings."

I was disconcerted. Not knowing what to think. What to believe. I looked around the coffeehouse. At the other tables. Each circled with faces in the glow of the candle lamps. Each a sun in the dark space of the room. A universe of conversations. With their own discussions and decisions. Assumptions and first principles. Each with their certainties. But in my life, my world, there seemed none. Nothing I was assured of, could count on. Not even the intentions of someone I cared for. The first, I thought, I ever cared for.

Hume was studying me. When he spoke, his voice was softer. Full of concern. Surprisingly.

"Why *did* you come here to see me this evening?"

"I d'no really know. Now."

Hume nodded. "If I may say so, keep in mind that you are no that much older than Jean yourself. She introduced you to me as her tutor. But I suspect your relationship with the university is much more casual. Let me see . . . you probably matriculated, what, three or four years ago. But your studies dinna really prepare you for the world. In fact, if anything, they only served to confuse you the more. So you've stayed on, in independent study as they say, reading on your own. I would guess in Law."

"Engineering."

"Ah. Yes, of course. Because you like to build things, don't you? You like to see the construct. The thing in itself. Not just the empty talk. And to be a success at the Law, one needs to love the talk itself, to be able to argue any truth for the sheer joy of discourse. No, from what little I know of you, that wouldna suit you at all. You care too deeply. About the answers. About adding up the sum of parts to reach a whole. That is probably what drove you to stay on at university. Because in the midst of your engineering studies, and your pursuit of answers, you stumbled into the realm of philosophy, the constructs of the greater reality. Which led you eventually to me. Does any of this have a familiar ring to it?"

"You say morals are based on sympathy," I blurted out. Not knowing beforehand that I would do so. Unaware the topic was urgent to me. "The recognition of shared sentiments and sensibilities among a people. No a universal that separate groups of people could reason to. But if that is true, then morals can change between groups of people. What is morally right for one group may not be morally right for another. We talked that night at dinner about the American Indians and how they treat their captives. The atrocious things the Indians do to others. If what you say is true, those atrocities could be morally right, at least to them. Because the savages all share the same sentiment. If that's true, then anything can be considered morally right, as long as everyone else in a group does it. Anything is possible. Cannibals are morally right among cannibals."

"Congratulations, Mr. Keating," Hume leaned back. Beaming. "You've described the problem exquisitely."

"Hang your exquisitely!" I shouted. Almost a scream. Causing others at nearby tables to raise up. Look over at us. "How can that be?" I went on. Trying to keep my voice down. A hiss.

Hume folded his hands across his great middle. Waited until I recovered myself. Before he replied.

"You are looking to me for answers. But I dinna know what your questions are. If your questions were the same as mine, the philosophy I have derived in my books would have supplied you. Or, if you did no agree with my answers, would have driven you to others with their answers. Which then would lead you to your answers. Obviously, your questions are different than mine. I do no presume that philosophy will stop and end with me. It is a growing thing, to be added on to by others. An accumulation. I have only written to answer my particular questions. You must discover *your* particular questions."

"But how do I do that? I've read and thought about these things until my mind is awash with ideas."

"Ideas are useful, of course, but they have depth and meaning only from the experience behind them. The problem is that ideas are reflections of the impressions that gave rise to them. They are an additional step removed from the world itself, and so are limited by the range of impressions that spawned them. You've heard me say before: we gain impressions only through our experiences. So that we are what we experience. In the last analysis, those impressions, those experiences, are all we have. To find your questions, you will probably need to experience more. Though I fear for you, Mr. Keating. I fear the search for experience to discover your questions will drive you further than any answers could."

When I was at university in Edinburgh, I remember reading or hearing about certain religions in the world. That believe the soul or spirit of the dead stays with the body for a length of time. Before departing for wherever the soul or spirit goes. Hovers over the body perhaps, or around the dying place, or is simply slow to leave the once-living form. For some, as I recall, it is a matter of hours. For others, days. I remember thinking such beliefs were strange. Almost ludicrous. Why would the soul linger? Why would the spirit hang on? Lonely for the body? Unwilling or afraid to let go? Or were such ideas merely the fabrications of the living who were left behind? Wishful thoughts. The living the ones unwilling or afraid to let the dead go. Desperate to yet be able to help the dead, after not being able to help the dying. Desperate to yet convey to the dead that they are loved.

Such ideas are not strange to me now. After Elizabeth took her own life, I sat with her through the remains of the morning. So she would not be alone. Closed her eyes for her. Watched as a cortege of sunlight from the musket ports paraded slowly across the floor. Up the opposite wall. Disappearing as the day progressed. Disappearing in the general gloom. Sat with her as the blood that flowed from her eventually stopped. Congealed. Violent red. Turning blackish as morning became afternoon. Wondering if she knew somehow that I was there. Kept vigil for her. Sometimes I talked to her. Repeated the Lord's Prayer. Yea, though I walk through the valley of the shadow of death. Told her of my plans, what I intended to do next. Told her things that, if still alive, we would have needed to discuss. In our life together.

Only once breaking down to tears. For her. For me. For all the creatures of the earth.

Then it was time. I got up and checked the gunports once again. The fires had burned themselves out by this time. Smoldering, blackened timbers. Small wisps of smoke still rising. A haze through the valley. But that was all. I found a blanket among the piles of stores. Spread it on the flagstone floor in the center of the room. Drew a fresh bucket of water from the springhouse. Then lifted Elizabeth from the tangle of bedclothes. Laid her on the blanket. Removed her clothes and washed her. Carefully, gently. Finding myself humming the lament I had heard Black Duncan play. At the graveside of Donald Fraser. "The Flowers of the Forest." To comfort her as I worked. To comfort me. Combing her thick black hair, freeing it of its snags and tangles. From the stores I took a bolt of muslin. Cloth to be cut up into swabs for cleaning musket barrels. I wrapped her in a length of the cloth for a winding-sheet. Lifted her again in my arms and carried her to the corner. Down into the springhouse. Murmur of the water in its pool. Like the voice of a mourner. Song for the dead. I laid her on the steps, arranged the winding-sheet neatly about her. Hoping the cool air and shadows would slow her decay. Beside her on the steps I placed her few personal items. A thin wristlet of beads. Her leather moccasins. Her comb. Small altar of remembrance.

From the spring I took another bucket of water. Rolled her blood-soaked bedclothes and pallet into a bundle and tucked them away behind some boxes. Scrubbed the best I could the bloodstains from the floor. The splatterings on the wall. From the force of her self-inflicted wound. Then stripped. Washed myself, standing naked in the center of the room. Before leaving to go upriver we had stored our large backpacks in the blockhouse. I rummaged through the kits, my own and the others. From Adam MacKenzie's I took new undergarments, Adam never bothering with them. In Donald Fraser's I found a clean pair of red-and-white-checkered leggings. From Duncan Murchie's an unworn blouse. In my own a new pair of shoes. My kilt and jacket I brushed clean as well as I could. Until I was the semblance of a proper officer. Soldier and subject of the King.

From the stores I took a flour barrel, standing it upright for a desk. Another for a chair. Found this uncut orderly book. Mixed ink powder and sat down here to try to write. The story of what happened here. Of this detachment of soldiers. The last days of a woman, a freed Indian captive named Elizabeth Cawley. When I started this journal four days ago, I believe I was taken for a time with a kind of madness. A madness from the events that transpired here. A madness at the madness of this world. But writing has helped lift this mania from me. I believe I am lucid now. Either that or my distraction is complete. Unable now to discern the sane from the insane. The world of figments from the world of figures. How do we ever know? as Hume has asked. Though I would say now that I'm not sure we need to know.

In the writing of this journal, I have had much time to reflect. On Elizabeth, mainly. What she told me as she lay here. Her life's blood running from her with the miscarriage. Telling me her feelings for me. Painting a picture of love and striving. Was that real? Or was it a fabrication? One of a number. To play out her further revenge on another soldier. A representative of those who dragged her away from her Indian life. A surrogate for the one who betrayed her through an act of supposed love. Or were her feelings for me true? "Ah, my love," she said to me. Before she aimed and fired. Was trying to kill me a way to try to save me? Believing that we'd never be rescued here? To keep me from what would befall me at the hands of the Indians were they to overcome this refuge? A supreme act of love. To kill one's love as part of love.

Or was it something darker still? That Elizabeth could not accept that she could love at all. Or be loved. After what had happened to her in her life. If not careful in this world, we kill what we most try to love. To free ourselves from having to love. Perhaps in the attempt to kill me, she was equal victim.

I have no answers. I know only that I will never know. There is only the memory of a woman named Elizabeth. A woman who in different circumstances I might have loved. Who might have loved me.

It is four days since I began this recounting. Still no sign of relief. But perhaps it is just as well. What needs done now is a solitary act. A singular effort. The journey back to Fort Pitt. To resign my commission as soon as possible. Then return to Scotland, to Edinburgh. To see if Jean is still there. If her feelings still exist for me. And mine for her. To see if it is too late to be worthy of her heart. A journey as uncertain of its outcome as the one I made upriver. For what can be more unsure than the search for love? More treacherous? Unknowable, as what may still lie in wait for me among these forests, among these endless trees. But none of that is important. What is important is to make the attempt.

Now I will close this book. Wrap it in oilskin and hide it, hoping it will survive. That someday it will be found and the story learned. I will stand, button my scarlet tunic, put on my belts of war, my pistol and basket-hilt sword. Take my musket in hand. Stand on the steps of the springhouse and say one last good-bye to Elizabeth. To her memory. Then go to the heavy oak door and open it. Afternoon sunlight flooding into this darkened room. My figure silhouetted momentarily against the view of the ruined buildings. The river and the green of the valley's hills. Light bursting about me as I step out into the day. To see what is there.

Thursday, 5 June 1766

IN THE SHADOW
OF THE VALLEY
II

1776

"Do you think the Indians were still out there?" Sara said.

Duncan closed the book. Rubbed the end of his stump over the cover in a kind of caress. Then pushed the book a little ways away from him, between them on the table. "Aye. Most likely. I d'no think anyone ever heard of Ensign Thomas Keating again."

Sara looked out at the darkness. The night was clear, with only a silver spit curl of a moon, a bank of clouds trailing over the distant hills like a lady's veil. The ripples of the creek caught the reflection of the moonlight, spilling pearls across the black water.

"I like to think the Indians weren't there after all. That they were gone. That he went out to face bravely what he thought was in front of him, and found it was only the goblins and demons within him."

"Then what happened to him?"

"He went back to Edinburgh, found Jean, and moved to the Highlands where they had a dozen children."

"A pretty dream it would be."

"Such things do happen," she said, pretending to pout, feeling surprisingly girlish for once. "People do live happily ever after."

"Aye, and pigs do fly, too," Duncan said, stretching, starting to untangle himself from the bench. "Handless men do learn to play the fiddle again." Then he stopped and sat down again, looking at her, concerned.

"Do you think still the woman was your mother?"

"Yes. I'm certain of it."

"I'm sorry it did no end better for her." Duncan raised his stump to brush a moth away. "'Tis a strange tale to be sure. Their end there together in the blockhouse. . . ."

"I guess she did what she felt she had to do. In the situation she found herself. It sounds as if that's what she did her whole life. She was a strong woman."

"Och. Strong is no the word for it."

"I didn't always think so. I thought the world had maybe worn her down. When she sent me away from Fort Pitt, I thought she didn't care enough about me to keep me with her. To fight to keep me with her. But I can see now that sending me away took real strength. The easy thing would have kept me with her. For company, if nothing else. Without me with her, she was totally alone, for all the men around her. And I would have fallen into the same life as hers. She didn't want that for me. She wanted me to have a chance at something better."

"I did no know her all that well, even though we traveled together up the river. But I felt at the time she was a good woman, for all that. And I would think your mother would be very proud of you. I would wager that she would think you living proof that she did the right thing by you."

Sara lowered her eyes. Touched beyond measure that he would say such a thing. High above in the darkness, above the dark canopy of leaves from the sycamore, a nighthawk whistled down the night sky. The moon had risen higher, farther from the veil of clouds. The dark hills defined the distance. But there was something else bothering her. Something else on her mind that, now that they were talking, she couldn't let go.

"So my mother had another child. I had a sibling."

"If you could call it thus."

"It didn't say whether it was a boy or a girl, did it?"

Duncan shook his head, studying her, obviously trying to decipher where this was going.

"And she lost it. Dropped it into the river and it was carried away."

"It sounded like the child was stillborn. It was dead when she delivered. That's why she had so much trouble with it. Why she bled so much afterward."

"Do you think she knew it was dead?"

"I am sure so. I would no think she could think otherwise. Why do you. . . . ?"

"I'm trying to understand why she tried to kill the ensign. Why she finally killed herself."

"Och, who can know such a thing? Maybe she was wild with the pain, maybe she knew she was going to die anyway. Maybe she blamed Keating . . . you canna know. It all depends on how she saw the world at that time, and we're no the one looking out at it through her eyes."

"But Keating loved her, and she loved him. He offered her a way out of her world."

"If they survived the Indians. And if she survived the aftermath of the stillbirth."

"Yes, but it was possible."

"No everyone can accept such possibilities when they come along, lass. 'Tis a talent that can take a lifetime to learn, and then there's no guarantee you have it right." Duncan smiled wistfully. "We could chase this around like a dog after its tail until the morrow. You need to get some rest now."

As she carried the betty lamp back to the blockhouse, she looked back as she had the night before. Again Duncan was standing away from the table, his back to her, looking off into the night, as if addressing the darkness, the hills. But this time she saw no wings extending from his back, there were no magic birds above him in the branches of the sycamore, no talking bears. Not that it would have mattered to her if she did. What she saw was a man. A man who, she found to her amazement and dismay, she trusted, trusted what he said, what he did. She had thought for days that it was this place that made her feel at peace, and it was peaceful here to be sure, beautiful, but she knew now that the peacefulness of this place for her came from the presence of this man. This man who was in equal measure strong and weak, self-sufficient and could use some help, open-minded and suspicious. This man who made her feel at one and the same time protected and protective. "No everyone can accept possibilities when they come along, lass," he had said, and she wondered if he was speaking of her mother. Or of her. Or of himself. And it occurred to her that when he spoke of her not being there for long, "No, you could no learn the fiddle, that's foolish talk, talk of the moment, you will no be here long enough," he wasn't speaking of her intention to leave, or of his desire that she do so. Perhaps his feelings had changed from when she first arrived. Perhaps he was speaking of his fear now that she would indeed leave. It was a possibility that she would need to not only accept but act upon. She knew what she must do.

In the morning she was up before sunrise and milked the cows and turned them out to pasture, fed the goats and sheep, threw out scratch for the chickens and slopped the pigs, while Duncan was still asleep. As she came from the barn carrying a bucket of milk, the sun making its first crack of light over the ridgeline of the valley, he appeared in the doorway of the barracks, rubbing his stumps into his eyes.

"What's this then?" he asked groggily.

"I've done the chores, but I expect you'll want to check that I did them the way you want."

He looked at her warily but didn't say anything, made his way to the creek and splashed water on his face, rubbing his dripping stumps through his thick black hair, and went off across the compound toward the barn. By the time he returned, Sara had taken the milk to the springhouse and was sitting at the wood table under the sycamore, the fiddle case open before her, working at tuning the instrument.

"I said you should put that back where you found it," Duncan said frowning. "I can see I should have also said for you to keep it there."

Sara ignored him. "I think I've got the tuning pretty close. What do you think?" she said, plucking each string in turn.

"Och. The last one is flat. No, turn it the other way. How did you know to tune it?"

"There was a fiddler or two in Carlisle. I used to hear them tuning up."

"And you remembered the tones? You must have the pitch then."

"You didn't know that about me. Well, now you do. So, what are you going to teach me first? 'The Black Bear' maybe, in honor of your Black Watch soldiers on the trail? Or maybe 'The Brown-Haired Maiden' in honor of me?" She took the bow and purposely scratched it roughly across the strings. At the screech, a half dozen crows took flight from the trees on the hillside, calling to each other as they winged down the valley over the river.

"No, no, lass, that's no the way you do it at all. Put your fingers on the fingerboard here, and stroke the bow gently. Like this."

She followed his direction and drew one long sweet tone from the instrument. The sound brought the crinkled smile to his face.

"There's something else you should know about me," Sara said.

"Aye, and what would that be?" he asked, bending over her to adjust her fingering with his stub, their faces inches from each other.

"Sara. My name is Sara."

THE BOOK OF LOVE
II

1817

The stone house sat on a rise above the ironworks, away from the other buildings but, in the clearing of the forest by the river, obviously part of it. Two-storied, L-shaped, with a gabled roof, a small front porch. The glass for the windows from one of the new glassworks at Pittsburgh, twelve miles up the Ohio River. Sitting among several centuries-old oaks and red maples and a lone sycamore that his father had spared for their shade. As Colin ran up the hill toward home, he kept low in the tall grass, away from the path, to keep from being seen. The Book of Love tucked inside his homespun shirt, held close to his side under his elbow. Lopsided like a damaged bird.

The heavy drapes were already drawn across the downstairs windows, to block out the growing heat of midmorning and hold in the coolness of the night before; he couldn't tell where anyone might be in the house. He avoided the front steps, the front door, and crouched against the foundation, scurrying along the side toward the back of the house. The kitchen windows were open. The air full of the smells of baking pies, bread, grease. Someone was inside, moving about, he thought it was probably Margaret the maid but he couldn't tell for sure. Rather than risk getting caught he squatted under the lilac bushes to wait and listen, hoping for something to indicate when it was safe to go inside.

The smell of the lilacs, sweet, mingled with those from the kitchen. The air alive with the sound of bees. A chipmunk two-hopped along the base of the house, under the bower of lilac branches, until it noticed the boy hunkered down there, decided it didn't need to travel that direction after all. The smoke from the ironworks eliminated any differentiation between sunlight and shadow, the light under the bushes as gray as the day itself. Though the house was less than fifteen years old, the fieldstone was already blackened and streaked from the smoke of the furnaces and the charcoal mounds, dark as granite. Beside him he noticed the scratches on the embedded stone he and Lydia had made another day in early spring. A day they hid here because they didn't have much time together, their parents and Margaret beginning to keep an eye on them. Scratches on the sandstone made with a piece of glass. A circle with two parallel lines through it, their secret sign. Exposing the tan core, the true color of the stone beneath.

"Are you still bleeding there?" he had said, sitting beside his sister.

"No. It was over a week ago."

"How long did it last?"

"Only four or five days. Margaret says I'm late starting. Most girls start younger."

"And it came from inside your cut?"

"Yes, but it's all right now." Lydia thought a moment, maybe waiting for him to say something. Resting her chin on her knees. When he didn't say anything, she said, "Do you want to put your finger in it again?"

"I was afraid I hurt you. I was afraid I caused you to bleed."

"No, silly. You didn't have anything to do with it. All women do it. That's what makes us different than boys. One of the things. Here, you can do it, I won't mind."

She straightened her legs and pulled up her long cotton dress, bunching it around her stomach. She looked at him as if to say What are you waiting for you? You know you want to.

Colin looked at her cut, at her face. Uncertain. "I thought the Book of Love said an acolyte of love had to be on his knees and say a prayer to the Goddess of All before he could put his finger in it."

"Well, yes. But the Book of Love also says a vestal virgin can give a special dispensation about being on your knees. If you kiss it three times first."

"When did it say that?"

"I read it. I just didn't translate that part for you. But if you don't hurry up and do it, the dispensation will be gone."

She opened her legs. He leaned over, sliding down a little for a better angle, but he still couldn't quite get at the flaps of skin. He kissed three times her soft tangle of hair, hoping that was good enough. He raised up again, propped himself on an elbow. There was a noise from the kitchen window above.

"Hurry, if you're going to," she hissed.

He kept his eyes on her eyes, looking for signs of encouragement or disapproval. Took his finger and felt around in her soft hair. Found the twin flaps. Worked his finger between them. Found the inner hole. Started to push his finger in. She winced.

"Wet your finger first," she whispered, not angry. "Like I showed you."

Her smell was on his finger. Dark. Like the smell of the animals the men killed in the forest. Deer and foxes. Bears. He licked it, stuck his finger in his mouth. Tasted her. The first time she ever had him do it, he was afraid he might gag. But the taste surprised him. Didn't bother him at all. Salty. Musty. Like nothing else in the world. He felt again now for the twin flaps. Her hole. She flinched, then smiled, as he pushed in as far as he could go. Sitting there looking up at her face. Marveling to himself, I'm inside her. Inside her. . . .

Plover, one of the many dogs about the place, stuck his nose under the bush. Bewildered by the boy sitting alone under a lilac bush. Colin shooshed him. "Go away, Plover, go!" he whispered. Flicked a stone at him to get him to move. There was a noise from the window above. Colin tucked himself closer to the wall of the house. Clutching the Book as if afraid someone would try to wrest it from him. He recognized his mother's footsteps as she bustled into the kitchen.

"Oh, thank you, Margaret. I would have gotten that."

"I needed to keep busy, m'um."

"Are you all packed?"

"Yes, m'um. Ready to go as soon as the coach gets here." There was the sound of movement, a knife blade scraping across the rim of a bowl. After a moment, Margaret said, "Is young Lydia okay?"

"Yes, yes, she seems to be fine. Taking it all in her stride. She's a strong young woman."

"Strong-willed, m'um."

"Yes, well, that too. Actually, she seems quite excited about going. Not at all the way I was afraid she'd take it after her father told her. It's a big step for a girl her age. She's never been around other children her age before. Only Colin."

There was silence for a moment. The boy could feel the look between the two women, even though he couldn't see them. He rested his cheek against his upturned knees. A comfort.

"Are you sure you can manage while I'm gone?" Margaret broke the silence.

"Yes, don't you worry. We'll do fine. The Simpson woman will take good care of us until you return."

"Because it's still not too late to change your mind, m'um. About sending the wee darling away and all. . . ."

"It is not my decision to make, or to change, Margaret. Her father said that the girl is going. And that's the way it is."

"Ah, m'um, I've asked myself a hundred times if I did the right thing. By telling you about finding them like that and all. I'm sure young Colin didn't mean—"

"Let's not discuss it further, Margaret. Her father says that had nothing to do with his decision. He says he had made up his mind a while ago that the girl needs a proper education. So that's that. Now hurry and get those parcels together. You'll need something to eat by the time you reach Pittsburgh. And make sure all your things are together, the coach should be here anytime. . . ."

He had let himself get distracted, listening to the two women. Wondering what they might say about him, about him and Lydia. Wicked wicked boy. He would have to hurry, he would have to take his chances getting caught. He crawled free of the lilacs and ran around to the front of the house, slinking quickly up the steps on all fours. The half dozen cats that lived on the front porch took one look at him, arched their backs, hissed and slunk away.

He eased open one of the double front doors, stepped into the vestibule, on into the front hall. The interior of the house cool and dark. His sister's and Margaret's trunks and suitcases stacked close to the door. From the back of the house came his mother's and Margaret's voices, the sounds of dishes being put away. He peeked into the dining room to the right, into the parlor to the left, to make sure no one was there. No one waiting to see the ironmaster, no one waiting to see Lydia off. Then he crossed quickly along the hall and started up the stairs. Keeping to the side of the treads close to the wall so the stairs didn't creak. Even so, on the landing halfway up, one of the boards gave a loud *Crack!* like a gunshot.

Silence. Then his mother called, "Hello? Colin? Is that you?"

He heard her start into the dining room. Stop. Listening. He pressed against the wall. Hardly dared to breathe. For a moment the house deathly still. Then he heard Margaret say, "I saw young Colin run down to the mill earlier but I haven't seen the lad come back. . . ."

He couldn't make out his mother's reply. But when he heard her turn back to the kitchen, he scurried on up the stairs on all fours, hoping her noise covered his.

Until a few months earlier, he and Lydia shared the same bedroom on the second floor, across the hall from their parents' bedroom. But since what was known as *the Trouble*, Colin had been moved to Margaret's quarters at the back of the house, and Margaret had slept in his bed in Lydia's room. Since the Trouble, there had rarely been a time when he was alone with his sister.

At the top of the stairs, his head barely above the level of the top step, he looked into his parents' bedroom. In the bars of gray light squeezing between the closed drapes, dust motes fell forever. Past the stern image of his grandfather over the mantel. The rocking chair his mother used to nurse both him and Lydia. The sleigh bed his father had shipped specially over the Alleghenies to please his bride. Otherwise nothing stirred. Across the hall, in the open door to her bedroom, Lydia crossed back and forth, getting ready. Dressed only in her petticoats, half a dozen layers. Tiers of white cotton flounced as she moved about. When she caught sight of him out of the corner of her eye, she gasped, both hands to her mouth, startled. Then dissolved into giggles.

"What are you doing there? Silly."

"I wanted to see you, before you left," Colin whispered.

"Were you spying on me?" she said, hands on her hips, like a schoolmistress, though with a glint in her eye.

Colin stood, checking down the steps behind him, and hurried over to her door. "I was making sure everyone else was downstairs."

"I'll bet you *were* spying on me. I'll bet you were trying to see me naked again, weren't you, one last time before I go. Well, sorry to disappoint you."

She turned away and went back to getting ready. Though with an extra movement to her hips, setting her aura of petticoats swinging. She was right in a way; he had hoped to see her naked again. Sometime before she left. He felt found out and embarrassed. Fallen from grace, beyond redemption. The drapes and windows were open, flooding the room with gray light. The room warm from the heavy air outside. Colin looked out the window. The men were still at work with the battering ram at the old blockhouse. A gaping hole in the back wall, like an open mouth. But his father was no longer there. While Lydia fixed her hair at the dresser mirror, Colin went over and sat on the edge of the bed.

"Are you excited about going?" he asked.

"Well, of course I'm excited. Who wouldn't be? It's just like Father says, it will open up a whole new world for me. It's not many girls out here on the frontier who have the chance to go to school in Philadelphia. I'll be a lady." She curtsied to her own reflection, and laughed a little to his.

He had almost forgotten. He dug the package from inside his shirt and held it out to her. She looked quizzically at it in the mirror. Turned for a better look.

"Oh. That old book." She turned back to the mirror, adjusting her hair. "What would I want with that old thing? Where I'm going I'll read all sorts of new books and learn all sorts of new things." Then she thought of something. She turned back to him. "But don't ever let Father or Mother see you with it. And don't ever tell them what I said was in it. You'll really get yourself in trouble then. Even more than you're in already."

They didn't have the Book of Love with them that day. The day Margaret found them by the pond. They hadn't done any of the things the Book instructed. It was a warm day in spring, he and Lydia had gone swimming together, naked, and when they got out of the water, had started to wrestle. Then just lay there, in the sunlight, for a while, holding each other, wrapped in each other's arms and legs. It had been the most beautiful day Colin ever experienced. More beautiful than when they did any of the things the Book instructed. Just holding her. Feeling her skin all about him. But then Margaret appeared from the forest. And everything changed.

Colin went back and checked out the window. Far down the river road, where the Allehela emptied into the Ohio, a coach-and-four was coming up the valley. To take her away. He didn't let on he had seen it.

"I didn't bring the Book to you as a present. Unless you wanted to take it with you." He turned away from the window to look at her again. Look at her as often as he could. "I brought it to ask you to read from it again."

She studied him in the mirror a moment. Then turned to look at him directly. "What are you talking about?"

"I want you to tell me what it says again. There are a lot of things I still don't know about. Everybody seems to want me to be grown up all of a sudden, but I don't know how. I don't know what that means. When I do what I think are grown-up things I get into trouble. I need you to tell me what the Book says."

"It was a game, Colin." She looked at him incredulously. Exasperated. "It was only a game. Didn't you know that? I made all that stuff up."

Now that she said it to him, yes, of course he knew it. Knew it from the beginning. But somehow it didn't seem to matter. "But the words . . . all the magic things. . . ."

"It isn't magic. It's Gaelic, or at least I think that's what it is. I've seen some of the same words in the letters Margaret gets from home and she told me what it was. But no matter. I made up all that stuff as we went along. It didn't mean anything."

"It meant something to me."

She came over to him. And for a moment he thought she was going to hold him again. But then she looked beyond him, something caught her eye out the window, in the distance.

"The coach is coming. I have to get ready." She turned away quickly, skipped back across the room and took her dress hanging from the door. Pulled it over her head, down over her body. Smoothing it out over her layers of petticoats. Laughing at her hurry, her efforts. Colin looked at the Book of Love, still wrapped in its oilskin, lying on the chenille spread. Useless. What did he think was going to happen? That she was going to stop getting ready and play their secret game again? Stupid. Evil. He tucked the parcel back inside his shirt again. To get it out of sight.

"Will you think about us when you're gone? Will you think about me?"

"Of course I'll think about you. You'll always be my little brother." As she hurried past him to get her sash from the chair and back to the mirror, she added, "My little baby brother."

He wanted to hurt her. He wanted her to hurt, as much as he hurt. "I should be the one going away, not you. I should be the one going away to school, not a girl."

She stopped what she was doing to look at him. Head tilted to one side. As if she were looking at an unfamiliar life-form. "You don't understand, do you? This isn't something special Father is doing for my sake. This is for your sake. They're sending me away to safeguard you from me. They're afraid as long as I'm around

I'll distract you from your lessons. From all the things Father wants to teach you about the ironworks. He'll send you away to school, all right, when you're older, when he thinks it's time, maybe even to England if he thinks that's what it will take to make you a first-rate engineer and ironmaster. He says he's sending me away to boarding school so I can become a polished young woman, but I know it's not that at all. They consider me a corrupting influence on you. And I guess maybe I am."

She gave a saucy wave of her hips, sending her petticoats rocking back and forth. A look on her face as if she were proud of herself.

"If that's the reason they're sending you away, why are you so happy about going?" He didn't say what he wanted to say. Why are you so happy to leave when it means leaving me? I thought you said we would be together always.

"Because this is my one chance to be something. Be somebody. This is my chance to have an education and become exposed to the wider world. If I stayed here I would always be second to you, even though I'm older. And what chance would I have, for anything? Father would never let me marry a workman, and how would I meet anyone else? I'd end up an old-maid aunt taking care of your children."

"Father won't let you stay there, you know. He'll bring you back."

She went once more to the window, looking down the hill at the ironworks. "I doubt that. He wouldn't even stop work today and come home to see me off. He said good-bye this morning at breakfast. I'm a nuisance to him, he doesn't know what to do with me because I'm a girl. Once I'm away, why would he go to any trouble to have me back? He'll find some relative there in Philadelphia for me to stay with after I graduate. Until I find a husband there to take me."

The gray light from the front windows washed over her face. Her eyes that he thought might tear. Colin was shaken. As if something surrounding him had given way. Lydia must feel about their father, the same way Colin felt toward her. Loved her father. The way Colin loved her. Realized in that moment there are longings in the world that can never be fulfilled. Leavings and neglects as final as death. Then just as quickly as Lydia's tears came, they went away. Herself again. Bustling about picking up her last things from the dresser. Hairbrush, pins, a porcelain figure of a dancer. Put them in her handbag. Checked to see if she had forgotten anything.

"Lydia," their mother called from downstairs. "The coach is here."

And before he knew it, she was gone. Her last minutes there a flurry of rushing about. The coachmen gathering her trunks, tying them on the back of the coach. Margaret and Mother making sure Lydia had everything. The dogs barking as they danced around the horses, the cats on the front porch scurrying away. Hurried good-byes on the front steps. Kisses for everyone. Tears. I'll write every day. Laughter as they helped Lydia squash her petticoats through the door of the coach. More laughter as Margaret struggled to mount the coach steps. The crack of the whip, the jingle of harness, the creak and groan of the carriage springs. Oh, good-bye, good-bye. Good-bye everyone. . . .

He ran behind the coach as it pulled away until he couldn't keep up, until it rolled away from him, down the road, dipping out of sight momentarily beyond the contour of the slope then reappearing again farther down the hill, heading toward the ford at the end of the valley, the post road to Pittsburgh. He walked up into the fields, his hand trailing in the tall grass, watching as the coach grew smaller and smaller. A miniature of a coach-and-four. A spiral of dust. Gone. Gradually becoming aware again of things around him. The chirring insects. Grasshoppers arcing away where he stepped. The birds, crows calling from the woods. From the hollow came the ring of the warning bell. The end of one heat at the furnace, the beginning of the next. With nowhere else to go he angled on across the fields in that direction.

He found his father at the casting bed, supervising the last-minute preparations to tap the furnace. The furrowing of the runners and casting trenches in the hard-packed sand in front of the hearth. The careful placement of the clay molds, buried except for their sprues and risers. His father came over and stood beside him.

"Did your sister get off okay?"

"Yes sir."

"Good." After a moment he said, "I thought it best to stay away this morning. Maybe it was the wrong thing to do, I don't know. But I'm sure Lydia will do very well for herself. She's a resourceful young woman. She's like her mother."

Colin didn't know what to say; he was confused. The two stood side by side, his father looking to where the boy was looking. After several moments with nothing to say, his father called one of the workmen over, took the man's spade and showed it to Colin.

"This is called a *ship*. Do you know why?"

The boy shook his head. His father turned it upright. "Because the blade is shaped in a V like the bow of a ship. It's to keep the sides of the channels from collapsing into the molten metal. Watch."

At a signal from his father, one of the workmen took a long chisel and held it against a clay plug in the front of the furnace; a second workman hit the end of the chisel with a two-handed hammer. After several blows the plug popped into the furnace and molten metal gushed from the tap hole. Traveling in glowing streams along the channels and runners, stewing and sputtering until it reached its final destinations in the molds, turning gray at the edges as it slowly began to harden. The heat rose against Colin's face, making him smile. As warm as the excitement coursing through him.

His father smiled too, watching him. "What's that inside your shirt?" he asked, noticing the lump.

Colin had forgotten about it. He touched the parcel through his shirt. Shook his head. "Nothing, sir. Nothing at all. Just an old book I found."

His father nodded, already thinking of something else, and set off to check the castings, stepping carefully over the trenches and runners. For a moment Colin had the idea to throw the parcel in the furnace. Get rid of the Book for good. Burn it. But he decided to keep it. A reminder, if nothing else. He readjusted its position inside his shirt and tailed after his father. Stepping in the packed sand where his father stepped over the hardening metal.

Acknowledgments

There are three people—friends, actually; dream catchers—without whom I could never have brought these books to publication:

Kim Francis
Dave Meek
Jack Ritchie

A big thank you goes to Bruce McAllister for his support, good thoughts, and encouragement during the early stages of the book. I also thank Eileen Chetti for struggling through my quirks of style and punctuation; Linnea Duly for writing a study guide; and Bob Gelston, who is always around to answer questions and take on anything else that's needed. And then, of course, there's my wife Marty. . . .

Richard Snodgrass lives in Pittsburgh, PA with his wife Marty and two indomitable female tuxedo cats, raised from feral kittens, named Frankie and Becca.

To read more about the Furnass series, the town of Furnass, and special features for *A Book of Days*—including a Reader's Study Guide, author interviews, and omitted scenes—go to www.RichardSnodgrass.com.

Made in United States
Orlando, FL
28 July 2023

35556555R00168